You Had Me

Holly moved on to the next box, where she found a slinky black skirt and a camisole that had cost her four weeks' wages.

She had been wearing that outfit the day she and Todd went on their first date. If anything would convince him, this would be it. Well, that and a bit of private bedroom information, though with Vince listening in on every word, Holly had decided that sex secrets would be used only as a final resort.

"You know, just because I don't care about my manly image doesn't mean I want to go around wearing a skirt." Vince took control of his hand and put the offending item back in the box.

"I don't quite think you have the legs for a DKNY pencil skirt," Holly retorted as she reached for it again. "Anyway, it's not for wearing. It's for sentimental purposes only."

"I hope you remember that," Vince said as Holly heard her stepmother coming up the stairs.

"Fine," she whispered as she quickly shut the box up. "As long as you're quiet, I'll do anything."

"Anything?" Vince sounded interested.

Stop it, she commanded just as her stepmother walked into the room. *Good grief.* Besides, what on earth did he think she could do when they were in the same body? Then a disturbing thought entered her mind, which she immediately blocked, but not before she felt some sort of movement in the trouser department.

Oh, my God. Vince, she hissed in horror. . . .

You Had Me at Halo

Amanda Ashby

NEW AMERICAN LIBRARY

New American Library
Published by New American Library,
a division of Penguin Group (USA) Inc., 375 Hudson Street,
New York, New York 10014, USA
Penguin Group (Canada), 90 Eglinton Avenue East, Suite 700, Toronto,
Ontario M4P 2Y3, Canada (a division of Pearson Penguin Canada Inc.)
Penguin Books Ltd., 80 Strand, London WC2R 0RL, England
Penguin Ireland, 25 St. Stephen's Green, Dublin 2,
Ireland (a division of Penguin Books Ltd.)
Penguin Group (Australia), 250 Camberwell Road, Camberwell,
Victoria 3124, Australia (a division of Pearson Australia Group Pty. Ltd.)
Penguin Books India Pvt. Ltd., 11 Community Centre,
Panchsheel Park, New Delhi – 110 017, India
Penguin Group (NZ), 67 Apollo Drive, Rosedale, North Shore 0745,
Auckland, New Zealand (a division of Pearson New Zealand Ltd.)
Penguin Books (South Africa) (Pty.) Ltd., 24 Sturdee Avenue,
Rosebank, Johannesburg 2196, South Africa

Penguin Books Ltd., Registered Offices:
80 Strand, London WC2R 0RL, England

First published by New American Library,
a division of Penguin Group (USA) Inc.

First Printing, August 2007

1   3   5   7   9   10   8   6   4   2

 REGISTERED TRADEMARK—MARCA REGISTRADA

LIBRARY OF CONGRESS CATALOGING-IN-PUBLICATION DATA:

Ashby, Amanda.
You had me at halo/Amanda Ashby.
p. cm.
ISBN: 978-0-451-22135-3
1. Angels—Fiction. I. Title.
PS3601.S54Y68 2007
813'.6—dc22   2006101085

Set in Sabon   •   Designed by Elke Sigal

Printed in the United States of America

PUBLISHER'S NOTE
This is a work of fiction. Names, characters, places, and incidents either are the product
of the author's imagination or are used fictitiously, and any resemblance to actual per-
sons, living or dead, business establishments, events, or locales is entirely coincidental.
    The publisher does not have any control over and does not assume any responsibil-
ity for author or third-party Web sites or their content.

The scanning, uploading, and distribution of this book via the Internet or via any other
means without the permission of the publisher is illegal and punishable by law. Please
purchase only authorized electronic editions, and do not participate in or encourage electronic piracy of copyrighted materials. Your support of the author's rights is appreciated.

I started writing this book three weeks after my dad died, and while he might not be here anymore, I'm certain that, in typical fatherly fashion, he's up there pulling a few strings.

GERALD FRANCIS ASHBY

(1935–2005)

Acknowledgments

I would like to thank my critique partners, Pat Posner, Sara Hantz and Christina Phillips. Their knowledge of when to crack the whip and when to administer chocolate is unerring.

I would also like to say a big thank-you to Jenny Bent, who is quite simply the best agent a girl could have and who is so gentle with my dreams.

To Anne Bohner and everyone at New American Library, I still can't believe how lucky I am, so thank you for all your patience and hard work.

Of course, I can't forget Penny Jordan, Susan Stephens, Amanda Grange and everyone else from my local RNA chapter in England. Not only are you all great writers, but you have the most excellent taste in pudding as well.

To Pam, who despite having a daughter who refused to get a real job, has been a great support. To Kay, who is nothing like the stepmother in this book, and to Nick and Liz, for never laughing apart from when they were meant to. Also, to all my other family, friends and writing pals spread out across the world—yes, you are expected to buy it, read it and answer questions. Sorry, but those are the rules.

Finally, to Barry, Molly and Arthur, I quite simply couldn't have done it without you.

You Had Me at Halo

One

"Unbelievable." Holly Evans shook her head as she peered down through the window to the scene below.

That was the problem with an open casket. It meant everyone's last memories of her would be with a puffy white face, the wrong color lipstick and a dreadful polyester dress. They always said the camera added five pounds, but no one ever talked about how fattening embalming fluid was.

"Sssshhh."

"What?" Holly kept her eyes focused on the service. "Oh, sorry. It's hard to be quiet when I have to look at myself getting buried in that outfit. I'm only twenty-two. So much to live for, yet there I am. Dead. You know I don't like to kick up a stink, but I most certainly didn't die of natural causes."

There was another angry hiss from behind, which Holly ignored. She'd been ignoring a lot of things since she'd died two weeks ago. And it had to be said that heaven wasn't nearly as much fun as she had been led to believe. All the rules, for a start.

Where were the fluffy clouds and peeled grapes? To

be honest the place looked more like terminal two at LAX than a celestial paradise. She pressed her nose up to the glass again. Here came the speeches.

Holly sniffed as she listened to Gemma's glowing tribute. Of course, she knew her best friend would come through for her. "And look at how everyone is crying," she said to no one in particular. "I'm really touched. Perhaps the dress wasn't such a bad choice after all?"

Now it was Todd's turn to speak, and if she didn't know better, she would say his eyes looked a bit moist as well.

They had been dating almost a year, and he hadn't even shed a tear when he broke his leg in three places while playing football. Yet here he was crying over her.

It just made Holly feel even worse about their fight. Todd had wanted to propose to her in front of everyone at the annual Baker Colwell ball, while Holly had wanted it to be a more private affair. He had refused to budge on the issue, and after three days of not speaking to him, Holly had finally come to realize what a fool she was. If he wanted to show his love for her in front of the entire company, it was hardly something she should argue. Especially since she had "accidentally" found the ring at the bottom of his closet a week earlier.

It was beautiful. And so big. If only she hadn't died, then she would've been able to apologize to him before the ball and by the end of the night it would've been hers. It wasn't fair. Especially when she thought of how much she'd spent on the pink bra and panties to complete her apology. Not that she had resented the cost, since it wasn't every day a girl got engaged. Besides, Todd had once said how gorgeous pink looked against her dusty brown curls and huge sloe eyes. Okay, so he hadn't used those words exactly, since he was more of a salesman than a poet. But Holly just knew he had been thinking it on the inside.

There was no use crying over spilled milk, or diamonds as big as her knuckle. She was in heaven now and she just had to forget about how much better the death notice would've looked if only it had said, "Loving fiancé, Todd Harman."

"But," she said with one final sniff, "there's no denying it would've been a beautiful wedding."

"I told you. No talking during a funeral."

"And I told you that since I'm only going to die once, I might as well make the most of it," Holly retorted to the person behind her. "Besides, how often do you get all of Baker Colwell's head office to turn up to your funeral? That includes the notoriously stuck-up corporate affairs guys from the fifth floor. Look, they spelled my name out in bright red roses and white carnations. What a nice gesture."

"Miss Evans," someone else said, and Holly reluctantly spun around to where Tyrone, her first-level tutor, was standing. He was tall and bald with a beaky nose, and when Holly had first arrived in heaven, she'd been under the mistaken impression he was God.

The fact that he had laughed hysterically at her mistake hadn't made Holly warm to him much. From what she had gathered, no one really got a good look at the big man, so who was he to say he didn't look like Tyrone? It was possible.

"Yes?"

"There have been complaints."

"Complaints?"

"Yes, Miss Evans. Complaints. About the talking. It's got to stop."

"I've hardly said anything," she protested. "Honestly I haven't. It's just that *some* people around here jump down your throat for even breathing . . . well, not that we actually breathe anymore. But still, they really should try to relax a bit. Anyway, it's easy for them to sit there looking smug, since most of them got to see the right side of seventy."

Tyrone gave her a patient smile. "Remember, I explained that these feelings are just temporary, and as soon as they're purged you'll be left with an overwhelming sense of joy."

Holly grunted by way of an answer, since the longer she was dead, the less joyful she was becoming. It wasn't that she wanted to cause a fuss, but she was still grappling with what had happened.

She had her whole life in front of her: a great new promotion with the eleventh-most-benefit-friendly employer in the country, a heap of friends, and a potential fiancé who was drop-dead gorgeous. Oh, yes, she had had it all to live for, but around here that didn't seem to matter.

"Look, Miss Evans. This will get easier as you go along. You just need to stick to the rules and do as you're told."

Holly was becoming more and more frustrated. She wasn't usually quite so petulant, but then she wasn't usually stuck in heaven either. "What are they going to do, kill me? Oh, wait, that's right. I'm already dead."

"Actually . . ." Tyrone cleared his throat. "I think you'll find there are quite a few fates worse than death."

"I find that hard to believe," Holly was stung into replying. "I've got to say it's pretty disorganized up here. All I keep hearing is, 'Of course you can't see your parents yet, Miss Evans; you need to wait until you're at Level Three for that. . . . No, Miss Evans, you can't go and haunt someone just because they took credit for one of your ideas last month. . . .' "

All around her she could see people catching their imaginary breath in an inward gasp.

That was another thing about this place: Everyone just seemed to sit around doing nothing. Tyrone said it was because on Level One people were still waiting for their security clearances before moving up to their higher destinies. Whatever the reason, it was pretty annoying to always have the peanut gallery listening in on what she was saying.

"I know you must be frustrated right now, Miss Evans, but try to be patient a bit longer," Tyrone said in a mild voice, which reminded Holly of just how pointless it was to argue with him. "So, please, no more talking."

"Fine." Holly felt the fight drain out of her as she let out a sigh and turned back to her own funeral. She would try very hard to watch the rest of it without opening her mouth, and— "Oh, great. This day just keeps getting better and better, doesn't it? First the horrible dress and now look. Why are Vince Murphy and all the other computer technicians down there? Don't they have anything better to do?"

Behind her Tyrone coughed, and Holly lifted her hand in an apology. "Okay, sorry. I was just a bit thrown to see them. Especially since I wasn't friends with . . . Oh, and why does Vince have all those purple flashing lights dancing around his head? I know he's weird, but that's just something else."

"If you'd read your manual properly you'd know purple lights mean the body in question is about to die," the same annoying person called out from the peanut gallery. Obviously she wasn't the only one who hadn't been filled with joy yet. This guy didn't seem to be feeling the love either.

"I suppose that's right next to the paragraph about no talking during funerals," Holly retorted.

"Actually it is. But since you were obviously too busy doing your nails instead of learning how to read before you committed suicide—"

Holly spun around and glared at the man for the first time. *"I. Did. Not. Commit. Suicide."*

"Of course not, and I guess those pills magically entered your system," said the horrible man (who Holly was very glad to note was incredibly fat). "Oh, yeah," he continued with a snigger. "You're not the only one who looks down at what's going on. I saw the hospital report and what it said. Apparently it's not the first time you've tried it either. Sounds to me like you're not only a big mouth, you're a—"

"Thank you, Mr. Michaels, that's enough," Tyrone interrupted before joining her at the window.

"I didn't commit suicide." Holly managed to keep her voice low. She could feel her body shaking, which was not in keeping with what Tyrone had explained to her. Once a person got to heaven, while their spirit still had the appearance of a body, it didn't actually work like one. As in, no feeding, no watering, no washing.

Or shaking.

Holly put it down to this purging business.

"It's no one's job to judge here, Miss Evans."

"Tell that to the fat guy behind me," she muttered in a sullen voice as her fingers unconsciously made their way to the scars on her wrist.

Tyrone coughed. "Again on the not being here to judge."

Holly bit her lip. "Okay. Sorry. He probably has a wonky metabolism or something. But . . ." She gulped as she stared out the window again. "Is Vince Murphy really about to die? What's wrong with him?"

"Probably missing your smart wit."

"Mr. Michaels," Tyrone said in a quiet voice, which somehow sounded more like a roar than a whisper as it echoed around the large glass-fronted room. "One more word and it's another month on Level One for you."

Serves you right, Holly wanted to say, but she wisely kept her mouth shut. Besides, Tyrone could be sort of scary. She watched him turn back to her.

"I don't know what's wrong with your friend, but it's true he's about to die," he said in a kinder voice. "However, Miss Evans, I have to insist there's no more talking, because otherwise the matter will be out of my hands. Do you understand?"

Holly nodded her head, lifted her fingers to her lips, and pretended to zip them together before returning her attention back to Vince. How odd that he would die as well.

She watched as her stepmother walked to the front of the church and smoothed out a piece of paper. She could just guess what was on it. *Holly Evans has been the bane of my existence for as long as I've had the displeasure of knowing her, and despite how much she denies breaking my favorite Clarice Cliff vase, I know she did it. . . .*

Of course, her stepmother was too clever to say these things aloud, but Holly would bet her beloved Miss Sixty jeans that her stepmother was thinking them on the inside. *Well, Mrs. Evans number two, you won't be burdened by me any longer,* Holly thought sullenly.

Her eye was drawn to Vince Murphy again. If she didn't know better she would say he was about to collapse. Holly could scarcely believe it as she spun around to face Tyrone, shooting him an accusing glare.

"You didn't say he was going to die *now.* As in, right in the middle of my funeral. I'm sorry, but this is too much. I don't get to make up with Todd, I don't get my wedding, and now I don't even get my own once-in-a-lifetime funeral?"

All of a sudden things started to get a little bit shaky, and she stretched out her hands to grab hold of the rail that was attached to the large window she'd been staring out of all morning.

Holly had been through a lot of strange experiences in the last two weeks—dying, finding out that heaven wasn't full of M&M's and *Friends* repeats, being told off every time she opened her mouth—but there was something different about this. For a start it felt as if she were falling. Down. Through a long white tunnel.

Then she opened her eyes as she realized she was hovering just millimeters from her own dead body, complete with puffy face, bad lipstick, and a polyester dress.

Oh, dear.

Tyrone hadn't been joking.

She really was getting kicked out of heaven.

Two

"Right, Miss Holly Elliot Evans, client number XY4588890. The time is two-oh-five, and this session will commence immediately. My name is Dr. Alan Hill and I'm here to help."

Huh?

Holly blinked and looked around her. This wasn't right. She'd been to St. Luke's Church on the corner of View and Elm plenty of times over the last twenty-two years; her most recent visit being a few seconds ago, when she'd seen her dead body. But wherever she was now, it wasn't church.

Everything, from the funny round beanbags in the corner over to the books in the floor-to-ceiling shelving, was white. Unlike in Level One, there were no windows anywhere to be seen. No wonder she was a little hot and flustered. Did she mention that none of this made sense? What had happened to her? Was she more dead then dead?

"It's all right to feel a bit confused, Miss Evans. It's perfectly natural after such a journey. Just take your time."

Holly blinked again. The man talking to her was sitting on a white leather chair, which was floating in the air. He had red hair, chubby fingers, and was wearing what looked like a pair of Nike sneakers on his feet. Gosh, commercialism really was far-reaching.

"What's going on?" Holly finally managed to speak. She just hoped that her voice didn't wobble too much. "And why was I flying over my dead body a minute ago?"

"Oh, well, that's part of the treatment to help you tap into your emotions."

"And why would I want to tap into my emotions?"

"Because it's part of the healing, of course." The man seemed surprised. "Surely you read about it in your rulebook when you first arrived in heaven?"

Holly shook her head. She had been given the book on the first day, but to be honest, she had been too annoyed to do anything more than thumb through it a few times. Besides, if they really wanted people to pick the thing up, then they should consider a more inspired title than *The Official and Unabridged Manual for the Recently Departed—Complete with References and a Fully Illustrated Appendix.*

"Oh." Dr. Hill seemed to be working out how to deal with this detour. "Well, I suppose I should give you a rundown of what's going to happen, then. You see, some people who die just don't quite manage the transition as smoothly as others, and that's where I come in."

Holly looked at him blankly.

"Hmmmm." The doctor ran his fingers through a strawberry curl. "Let me explain it another way. When you first die, you get purged of all your human baggage and worries, so that you can be ready to take on the divine joys of heaven. But sometimes it doesn't work and you need a bit of . . . prompting."

Holly groaned as she dropped down onto the long white couch she had suddenly noticed was beside her. "You're a shrink, aren't you?"

"Well, I prefer to use the term spiritual realigner," Dr. Hill admitted.

"A shrink," Holly repeated in disbelief. "I've been kicked out of heaven and sent to a shrink because I was talking too much?" Could today get any worse?

"This is not a punishment. I'm here to help."

"Look, I think there's been a mistake. Yes, I was a bit upset about the whole dying thing. But trust me on this: I'm not crazy. I went to one of you guys when my dad died, and he said I was fine. *Fine.*"

"Well, that's good." He clapped. "Because that means it won't take long to remove all of your earthly issues and send you back to Level One in shipshape condition. So how about we start with something basic? Like ink blots."

"But I'm fine," she repeated as the man shuffled over to his white filing cabinet and pulled out a large stack of cards. "You can ask any of my friends. They'll tell you that I'm the most together person they know."

"Okay, Miss Evans. When I hold up the first picture, tell me what you can see, and don't be afraid to say anything you want."

Holly folded her arms and glared at him, but this didn't stop him from waving the ink blot and giving her an encouraging nod. She let out a disgruntled snort. "Okay, so perhaps I was a little mad before, but surely you can't hold that against me. For a start, did you see what Rochelle Jackson was wearing to my funeral? Where's the respect?"

"Ah, see? Now, that's progress." Dr. Hill gave an enthusiastic smile. "So how about this one?"

Holly didn't even look at the picture as the gnawing frustration that had surrounded her since she first arrived in heaven once again surfaced. "And it's not just that my funeral was ruined; this whole dying thing has pretty much screwed up my life as well. I had plans, Dr. Hill. Lots and lots of plans."

"Okay, and this one?" The doctor seemed to be inching away from her with a fearful expression on his face as he held up another card.

Holly ignored it. "For the last few years I've been working so hard to make something of myself. Just as it all starts to come together, I suddenly wake up and find myself dead. Poor Todd probably thinks that I'd rather kill myself than marry him. Which is so untrue. There's nothing I wanted more than to be Mrs. Todd Harman, and now he'll never know."

"Hmmmmm. I sort of thought it looked like a cat, myself," Dr. Hill said in an overbright voice, but Holly was beyond noticing.

"What's even more annoying is that I didn't take any pills. Nothing. Tyrone keeps assuring me I don't have to worry about it, because it's all in the hands of divine justice, but I've got to say that judging by the way this operation is run, I'm not sure I trust divine justice to get the job done. Someone must know how I died, so why aren't I getting any answers?"

"You're not talking about the inkblot, are you?"

Holly got up from the sofa and looked at him in astonishment. Had she really just revealed all of that information? Normally she was a lot more controlled. Then again, she had never been dead before. It obviously brought out her inner bitch. "I guess you were right. I did have some issues, after all. You've got to understand that I don't want everyone to think I screwed up when it wasn't my fault. But I can't clear my name on earth, and I can't even tell my dad because he's on Level Three. I'm stuck, and there's nothing I can do."

The doctor scrambled to his feet and started to speak into a credit card–size piece of plastic. "We've had real progress with this session, and Miss Evans has definitely turned a corner." Then he put the small machine back on the desk, and Holly spun around to face him.

"I have?" She tried to hide her surprise. "Wow, I must say I didn't really think those inkblots would work, but once I started talking I just couldn't stop."

"See." He beamed. "I told you it wouldn't be so bad."

"So does that mean I can return to Level One and be purged?"

"Er, no."

Holly felt her lip start to quiver. "But you just said I'd turned a corner."

"That's right. A big corner. You've acknowledged you have things that need to be sorted out. Which is why you're ready for a manual purge. Tyrone said you might need one, but I had been hoping to avoid it."

"Me too," she agreed, since there was nothing good about the words *manual purge*. She'd never had a colonic irrigation, but this sounded similar.

"I'm afraid it's going to be necessary. But don't look so frightened; they're not too bad. Just a bit extreme. Now, just let me have a peek on the computer and I'll see what's available."

Tyrone was right: She should've just kept her big mouth shut. In the past Holly had been an achiever. Good marks at college? No problem. Getting a job with Baker Colwell? Easy. But dying and getting sent to heaven? Must try harder.

"Ah, well, isn't that lucky?" Dr. Hill seemed to be talking to himself. "There's an immediate opening. It's so much better if you don't have to wait."

"W-wait for what?" Holly finally dredged up the courage to ask.

"Wait to go back to earth to confront your past life, of course." Alan Hill shot her another strange look. "Miss Evans, haven't you read *any* of your rulebook?"

"You mean you're sending me back home?"

"That's right. Only for two days, and it's just to help you accept your recent death. You see, right now you're still bound to the earthly plane by your issues. But as soon as they're resolved, you'll be more receptive to moving back up through the levels."

Holly stared at him. "This is amazing, and look—I'm sorry about all the rude things I said before. I guess I was a little bit fired up, but this is beyond anything I could've hoped for."

Dr. Hill looked a little bit concerned. "So you do understand what you've got to do?" he asked. "This isn't just for a social visit. You need to get your problems sorted out so you can be purged."

Holly reached over to his desk and grabbed a pad and pen. "That's right. So let's see . . . Obviously I need to find out how I died, and then I need to let everyone close to me know what really happened so that they understand I loved them and would never purposely kill myself." She looked up and grinned. "They're my earthly issues, and once I sort them out I can kiss Level One good-bye and get one step closer to seeing my parents."

"Er, yes." He still looked a little bit surprised. "And I must say, it's nice to see so much enthusiasm. Some people aren't quite as keen. Though since I'm almost ready to send you back, it's probably good you're so excited."

"Are you kidding? This is brilliant. I still can't believe I'll see Todd again. Oh, and this means I'll hear his proposal."

"Actually"—he started to cough—"the thing is—"

"Because"—Holly started to grin—"I'm sure a lot will be forgiven once I get that ring on my finger. Wait until you see the size of the rock—I'm not just talking big; I'm talking enormous. . . . Oh, and I hope my roommates haven't moved my stuff out of the apartment yet."

"Miss Evans—"

"My rent's paid up until the end of the month, so—"

"*Miss Evans.*"

"What?" She blinked at him in surprise. "Why are you shouting?"

"Because it's the only way to stop you from talking."

"Oh." She winced. "I'm sorry. I tend to talk a lot when I'm excited."

"Yes, but that is the thing." Dr. Hill gnawed on his bottom lip and looked a bit uncomfortable. "You know, you really should've read the rulebook, because it would've made this a lot easier."

"Made what a lot easier?" Holly said slowly, not liking the way he was avoiding eye contact. That couldn't be good.

"Miss Evans, you're not going back to earth as yourself, because your human body is now officially dead."

"That's right," she agreed. "I just saw myself in the coffin. That's why you need to wave your wand or twitch your nose to give me a new body."

"Indeed we do," he agreed. "When a soul dies, the human body can still function for up to two days, so when we send people back for a manual purging, we use a body where the soul has gone but the flesh hasn't, so to speak."

"Ew." Holly felt her whole face wrinkle in disgust. "That's revolting. And it means that I could go back as anyone. A tramp, an old woman, a dog . . ."

"Technically that's right," Dr. Hill said. "But on the bright side, you'll be pleased to know it's not that random. I've managed to find you a body that's almost the same age as you, and even works for your old company. Isn't that wonderful?"

"I don't know." Holly cautiously peered at him from under her lashes. "What's her name?"

"It's not a her. It's a him. And his name is Vince Murphy."

Holly's spine stiffened. "That doesn't make any sense. You can't put me in a guy's body. Especially not someone like him. How will I be able to find out what happened to me? Speak to Todd? Get my engagement ring? I don't understand."

"I'm sorry." Dr. Hill shrugged. "But that's the best I can do for you."

"No." Holly folded her arms in front of her chest and shot him a mulish look. "This is ridiculous. You can't send me back as a guy. There must be some alternative. How about more inkblots? Hypnosis? Anything."

"There is one alternative."

"I knew it." Holly felt a flood of relief run through her. "Once when I tried to return a navy skirt to that shop on Maine Street, the sales assistant refused because I didn't have a receipt. But there was no way I was giving up. You should've seen what happened to it in the wash. Sometimes you just need to keep asking until you get what you want."

Dr. Hill scratched his head. "Er, right. So, anyway, the reason I didn't mention this alternative is because it's not very good. Can you imagine what hell looks like?"

"I have a rough idea," Holly answered cautiously.

"Well, take that image and double it. Then double it again. Hell is two levels down, and it's a long, sweaty way to get back up to where you were."

"Oh." Holly chewed on her lip and gulped. "You see, that didn't happen with my skirt. The manager just ended up giving me a gift voucher."

"I'm sorry, Miss Evans, but this is a bit different."

Yes, so it would seem. Holly blew out a column of

imaginary air and tried not to panic. She really had managed to get herself between a rock and a hard place on this one, and she couldn't help but think how much easier it would've been if she'd just kept her mouth shut during her funeral. "So there really isn't any other option?" she double-checked, but Dr. Hill shook his auburn head.

"I'm afraid not. What's it going to be?"

Holly closed her eyes. She couldn't believe she was about to agree to this, but it didn't seem like she had much of a choice. Besides, perhaps he was right? She would feel a whole lot better when she found out what had really happened.

"Fine."

"I think you've made the right choice." Dr. Hill nodded as he tapped something into the computer. "Now, you might want to close your eyes for this. It can make some people a little bit . . . dizzy."

"Oh, but there's one other—" Holly started to say before once again she felt herself falling through a long white tunnel, where no doubt Vince Murphy's body was awaiting her. Who would've thought that it could get worse than dying?

Three

The first thing that hit Holly was the smell. She took in a lungful of air and tried to untangle the different bouquets around her. Ah, that was the aroma of fragrant roses drifting past her. Yes, and there was the tang of perfume and aftershave mingling in the air, and then there was . . . the disgusting smell of male body odor.

"Come on, Vince, what do you say?"

Holly blinked and realized she was surrounded by a group of computer geeks from the Baker Colwell technical department. And judging by the stench, they seemed to prefer to bathe in sweaty old gym socks rather than in water.

She tried to work out why she was feeling so disoriented when one of them hit her on the arm. If they kept that up then they'd get a squirt of pepper spray that they wouldn't forget in a hurry. Before she could look for it, another one started to speak.

"If we want to get this consolidation project finished by tonight, we'd better head off."

Since Holly had no idea what a consolidation project was, she stared at him blankly before glancing around in an attempt to figure out what was going on. The first things she caught sight of were all the gravestones in the background. Perhaps it was a Halloween party? That would explain why the guys in front of her were so badly dressed.

"Well, Vince?" The tallest of the guys shot her a questioning look. "Are you coming or what?"

Yeah, right. Holly snorted. As if she'd hang out with them. And why were they calling her Vince?

"Just leave him here, man," another one said. "He can catch up with us later."

Holly winced as four sets of hands thumped her on the back by way of good-bye before a small glimmer of something ridiculous forced its way into her brain. In fact, it was beyond ridiculous. Beyond crazy. But it wouldn't go away, so she peered down at her shoes for confirmation.

Her feet—once a nice size seven—were now about a ten, and they were covered in a pair of black Doc Martens.

She stretched out her hands and almost screamed. They were so big and . . . *How disgusting!* Was that grease on them? Then she touched her chest as the familiar feel of her heartbeat rapped out a tattoo. She'd forgotten how loud it could be. As for the fact her boobs were no longer there, well, she was going to totally ignore that, because surely no good could come from it.

Holly took a moment to digest everything. She was dead and had come back to earth as Vince Murphy. It was not great news.

All around her people were milling about in groups.

After the relatively silent surroundings of Level One, Holly found their voices loud and grating and could finally start to appreciate why her constant commentary had been driving people crazy.

She was just about to look for some peace and quiet when she caught sight of Gemma walking straight toward her.

Thank goodness for a familiar face. Especially since it helped jog Holly's memory of why she was back down on earth. She had a job to do, and she didn't have much time.

"Gem," Holly squeaked as she stuck out her arms and launched herself in her friend's direction. "Oh, my God, I'm so pleased to see you. You won't—"

"Are you insane?" Gemma demanded with the glacial-bitch stare she'd spent all of last Christmas perfecting.

"Of course not." Holly wrinkled her nose as she dropped her arms back down to her side. "It's just . . . I've been dying to—"

"Make a pass at me just seconds after Holly's coffin has been lowered into the ground?" Gemma interrupted with a stamp of her foot. "Honestly, what is it with you technicians? I just can't believe you would try something like this today."

"What?" Holly said, but before she could even finish her sentence, Gemma turned on her gorgeous pink suede wedges and headed toward the graveyard gates.

Holly hurried after her, but as the weight of the Doc Martens combined with the length of her muscular legs hit her, she suddenly remembered what had triggered Gemma's apparent visit to Crazyville.

She was Vince.

Well, no, she was Holly. But to the outside world she was definitely Vince.

What a nightmare. And what was the point of this whole manual purging if she couldn't even convince her best friend who she was? It just seemed to be yet another example of a celestial screwup. Well, Holly had worked under bad management before, when she'd done a summer internship in her first year of college, and she'd quickly learned that the only way to succeed was to just get on with it as best you could.

She pushed her way through the crowd of mourners. Ah, there was Gemma, over by that strange-looking mausoleum . . . *talking to Todd.*

For a moment Holly's heart skipped a beat as her eyes feasted on how divine he was: all rippling muscles and square jaw. He was wearing the chocolate brown suit he'd bought for his sister's wedding last month, and the white linen shirt he had underneath looked cool and crisp against his olive skin.

Sometimes Holly had to pinch herself at how lucky she was. Not only was Todd gorgeous, but he was also going places. Everyone knew that if you got promoted to senior account manager on the fourth floor then you could virtually rubber-stamp yourself a six-figure salary by the time you were thirty. And Todd, at twenty-four, was the youngest employee at Baker Colwell to be promoted to that position. Brains and a hot body. What was there not to love?

Holly realized he was looking at her, so she made her way toward them.

"Gemma, Todd, you won't—"

"Save it," Todd cut her off. "We may work together but we're not friends. As for hitting on someone at a funeral, well, that's just—"

"Todd, you don't understand," Holly started to explain. "I know Gemma thought I was trying to . . . well whatever . . . but the thing is, it's a bit more complicated, and—"

"That's where you're wrong, buddy," he growled. "So just get lost, okay.

Holly stared. This situation was intolerable.

All she wanted to do was tell him how sorry she was about their fight. That it was stupid and completely her fault, and, if he happened to have the ring in his pocket, perhaps she could just try it on once for size? But instead she was standing right in front of the love of her life and unable to explain anything.

"Well?" He glared, and Holly accepted that there was no use trying to talk to him in this mood. Besides, she'd just caught sight of her stepmother over by a beech tree, and it dawned on her just how totally unprepared she was for this whole situation.

"Fine." She raised a reluctant hand. "I didn't come to cause a scene, so I'll get going."

"Good. Make sure you do."

Holly turned and headed away from where her body was buried. Finding out that her boyfriend wouldn't give her the time of day was the icing on the cake.

Holly tapped her fingers impatiently. She had spent the last of Vince's cash on a hamburger and fries. Funny—

after almost two weeks of not eating, she thought this would taste better. Then she had headed back to her old apartment, only to discover her roommates were all out (no doubt at her funeral), and the spare key was no longer hidden under a brick near the trash cans. Next time she died and came back to earth, she really must remember to bring her door keys with her.

Now Holly sat on a bench underneath the huge syca-more tree outside Gemma's apartment.

Surely her friend couldn't be too much longer. Holly hadn't quite figured out the finer details of how she was going to convince her of the truth, but she was certain she would figure something out.

They'd been friends ever since they'd both turned up on the first day at Baker Colwell wearing identical suits and black stilettos complete with little bow detailing. They had had so much in common, there was no way Gemma wouldn't recognize who she was now. Or at least eventually.

Ten minutes later her friend turned the corner and came into sight. She was limping slightly, probably thanks to her new shoes, but apart from that she looked exactly the same as she had thirteen days ago. Well, per-haps she was a bit more pissed off than she had been back then. . . .

"What the hell are you doing here?" Gemma de-manded as she put her hands on her hips and glared. "You know there's a strict company policy on stalking."

"What?" Holly said, before remembering that she couldn't be distracted. She was on a mission here and needed to concentrate. "I mean, I'll tell you why I'm here. And . . . well . . . I don't really have much time and there's not an easy way to say it, so I'll just spit it out. I'm Holly."

Gemma let out a bark of laughter. "Jeez, what is wrong with you? Have you been drinking? I know funerals make people a bit weird, but this is a ten on the Richter scale. It's not funny."

Boy, she could say that again. Holly took a deep breath. "Gem, it's true. It's me. I know it sounds ridiculous, but the Cliff's Notes version is that I've been sent down from heaven for two days in someone else's body."

"You're damn right it sounds ridiculous." Gemma folded her arms and glared.

Yep, it was really going well. "Okay, so why don't you ask me any question you want?" Holly licked her lips and tried to keep the desperation out of her voice. "Something only I . . . I mean, something only Holly would know the answer to, and then you'll see."

"I'll see you getting arrested," her friend retorted.

Oh, crap. Holly winced. So much for her brilliant plan.

"I mean it." Gemma fumbled around in her purse, presumably for her phone.

"Your last serious boyfriend was Gavin Rivers, but you broke up with him at Christmas because he had been cheating on you," Holly blurted out in a rush.

Gemma lowered her hand and stared. "Who told you that?"

"You did."

"Yeah, right, because I tell you technicians about all my dates."

"No, you tell Holly Evans about all your dates. What about the fact that you have a secret crush on Simon Trimmer, and when he accidentally touched your leg in the staff cafeteria last month you sent me a text message to tell me how hot he was? You have high hopes he's going to ask you on a date any day now."

"Oh, my God. So you're the creep who stole Holly's phone the day after she died, and now you think it's funny to have read her text messages. Well, I can tell you something for nothing, Vince Murphy: You're one sick guy."

"No." Holly scowled in frustration. "Of course, I . . . wait . . . someone stole my phone? Oh, man, I hope they didn't see the photo of us lifting up our shirts after we'd drunk that bottle of wine, because I looked so fat in that. How embarrassing."

Gemma's mouth fell open and she widened her eyes. "Okay, so now you're starting to freak me out. I deleted all those photos before the phone was stolen. So if you did steal it then there's no way you'd know about them."

"Unless I was Holly."

Gemma narrowed her pale blue eyes and folded her arms tightly around her waist. "Fine, so if you really are Holly, you won't mind answering a few questions then."

"Shoot."

"Do I prefer George Clooney or Brad Pitt?"

"Trick question, because you don't like either of them; your heart always has and always will belong to David Boreanaz."

"What's my favorite color?" Gemma demanded in a firm voice.

27

"Green, because you think it suits your hair, but to be honest I've always thought blue looked better on you. Especially that Gap blouse that you like to wear with your True Religion jeans."

Gemma started to look a little less comfortable. "A-and what was the name of the concert Holly and I went to see last November?"

Holly felt a lump form in her throat. "We went to see U2 and you still have the ticket stubs at the back of your drawer, along with the pressed flower your very first boyfriend gave you. It was a yellow rose."

"H-Holly?" Gemma said in a whisper. "But I don't—"

"Me either," Holly finished. "None of this makes any sense at all. Especially the waking-up-dead part. But it really is me." Holly could feel the tears pouring down her face.

"How can this be happening?" Gemma said in a shell-shocked voice. "I saw you in the coffin; how could you now be alive?"

"That's because heaven is complicated. It has even more rules than a Baker Colwell Staff Incentive Fun Day, and it's twice as boring. But the thing is, I still have some earthly issues to get sorted out, and until I can do that they won't let me move up through the levels."

"Heaven? Levels? I think I'm struggling here." Gemma shot her a bewildered look as she dropped down onto the bench next to Holly. "I want to believe you, but—"

"But it doesn't make any sense," Holly finished with a sigh. "Tell me about it. And you haven't even heard the rest of it yet. . . ."

✝

"So let me get this straight: You've been put into therapy and given a two-day pass back to earth?" Gemma said several minutes later, once Holly had explained it as best she could.

"I guess you could say that."

Gemma shook her head. "The whole thing is extraordinary. Who knew that heaven was such a bureaucracy?"

"Yes, and they certainly keep all this body-swapping business quiet." Holly snorted.

"It does take a bit of getting used to," Gemma agreed. "Oh, Lord, I feel so bad that I didn't believe you sooner."

Holly sniffed. "I probably wouldn't have believed it either, but at least you know now. That's all that matters."

"Er, I'm afraid that's not exactly true." Gemma winced as she searched for her phone and frantically started to stab in a number. "You see, when I saw you sitting outside my apartment I panicked a bit."

"It's okay," Holly tried to reassure her. "I'm honestly not mad."

"I thought you were stalking me, which is why I called Todd. He should be here any minute," Gemma said miserably. "And he didn't sound happy."

Of course he didn't. Holly groaned. On a day like this, it made complete sense.

Four

"This will be him," Gemma said ten minutes later as some-one knocked on the apartment door. Despite her urgent calls, Gemma hadn't been able to get back through to Todd's cell phone to let him know everything was okay. "So what do you want to do?"

She really should have just kept her big mouth shut when she was up in heaven and then none of this would be happening. Tyrone had certainly warned her enough times. Why hadn't she just listened to him? Perhaps if he'd given her a heads-up on the whole being-shoved-into-a-guy's-body thing, she might've paid a bit more attention.

There was another knock on the door. "Well?" Gemma said.

Holly twisted the fringe of Gemma's bedspread as she tried to decide. Half of her longed to throw herself at him, but the other half (possibly the half with the better self-preservation skills) wasn't so keen on the idea of get-ting punched.

"Just tell him you made a mistake and that I'm not here."

Gemma raised an eyebrow. "Since when do you lie to Todd?"

Holly twitched her lips before glancing down at her long, lean legs.

"Oh, yeah, good point," her friend conceded. "But perhaps you should explain it now and get it over with?"

Holly had been thinking the same thing, but had reluctantly dismissed the idea, since it was becoming more and more obvious that she wasn't going to get very far on her mission if she didn't have a bulletproof plan. The only thing worse than not talking to Todd now was talking to him and screwing the whole thing up even more.

"I'm sure," she said firmly. "Now go and tell him . . . but act casual . . . and smooth down your blouse; it's wrinkled on top."

Gemma snorted. "Well, at least I know you're definitely Holly; only she would say something like that at a time like this."

Holly sighed as her friend left the room. If only it would be so easy to convince Todd.

It was no good. No matter how hard Holly tried, she couldn't hear a damn word that was being said, and unless she wanted to open the bedroom door and risk getting her face punched by the man of her dreams, she was just going to have to wait until Gemma came back.

She padded back across to the dressing table, just like she used to. *Gosh, that's a nice lipstick. Sort of like a lip gloss but with a matte finish. Interesting.*

"It's all done." Gemma pushed the bedroom door

open. "I just told him I'd made a mistake and . . . Holly, what are you doing?"

"I'm trying on your lipstick. Is it new? Anyway, tell me everything. Did he . . . *What*? Why are you looking at me like that? Is there a problem?" Holly frowned. It wasn't like Gemma to worry about a bit of makeup.

"Yes, there's a problem. I don't think Tropical Pink Crush really goes with your stubble."

"What . . . ? Oh, crap." Holly groaned as she looked in the mirror. This was ridiculous. She could not spend the next two days in Vince Murphy's body.

She reached over for the makeup remover and quickly smeared it on her face. Except it wasn't her face at all. Gone were the brown eyes with the heavy lashes, the pointed chin, and the nose that was slightly crooked. And instead staring back at her was Vince Murphy.

It was going to take a bit of getting used to. Though, really, if you took away the attitude he wasn't such a bad-looking fellow. He could use some sun, but despite his pale face he had a nice pair of blue eyes and light brown hair that flipped and flopped all over the place. She puckered her lips. They were quite full, weren't they? Weird that she'd never noticed before.

"Are you okay?" Gemma was looking at her strangely, and Holly realized she'd been checking out her own face. Well, Vince's face. Which was sort of her face, since she was the one inside. She finished wiping the makeup off and quickly turned away from the mirror.

"Just pretend you didn't see that," Holly advised as she sat back down on the bed.

"It's forgotten," Gemma readily agreed. "The good

news is that Todd seemed to believe I'd made a mistake, which means we can now get down to working out a plan. What should we do first?"

Holly paused for a moment and rubbed her chin, trying to ignore Vince's one-day stubble. He could've at least shaved for her funeral. "Well, the sooner I can find out just how I really died, the sooner I can start convincing everyone of the truth. Especially Todd, so I suppose we'd better figure out how those pills got in my system."

Gemma blanched as she reached for a diamante-studded diary next to her bed. "So pills it is. We need to work out whether someone purposely gave them to you, or if you took them by accident."

Holly sighed. Not that she'd really remembered too much of it at the time, but when she first arrived on Level One, disjointed images had started to come back to her. Dying wasn't much fun. It was very uncomfortable.

"Your stepmother told me they'd found Dimen-hydrinate in your system, and apparently the drug is most commonly used in motion-sickness pills. Here." Gemma ripped the page out and handed it over. "These are my notes. They couldn't be certain of the dosage, but thought it was probably the equivalent of about four pills—not enough to kill you, just enough to make you drowsy. Oh, and they're not prescription, so anyone can get them."

"Great." Holly shoved the piece of paper into Vince's jacket and thumped in frustration the heart pillow she had been hugging. "This narrows it down to just about anyone."

Gemma reached over and grabbed the cushion from

Holly's tight grip. "I'd better take this. Now that you have this man-strength, we need to be careful with you."

Holly looked at the misshapen cushion and blushed. "Sorry, it's just so frustrating."

"I know. I mean, you're dead. You've got every right to be frustrated. It's not really all doom and gloom, since the person who gave the pills to you—either intentionally or otherwise—might still have them. After all, why would they get rid of them when there's no need to? It's not like the cast of *CSI* is going to come crashing through their door with rubber gloves and fingerprint kits."

"Good point." Holly brightened up. Okay, so it was a long shot, but at least there was still a chance, and if she had to search everyone's desk to find the pills, then she would do it. She sent her friend a grateful smile. "Gem, thanks for this. It's so nice to be around someone who's on my side. The people in heaven were saying I'd killed myself, and I guess I was starting to believe it. Especially after, well . . ."

"Hey," Gemma said firmly. "It's got nothing to do with this. For a start it was six years ago. A lot of kids do weird stuff when they're teenagers. It's just the hormones. Try to just forget about it."

"I thought I had," Holly admitted as she looked down at the smooth skin on her wrists. Well, that was one advantage of being in Vince's body: She didn't have a constant reminder of a past she would rather forget.

The shrinks had called it self-harming, but to Holly it had been the only way that she could get out all the frustration trapped in her body. The worst thing was that she'd worked so hard in the last few years to make amends for her lapse in wisdom, and now it had all been undone in one fell swoop.

"It's true," Gemma insisted.

"It was hard enough convincing people that I didn't do it intentionally back then. This time the evidence is sort of compelling, and people begin to think, Where there's smoke there's fire."

"For a start, hardly anyone knows about what you did back then anyway. When you were alive you couldn't even see the scars unless you were looking, so enough of the self-pity here. Of course it's going to work out. It always does. Remember what we always do when things look bad?"

"Accessorize?"

"No." Gemma glared. "We rise above it. We're going to work out how the pills got in your body, figure out a way for you to make up with Todd, and then you can prove all those people up on Level One wrong."

"You're right." Holly perked up at the idea. Okay, so perhaps revenge wasn't the best of motives, but it was satisfying. She was sure even Dr. Alan Hill would approve. In fact, it might be a legitimate part of her therapy.

"Okay." Gemma chewed on the end of her pencil for a moment. "The first thing we need to do is find out how long the pills were in your system before you died, and then we need to retrace your steps to work out who you came in contact with around that same time."

Holly stood up and padded across to where Gemma's laptop was perched. "That's a great idea. I'll get on the Net and see what I can find." But before she even powered the computer up, the door opened and Gemma's roommate, Irene, poked her head in.

"Hey, Gem, I know you've just come back from the funeral, but I was wondering . . . Oh, I didn't realize you had company. . . ." Irene trailed off in a mournful voice.

"Hey, there!" Holly said in the same overbright tone she always used when she met Irene. Not that it ever worked, since Gemma's roommate was in a permanent state of misery. Holly studied the girl's droopy mouth and doleful-looking eyes. In fact, the only things that were upbeat about Irene were her trust fund and her great taste in soft furnishings.

"Hello." Irene let out a heartfelt sigh before turning to Gemma. "I didn't mean to interrupt. I'll go into my bedroom so I don't disturb you."

"Irene, of course you don't need to go into your bedroom. It's not like we're using the living room or kitchen." Gemma jumped to her feet and hurried over to her roommate, gently directing her toward the door.

"No." Cue another drawn-out sigh. "I'd only be in the way, and I'd hate to stop anyone else from having fun. . . ."

"Don't be stupid . . ." Holly started to say before Gemma gave a warning shake of her head and mouthed, *No.*

"It's true." Irene's bottom lip started to tremble as she escaped from Gemma's clutches and dropped down into the cane chair by the dresser. "I'm always in the way. That's what my ex-boyfriend Dave used to say. And my other ex-boyfriend Ethan, and—"

Oh, yeah, Holly had forgotten that Irene wasn't just miserable; she liked to talk about her misery. A lot. Irene got comfortable. So much for Holly's plans to stay here and do some research. At this rate the only thing she would be researching was just how tough Irene's full-expenses-paid-by-her-parents life was. Well, she should try being dead for a while and then see what misery was all about.

Holly coughed. "Actually, Gemma, I'd better go."

"See?" Irene wailed as she threw herself prostrate on the floor. "I told you I was in the way. Why does everyone hate me?"

Holly figured this was as good a time as any to leave.

"Sorry she freaked out like that," Gemma whispered as she walked Holly outside. "She's just a bit—"

"Insane? Miserable? Passive-aggressive?"

Gemma's shoulders slumped. "Yes to all three."

"You know, Gem, you really can't keep living here, no matter how cheap the rent or how great the free cable is."

"Yes, well, that's easier said than done, since the person I was going to move in with died recently."

"Oh, God, I'd forgotten about that." Holly moaned as she thought about how they'd planned to move in together when their current leases expired. While Holly's roommates might not be as bad as Irene, they had a few funny ideas when it came to how the phone bill should be split.

She and Gemma had even started apartment hunting at some of the cute places down by the river. Then, when she and Todd got married, she would move in with him and Gemma would no doubt be planning her own wedding. It had been absolutely foolproof. Well, so she thought. Once again, this whole being-dead business had ruined everything.

"Don't be so hard on yourself," Gemma advised. "Besides, there will be plenty of time to worry about my housing situation after we've sorted out your issues. I'm just sorry you can't stay here while we come up with a plan. Irene is going to freak when I tell her I have to go out."

Holly shuddered at the idea of a freaked Crazy Irene. "Look, it's probably best if you stay in, because otherwise she might make your life hell."

"Yes, but you don't have much time to clear up everything. Do you really think you can do it on your own?"

"Yes."

No.

She had to admit that after convincing Gemma of who she was, she'd thought things would start to get easier, but Irene turning up had thrown a wrench in those particular works.

"So where are you going?"

That was a tough question. Obviously Todd's house was out. Her roommates wouldn't be back yet, and there was no way she was going to her stepmother's house. Which left only one place.

"I suppose I could go to Baker Colwell. Vince's ID badge is in his pocket. At least I can use the computers and do some research on the Internet before working out what my last steps were. Then I could make a list of anyone who might have a grudge against me and check out their personnel files. You never know; someone might be married to a pharmacist or a pilot who uses the pills himself when he's traveling."

"I didn't think you were allowed to go through the personnel files like that," Gemma protested with a frown.

"Well, you're not allowed to slip pills to other people either, but that didn't stop someone from doing it," Holly retorted. "Besides, I only have computer clearance to look at the basic stuff. But you must admit, it's a start."

"You're right," Gemma apologized. "And if we need it, tomorrow I'll go and see Jeremy about clearance. He owes me a favor, since I organized weekly neck massages for all of his department."

"Thank you."

"I knew I'd moved to human resources for a reason." Gemma grinned.

When her friend had first decided not to stay in the more competitive executive training program, Holly had thought she was crazy. Now she was just grateful that Gemma wasn't as ambitious if it meant she could call in a favor.

"Thanks, Gem. You're the best." Holly reached over and squeezed her hand.

"It's nothing," Gemma said gruffly. "If I'd come back from the dead in someone else's body and I wanted to sort my life out, I know you'd do the same for me."

"Of course I would," Holly agreed as a loud wailing noise came from the upstairs apartment. Holly quickly let go of her friend's hand as she realized Irene's woe-stricken face was pressed up against the windowpane.

"You'd better go, before her head starts spinning around."

"I just feel so bad that you can't stay."

Holly crossed her legs and shook her head. No way did she want to be in the same house as Irene and her misery. She'd seen Kathy Bates in that Stephen King movie, and it was a slippery slope. "I'll be fine. After all, I've been kicked out of heaven, turned into a guy, and my fiancé almost beat me up. I'd say the worst of the day is over."

Five

Holly waited until Gemma had shut the door before turning and heading for the Baker Colwell head office. The August evening was sultry and warm, and she shrugged off the heavy black jacket that Vince Murphy seemed to have surgically connected to himself. Ah, that was better, though, boy, the gray T-shirt seemed a bit tight. Holly neatly tucked it in, then glanced at her arm and was surprised to see a bulging biceps staring back at her.

Vince Murphy worked out. *Well, how about that?*

Then she wondered if it was weird to be staring at her own arms. Actually, this whole thing was still a bit too weird for her liking. Thank goodness she had convinced Gemma of the truth, but how on earth was she going to explain it to Todd when she saw him tomorrow? And what was she going to say to her roommates when she went back home to sleep? It probably would've been better all around if Irene had been away on business for the week.

She slung her jacket over her shoulder. Actually this man-strength was quite handy, because it felt as if she were holding only a flimsy bit of cotton rather than half an animal hide.

And was someone *following* her?

Holly glanced around just in time to see two strange guys waving frantically at her. She increased her pace, but the next time she looked back they were still there, and so she sped up some more. *What the . . . ?*

The panic flooded through her as she remembered each and every one of her stepmother's boring lectures on being careful when she was walking on her own. Not that Holly had ever bothered to listen to them, since stuff like that happened only to other people.

Normally in the movies.

Of course, that was what she used to think about premature death as well. She quickened her pace as the reality started to hit home. Had she really come all the way from heaven just to be mugged?

Behind her she could hear them calling out to her, but she had no desire to turn back and see what they were saying as she dashed across the road. Fortunately, at that moment a truck drove past, and while their vision was blocked she darted around the corner, down Grafton Street, and into the corporate splendor that was Baker Colwell's head office.

That was a close call, but at least she was out of danger, and she fumbled around in Vince's jacket until she found his ID card and ran it through the machine. She was further relieved when the night watchman did nothing more than shoot her a cursory glance before returning his attention back to the game on TV.

It wasn't until she was in the elevator that she felt herself start to relax. Honestly, this was just getting ridiculous, and she was starting to wonder if she really had been sent back to earth at all. What if she was in some sort of alternate-reality game and a spotty fourteen-year-old kid called Kevin was getting to platform ten by making her suffer through all these things? It sounded a bit extreme, but as she stared down at Vince's long legs, it was no less realistic.

She stepped out of the elevator and was pleased to see that the third floor was virtually empty. She would like to think it was out of respect for her funeral that there were none of the regular "working eight till eight is great" crowd, but she had a feeling it was because the CEO was out of the office for the next week. Even the most dedicated Baker Colwell workers tended to take it easier when the head honcho wasn't around to witness their dedication.

At least there was something soothing about being back here. For the last year her life had revolved around Baker Colwell, and even when she wasn't working she was normally with either Gemma or Todd, so the conversation often drifted back to the place. She tried to fight back the nostalgia as she hurried across to her cubicle. The last time she had been here was when she was alive.

Her desk was just the way she had left it: pens lined up, stapler to the left, and her neatly written to-do list ready for when she came into work on Monday morning. Except there hadn't been a Monday morning, or a to-do list. It was all Level One rules, dead people, and manual purges. Life seemed a whole lot simpler when she'd been alive.

She sat down at her chair and adjusted it for Vince's

larger frame. She might not have a chance to do all the tasks that were written on her list, but she was definitely going to make sure she got her issues sorted out. Okay, so there wasn't much time, but she had always prided herself on being organized. It was what had helped her achieve so much.

Holly flicked on her computer and entered her password, only to be greeted with a flashing icon telling her that her user name wasn't valid.

Well, that couldn't be right. She frowned for a moment before realizing she had been taken off the system. So soon? Of course, the Baker Colwell motto was that efficiency was the way of the future. But still, shouldn't there be a period of mourning before these things happened? And why change her password but not pack away her desk?

Luckily she knew Gemma's password, and she tapped it in. Her first stop was the Internet to look up the motion-sickness pills, but all she could discover was that taking too many could result in illness and occasionally death. Like, tell her something she didn't know.

She scanned down the page. It seemed that the effects of the pills could last from four to eight hours, so it looked like she was going to have to map her movements for most of the Friday. Hmm, well, that shouldn't be too hard. She opened up a Word document.

Ten minutes later she printed it out and had to say that it didn't look promising. Nothing really stood out at her to announce that it was at this point she'd ingested four motion-sickness pills, which had led to her falling asleep in the bath and ruining her life forever.

Perhaps Gemma would be able to make more sense of it tomorrow? She shoved it into the pocket of Vince's jacket and decided that while she was here, she might as well have a snoop through the personnel files and see what she could find.

She entered a search for anyone with a criminal past and a particular preference for drugging people.

Unsurprisingly she didn't get any results.

Holly chewed at her bottom lip as she tried to figure out who would do this. Perhaps she had accidentally spilled something on the cafeteria floor and the cleaner had taken an unwholesome dislike to her from that moment on? Or someone had taken exception to the way she poured her milk into her coffee cup before adding the hot water, or . . .

At that moment Holly glanced over to her to-do list again and caught sight of her neat handwriting reminding her of her presentation on Monday. Holly had been in her new job for only a month, so this was her first important project, and she'd worked extra hard to make sure everything about it was perfect. Pity she hadn't factored in dying.

She sniffed again. It was such a great job as well—okay, so finance operations was a little on the hard side, but still great. Gemma had thought Holly was rushing things, applying for a promotion only a year after joining the company, but Todd had said it was important to show her bosses that she was a player who wanted to make something of herself.

Holly agreed, especially since she *had* wanted to make something of herself. Which was why she'd bought the most adorable black ankle-strap shoes to celebrate. After all, how could you climb the corporate ladder without a good pair of heels?

Oh, and she'd bet Tina MacDonald was finding it hilarious that Holly didn't manage to do her presentation, since it was no secret Tina thought the promotion should've been hers. She'd even gone as far as complaining to personnel about an unfair interview process. *Yeah, right.* As if Tina had the calves for ankle-strap shoes, and—

Oh, my God.

Motive.

Holly was perfectly still as she realized she had just figured out who had slipped her the pills. Good-bye, earthly issues and Level One. She knew all it would take was a little application and organization. Wait until she told Gemma about it.

Oh, and it made even more sense, because she specifically recalled that the morning she died—on the pretense of being nice—Tina had given Holly a cup of coffee when they'd been in the staff room. Even though at the time it had tasted perfectly normal, it was now obvious Tina had laced it with pills so Holly would be forced to cancel her presentation and perhaps risk getting demoted. It all added up nicely.

She turned off her computer, tidied up her desk, and, out of habit, reached into the bottom drawer to grab her latest *Bride and Beauty* magazine (in case she had problems sleeping) and headed toward the elevator.

It wasn't until she was outside the building that she congratulated herself on being such a genius in working it out. Of course, she had always been clever. She thought back to *The Rich and the Restless,* her favorite soap opera, where everyone was convinced Joanne and Carlos were going to get together, but Holly had been adamant Lee would win out in the end. And she had been right.

Being right was such a nice feeling, and she was still basking in it as she sat down at the nearby bus stop and searched Vince's pockets to find a cell phone to call Gemma.

It didn't take long to stab in her friend's number, but there was no answer, and Holly cursed. The sooner she got Tina's address, the sooner she could confront the girl and put a stop to the suicide rumors. Then tomorrow she could concentrate on clearing the air with Todd. Well, it wasn't her typical to-do list, but then, it wasn't a typical day.

"In fact, it's probably been the weirdest day of my life," she muttered to herself as she drummed her fingers on the magazine.

"I'll say," a disembodied voice replied.

"What? Who said that?" Holly jumped back to her feet again and spun around, only to see nothing except an empty street and a candy wrapper blowing in the breeze. Well, that was strange. And why did she suddenly feel so . . . *weird*?

"What's going on?" the same voice demanded.

"That's what I'd like to know." Holly tried to stay calm. After all, she was dead. Technically nothing bad could happen to her. Could it?

"Ideas would be welcome," the voice continued with a hint of impatience.

"Who are you?" Holly croaked as she clutched at her throat. It almost sounded like the words were coming from inside her. But that was just impossible.

"I'm Vince; who are you? And more important, what the hell are you doing in my body?"

"What do you mean, you're Vince? Vince is dead," Holly said into the thin air, feeling more than just a little bit silly (and considering the past two weeks, that was really saying something).

"I'm dead?" The voice sounded surprised. "Are you sure? Because I don't feel dead. Perhaps I'm just having some sort of weird dream? I get them sometimes."

"No, you're definitely dead."

"Oh, so this is heaven? Because I've got to say, I expected more. This place looks like the bus stop outside Baker Colwell."

"Of course it's not heaven," Holly scoffed. For a start there were no dead people around. Sort of a giveaway. Though she still wasn't quite sure why she was having a conversation with Vince's body.

"So it's hell then?" the voice continued to probe. Was Vince's body always this annoying in a conversation?

"No," she explained. "It looks like the bus stop outside Baker Colwell because it *is* the bus stop outside Baker Colwell."

"Right. So how did I get from the funeral to here?"

Wait. This was getting ridiculous. Surely she wasn't really having this conversation. Perhaps if she closed her eyes, the voice would go away.

The problem was, not only did the voice make her feel weird, but something strange was happening to her leg as well. It felt . . . *twitchy*.

An uneasy feeling lodged itself in her stomach, which she tried to ignore. Surely this was just a side effect from

Dr. Hill's plan, and no doubt if she'd read the rulebook she would know all about strange voices and twitchy sensation in her leg.

She gave her thigh a wriggle.

"Hey," the voice said. "How did you do that?"

Holly started to sing the latest Coldplay song in her head. It had come out only a week before she died, so she didn't know all the words, but at least it would stop this voice from talking.

Then her other leg wriggled. All by itself.

Holly stopped singing and clutched at her thigh. And now spasms? This was so not her day. "What the hell's going on?" she croaked as she found herself sitting back down on the bench.

"That's what I want to know. One minute I'm at Holly's funeral, and the next minute I am at the bus stop outside Baker Colwell. It doesn't make sense."

Holly felt her hand reach up to her lips and gulped as a thought too startling and dreadful for words entered her head.

No.

It wasn't possible.

It couldn't be happening.

"Actually it is," another voice said, and for a moment Holly clutched at her head.

"Don't tell me there's someone else inside here too, because I don't think I'm going to handle it very well," she said.

"Of course not." Dr. Hill appeared from nowhere and sat next to her at the bus stop. "I'm right here."

Holly let out a sigh of relief. "Boy, am I glad to see

you. You won't believe what's just happened. For a moment I was starting to think Vince Murphy was still alive and in my body."

Her leg shot out from under her and there was a growling noise from her throat. "Actually I think you'll find it's *my* body. Can someone *please* tell me what's going on?"

"Of course." The doctor gave a small cough. "It's quite simple. Miss Evans, it appears that Mr. Murphy is in his body with you. At first it wasn't obvious because he was in a catatonic state, which made us think he was dead, but, well . . . the good news is that he's all better."

"And the bad news?" Holly could now feel the disbelief oozing out of every pore of her body. *Oh, no, wait. Make that Vince Murphy's body.*

"I don't think you're going to like the bad news." Dr. Hill let out a sigh as he started to explain what had happened.

Six

"What do you mean, you've stuck me in the body of someone who was only *nearly* dead?" Holly wasn't sure whether to laugh or burst into hysterical tears once Dr. Hill finished explaining everything. "How is this possible?"

Vince coughed. "Actually, I know the answer to that. I think I fainted."

"You fainted?" Holly echoed as she turned to Dr. Hill in disbelief. "So Vince isn't sick at all, and this whole mess is because my *spiritual realigner* couldn't tell the difference between a faint and death?"

Dr. Hill started to fiddle with the fancy cuffs at the end of his white shirt. "Okay." He suddenly threw his hands up in the air. "I admit it. I made one tiny little mistake. It could've happened to anyone."

Holly could only stare at him. "I'm sorry; I'm trying to stay calm about this whole thing, but it's not working. Don't you think it's hard enough for me to have come down here for two days to try to sort out all of my earthly issues while stuck in a guy's body, without now telling me I have to share the body *with* the guy?"

"I think we're forgetting who's the victim here. I fainted for, what—a *second* or two—and wham, my body gets snatched."

Holly uncrossed her arms and put her hands on her hips. "Okay, so I know this might be a shock, but at least you only looked like you were dead. I'm going to *be* dead forever. Surely letting me use your body for two days isn't really so bad in the big scheme of things?"

"Not if you want to tuck my shirt in like this. And don't think I can't smell the perfume either," Vince retorted.

"It was a mistake," the doctor repeated. "It does happen from time to time, you know. After all, I'm only human."

"No, you're not," Holly reminded him. "You told me you'd been dead for two hundred years. And you still haven't said what you're going to do to fix this mess."

The doctor rubbed his temples. "That's the whole problem. There isn't anything I can do. The technology we used to get you into Mr. Murphy's body is very exact—"

"Apart from mistaking him for dead," Holly cut in, and she could feel Vince nodding his head in agreement.

"Yeah," he said.

Dr. Hill ignored them. "I'm sorry, but it can't be changed or altered. You won't leave his body until the planned time—the day after tomorrow at one o'clock in the afternoon."

"But that's ridiculous," Vince said.

"Impossible," Holly agreed. "You must be able to do something."

"Sorry." Dr. Hill shot her an apologetic look, which seemed to be aimed at both of them. "There's nothing I can do, except perhaps advise you both that the more you bicker, the worse this thing will be. You should be pleased you're body-sharing with someone you know."

"We went to school together for two years way back when. I know my mailman better." Holly failed to hide her disbelief.

"So think of this as a chance to catch up on old times then," Dr. Hill said with an overbright smile. "Oh, and would you look at the time? I really have to fly. I'm late for a meeting."

"No." Holly's disbelief was replaced by horror. "You can't go. You've got to help me. Please."

Dr. Hill twitched his lips before reluctantly admitting, "There is one alternative."

"Yes?" Holly snatched at his words like the first in line at a chocolate convention.

"First you have to imagine what hell looks like; then you need to double it and—"

Her excitement waned as she folded her arms and shot him a mulish look. "Is this going to be your alternative for everything?"

"I'm sorry, Miss Evans. I don't make the rules. So what's it to be?"

"Fine." Holly let out a reluctant sigh. She had the feeling it would be a bit harder to find Tina MacDonald and make up with Todd from the burning depths of hell.

"Excuse me," Vince interrupted. "I'm not so sure I

want to go along with anything this guy says. God knows who he might stuff in here next."

Holly put her hands on her hips. "I know this isn't ideal, but we'll just have to work around it."

"Work around what? The fact that there's another person in my body?" he demanded as once again she felt her arms being crossed.

"There's no need to get snotty," Holly retorted as she turned to finish her conversation with Dr. Hill, only to find he had disappeared from sight. "He's gone."

"And I didn't even get to thank him for putting someone else in my body." Vince's voice was laden with sarcasm.

Holly got up and began to pace.

"Okay, now is so not the time to panic," she instructed herself. "We just need to think this situation through. Yes, it's going to make getting back to heaven a bit more difficult, but with a bit of planning—"

Holly suddenly found herself moving back to the bus stop and sitting down with a thump.

"Stop all of that walking so I can get this straight," Vince said. "Are you seriously trying to tell me you've been in heaven and they've sent you down for a . . . a . . . well . . . *why* have they sent you down?"

Holly let out a sigh as some of her anger evaporated. "I guess this is even weirder for you than it is for me. The thing is, I sort of got kicked out of heaven. Don't laugh."

"Sorry," he said in a contrite voice as she felt him bite down on the fleshy part of his lip. "So coming back to earth is a punishment?"

When I'm stuck in someone else's body it is, she wanted to mutter, but sensing that it wouldn't help relations, she kept her thoughts to herself. "You see, the thing is, after I got kicked out I was sent to Dr. Hill. He's a—"

"Shrink?"

"Yeah. Though he calls himself a spiritual realigner. A spiritual screwup is more like it. Anyway, I didn't quite manage to shed all of my earthly issues when I died."

"What does that mean?"

Holly sighed. There was no point being coy about this, since she and Vince would be sharing more than just secrets. "I still get a bit annoyed when anyone says I committed suicide," she admitted. "Apparently it's a problem."

"I can't imagine anyone who knows you would believe that you committed suicide," Vince instantly said. "You're probably just sensitive because of that thing a few years ago, after your dad died."

"How did you know about that?" Holly couldn't hide her surprise. Until she started working at Baker Colwell she hadn't seen Vince for at least twelve years, and her self-harming was not something she liked to talk about very often. Or ever, even.

"I kept in touch with a few people after I moved away. Word gets around," Vince said in a gruff voice.

"Well, thanks for not believing I did it on purpose. But even though most people don't know about what happened back then, they still seem to think I killed myself this time. Which is why I need to rectify the situation. I also need to explain to Todd what really happened."

"Good luck with that. He's a jerk."

"Of course he's not." Holly felt herself bristle again. "You're just saying that because you're jealous of him. He's wonderful."

"Yeah, right," Vince said with what was obviously jealousy. Not that Holly was surprised, since Todd was just that sort of guy. Girls wanted to be with him, and guys wanted to be him. For a moment she was lost in how wonderful Todd was before she caught sight of the watch on Vince's arm and remembered just how little time she had left on earth.

"Gemma," she said out loud as she got to her feet and turned in the direction of her friend's apartment. "It's almost nine at night. I've got to get back around to see her so we can find Tina MacDonald."

"Nine? Shit, I'm supposed to be somewhere." Vince turned and headed back toward the building.

Holly dug her heels in and forced him to stop. "Did I not just explain why it's so important that I get all my problems worked out? I only have two days. Tick-tock, heavenly clock and all of that."

"Well, you're not going to find Tina MacDonald at this time of night, so why waste time? This is my body, remember, and I have a life. You can't just come in here and take over."

"Possession is nine-tenths of the law," she reminded him as she tried to head back in the other direction. "Hey, you might learn something."

"That you're insane? I think I've already picked that one up, thank you very much. Now if you don't mind—"

"I do mind." Holly gritted her teeth. "Why can't you just work with me on this?"

"Well, let's see. For a start you seem to think that my problems aren't as important as yours. Second, because it's too late to go running around playing Nancy Drew. Third, but most important, because you didn't even ask or say 'please.' "

Holly dropped her jaw for a moment. Of all the ridiculous, stupid, selfish reasons, that was just the bottom drawer. In two days' time she could curse Vince Murphy all she wanted, but in the meantime she was just going to have to go along with it.

"Please, can we go back to Gemma's place so I can get Tina MacDonald's address?"

"If we must," Vince grudgingly relented. "Since I'm probably too late. But first I need to make a call, and can I just ask, Is this what it's going to be like for the next two days?"

"Hey," Holly responded, "you know, I'm sure there are a lot of other guys out there who would be thrilled to have someone like me in their body."

"Yes, I'm completely delighted at the experience. Just what I've always wanted. A dead girl to talk to," Vince retorted as he pulled his phone out of his pocket.

Holly was about to say something when the door to Baker Colwell opened, and her back stiffened as she recognized the two guys who had been following her earlier on. Had they been in the building trying to find her? What creeps. Not that they really looked like your normal run-of-the-mill thugs. In fact, they looked more like computer geeks than . . . *Uh-oh*. Holly winced as once again she realized she had forgotten just whose body she was in.

"Vince." The taller of the two spoke as they made their way over. "Where the hell have you been, man? You know we all had overtime."

"It's a long story," Vince said. "I was just about to call to explain why I'm late. Is Bob still inside?"

The shorter one shook his head and pushed his glasses back up his nose. "No, we've just finished, but he wasn't happy with your no-show."

"That I can believe, and trust me, I had every intention of being there. It's just . . . well—"

"What's going on, anyway?" Tall Guy asked. "First you were weird at the funeral, and then when we saw you before, you ran away from us."

"Ran away from you?" Vince blinked, and Holly winced some more. Besides, how would she know who Vince Murphy hung out with? Or that he even had any friends? Certainly when they were in school together, she didn't recall his being Mr. Social.

"That's right, and why do you have a bridal magazine in your hand?" the short guy said. Luckily, before Vince (who did seem a little speechless) could answer, the tall guy's cell phone started to beep, and after glancing at the screen he just shrugged his shoulders. "Look, we've got to go, but we'll see you tomorrow."

"A bridal magazine?" Vince stared down at his hands after the two guys had disappeared down the street. "Let me guess—tomorrow we'll be shopping for handbags and getting our nails done?"

"Look, I'm sorry about the magazine, and about running away from your colleagues. I met a few of the ge . . . I mean, computer guys at the funeral, but I didn't recognize those two. Besides, it could've been worse."

Vince made a choking noise in the back of his throat, and Holly closed her eyes for a moment to try to block everything out. Unfortunately, thanks to the fact that there was another person in the same body with her, she failed miserably.

"Okay," she admitted with a small gulp. "You're right. This is about as bad as things could possibly be."

"Thank you, and I know you wanted to see Tina, but I think it might be best if we go back to my apartment and get used to the idea. I have a feeling tomorrow is going to be a big day."

His place?

Holly was just about to retort that if he thought she was staying the night with him, then he had another think coming, when she realized she had no choice in the matter. She groaned. For some stupid reason she had just assumed she would be going back to her own place to sleep tonight, which, just like everything else she wished to do, would be impossible.

She rubbed her chin, but the feeling of bristles under her fingertips only served as a reminder that she'd come back to earth in a guy's body. A computer-geek guy at that.

She doubted Tina MacDonald would even open the door to Vince, let alone burst into tears and admit to spiking Holly's coffee. (Okay, so perhaps that scenario was a bit far-fetched but up until now the image had been keeping her relatively sane.)

"Fine." She reluctantly nodded her head in agreement. It wasn't ideal, but Holly was starting to discover that not much was these days.

Seven

Thirty minutes later she let out a sigh of relief when Vince opened his front door to reveal a neat and unassuming apartment. It wasn't anything like Todd's cutting-edge bachelor pad, but it didn't have anybody else in it trying to ask difficult questions, and for that she was truly thankful.

A bit of peace and quiet was what she needed to try to figure out a new plan on how to contact Tina MacDonald.

It was only ten at night, but when Vince walked past the tidy living room and into the only bedroom, Holly was too tired to complain. She sat down on the bed and started to pull the horrible boots off.

"What are you doing?"

"These things weigh a ton. What's in them? Cement?"

"They're steel-toed. In addition to sitting down in our workshop doing *geeky* things, sometimes we're actually let out in public to install systems. They're for protection."

"Oh." Holly tried not to flush as she realized he must've heard her start to call him a geek earlier. "Well, they're sort of heavy."

"I guess I'm used to them," Vince said, but Holly noticed he didn't stop her as she tugged them off.

"Ah, that's better." She wriggled her toes for a minute.

"If you say so." Vince didn't sound impressed. "What are we going to do about this situation then?"

Well, for a start, when Holly got back to heaven she would definitely be filing a report against Dr. Alan Hill. After all, what sort of bogus health professional would send an innocent girl into such a dangerous situation?

An experience like this could knock years off her life, if she were still alive. There should be consequences. And compensation.

"I guess we just need to play it by ear. You can talk when we're around your friends, and I'll talk when we're around my friends."

"Except I doubt any of your friends would hang around long enough for me to open my mouth."

"Gemma will, because she already knows."

"What do you mean, she already knows? How did you manage that?"

"With great difficulty. She thought you were trying to hit on her in the middle of my funeral."

"Great, as if my life weren't bad enough." Vince lay back down on the bed and put his hands behind his neck.

"But now she knows the truth." Holly wriggled him back up into a sitting position. "And tomorrow I'll explain everything to Todd."

"I'd like to see that." Vince snorted as he lay down again.

"Unfortunately, you will." Holly sat up and peered around his room. There wasn't much in there apart from a bookshelf with a pile of books, a small collection of coins, and a moth-eaten teddy bear. Then she caught sight of a Baker Colwell Platinum Merit certificate. Boy, those things were hard to come by. Vince must be good at his job. In fact, she and Gemma had both been hoping to get one, but so far they hadn't managed it. Gemma said—

Holly jumped to her feet. *Gemma. Of course.* All she needed to do was ring up her friend and get *her* to see Tina MacDonald. Why hadn't she thought of that sooner? All this body-sharing was obviously playing havoc with her brain.

She looked at her watch. It was after ten, and normally she would've waited until the morning, but this was a matter of life and death. Or was that death and life?

"Vince, can I use your phone?"

There was no answer, and Holly frowned.

"Vince. Can I use your phone, *please*?"

But there was still no answer. Was he ignoring her? She was just about to pinch his arm before realizing that not only would it hurt her as well, but perhaps he was asleep. After all, he'd had a pretty rough day, what with having his body snatched and all.

She fumbled around in his jacket pocket until she found the phone and prayed the battery wasn't dead. Actually it seemed quite outrageous that Dr. Hill hadn't provided her with an expense account when he'd sent her down here. She was going to have serious words when she got back up there.

"Hello?" Gemma's voice sounded cautious. "Who's this?"

"Gem, it's me. I'm using Vince's phone."

"And Vince's voice. Holly, can I just tell you one more time that this is seriously weird?"

"You don't know the half of it. Anyway, did Irene settle down?"

"Only after I let her tell me all about how her fifth-grade teacher humiliated her in front of the whole class by asking her to spell 'wheelbarrow.' Honestly, she's getting worse. But enough about her; how did you do?"

"I found out how the pills got in my system," Holly told her in a triumphant voice. "It's such a relief, because this whole mission was starting to look a little bit impossible. So now I just need you to go around and confront them."

"Oh, my God. Of course I will," Gemma squealed from the other end of the phone. "So, who is it?"

"Tina MacDonald," Holly informed her proudly. "In fact, it's so obvious I don't know why I didn't think of it sooner."

"Oh." Gemma didn't sound convinced. "Are you sure?"

"Of course I'm sure." Holly was stung by her friend's doubt. "Don't you believe me?"

"You know I do," Gemma said in a rush. "It's just that I can't really imagine Tina doing that. I mean, what would be the point?"

"Because she was jealous of my promotion, of course, so she was trying to sabotage my presentation," Holly said in surprise. "She gave me a cup of coffee on Friday morning, which is when she must've slipped me the pills. Can you believe it?"

"Holly, that doesn't really make sense," Gemma said in a tentative voice.

"What do you mean, it doesn't make sense? Of course it does. She couldn't bear the idea of losing out, so she decided to drug me up."

"Yes, but what would be the point of giving you only four pills? I mean, all she would've ended up doing is making you fall asleep for a night. It hardly would've stopped you from doing your presentation on Monday morning."

"Apart from the fact that I'm *dead*."

"Holly . . . look, all I'm saying is that Tina would have to be pretty stupid to think anything much could happen with only four pills."

Holly felt some of the wind go out of her sails. "Well, perhaps she was just hoping I would fall asleep in the bath and drown? After all, that's not so silly, since it really did happen."

"Perhaps." Gemma sounded doubtful. "But to be honest I think the whole thing was either an accident or the person we're looking for had a particular reason for wanting to make sure you didn't go out last Friday night."

She's right, you know. Vince suddenly spoke, and Holly almost fell off the bed in shock. *Besides which, I don't think Tina's clever enough to do it.*

Holly reached up to her lips. Had her mouth moved? She was pretty certain it hadn't, but to be honest she couldn't quite recall. Since being turned into a guy and then finding out she was body-sharing with the same guy, she'd found that her short-term memory seemed to be a bit up the wall.

I think we can speak telepathically, Vince informed her, the sound of his voice reverberating inside her head . . . his head . . . their head.

Did you just read my mind? Holly tentatively tried to speak to him. And could she just say that it was the perfect ending to a perfect day? Not only was she trapped in his body, but he would soon have unlimited access to all of her dark, dirty secrets.

I don't think so, Vince replied. *Unless you were thinking about why one of us can go to sleep while the other one is still awake.*

Holly let out a sigh of a relief, since that particular problem was way down on her list right now. Which meant that at least her secrets could stay dark and dirty.

S-so you mean we can speak to each other without moving our lips?

My lips, Vince corrected. *But yes, that seems to be what's happening.*

"Holly?" Gemma was saying. "Are you all right? You're so quiet."

Holly realized just how hard this was going to be. *Especially when I have to share a body with someone who has no idea of boundaries,* she muttered to herself.

I heard that, Vince sang out, but Holly was too depressed even to comment, as it occurred to her she was right back to the beginning again.

At this rate she was going to spend the rest of her life in Level One, having to put up with all the horrid rejects, while people like her parents were up on Level Three probably wearing lovely white linen togas and bathing in chocolate. How had she managed to screw up her death so spectacularly?

"Holly . . . Holly. Are you okay?" Gemma asked on the other end of the phone. "I know you're disappointed, but I think you're turning a molehill into a mountain. We'll get through this thing. We always do."

Holly sighed. Oh, yes, and apart from not getting invited to any heavenly chocolate orgies, she still had to freak Gemma out once again by filling her in on Vince's reappearance. Suddenly *impossible* was taking on a whole new meaning.

Eight

"Okay, so here's the plan," Holly announced the next morning as she tapped her pen against the kitchen counter. "I'm up against the clock, so we need to prioritize. Since Tina is a dead end, the most important thing is to retrace my steps until we get another clue. Then I can explain everything to Todd and apologize for our stupid fight."

Holly was proud of how organized she sounded. Especially since she'd stayed awake for half the night panicking. Fortunately she'd then remembered that the trick was to pretend she was focused and confident, even if she wasn't. That was how she'd managed to get her promotion, after all.

"So, what do you think?" She double-checked with Vince, who still hadn't answered her.

"Great," Vince mumbled as he rubbed his eyes. "Now can I have some coffee?"

Holly put down her pen and let Vince flick the coffeepot on. Perhaps she wasn't quite as organized as she thought. "Sorry about that. I'm still getting used to this body-sharing thing."

"Yes, I'm having some problems with that myself. So what are your thoughts on having a shower?"

Holly glanced down at his pajama-clad body and wrinkled her nose. When going to the bathroom and getting changed, she had squeezed her eyes shut and sung as loudly as possible to distract herself from what was going on. But a shower would require full nudity, and to be honest, she wasn't quite sure she had room in her head for any more nightmares right now.

"How about we just have a thorough wash instead?"

"Good idea." Vince sounded almost as relieved as she felt, and as he busied himself pouring the coffee, she tried not to think about what it would be like if he did take all of his clothes off. *No, scratch that thought.* She wasn't quite ready to be looking down anyone's else's trousers yet. Especially not Vince Murphy's.

"This is so strange that I'm getting ready for work and not putting on any makeup," Holly said twenty minutes later as she admired the way Vince carefully shaved the contours of his chiseled jaw. He definitely looked better without stubble.

Vince held the razor away from his face. "You know, it's easier to do this when you're not talking."

Sorry, Holly mentally apologized. *I don't think I'm ever going to get used to this.*

Me either. It's certainly not something I ever thought would happen. I'm still trying to adjust to the fact that you decided to work for Baker Colwell, let alone now live in my body.

What does that mean? She bristled. Not that she

cared what he thought, of course, but his pretense of knowing her well was irritating. When she first started working there he had even asked her out on a date—to catch up on old times, he had said. *Yeah right.* As if Holly had wanted to do that.

He shrugged as he washed the razor under the tap and splashed some aftershave on his face. Holly winced at the sting. "I don't know," he said aloud. "I guess when we were at school I always had you pegged as doing something a bit more creative."

"That shows how much you know about me. I've always wanted to join Baker Colwell. My dad used to work there as a senior analyst, so I guess I'm following in his footsteps."

"If I followed in my father's footsteps I'd be in prison for robbery."

"Oh." Holly felt her eyes widen as she tried to digest this information. Prison for robbery. Wow. "I didn't know that."

"It's no biggie." Vince roughly ran his hand through his hair and then turned for the door. "Anyway, if we have a hope in hell of getting through the day, we should probably leave already."

"Sure," Holly said as an awkward silence enveloped them. She wanted to say to him she was sorry for acting surprised, but she could tell by the set of his mouth that he didn't want to talk about it. Which was crazy.

Just because his father was in prison, that didn't mean Vince had done anything wrong. In fact, from what Holly had seen, the opposite was true. He had a good job, a nice apartment, and when he wasn't being annoying, he was an okay guy.

Holly glanced at her watch. She'd arranged to meet Gemma in the reception area before the weekly staff meeting, but there was still no sign of her, which was a nuisance, since some of her "last steps" had involved the ladies' room, and there was no way she could re-create them without Gemma's help.

Vince seemed unnaturally quiet as they watched everyone hurrying past them, and Holly could only guess he was finding this just as hard. Once, at Todd's bequest, she'd worn some skimpy lingerie underneath her black suit. It had felt sexy and exciting in equal measures to be walking around with such a secret on underneath, but nothing prepared her for how it felt to be walking around with a secret like this.

"Sorry I'm late." Gemma panted as she careened to a halt in front of them, and Holly was grateful to be jolted from her thoughts. Thinking of skimpy underwear and Vince Murphy in the same sentence was just disturbing.

"I was wondering where you'd gotten to," Holly told her friend.

"I had a rotten sleep last night."

"I know the feeling," Holly agreed.

"You poor thing." Gemma flushed as she reached out to give Holly's hand a squeeze. "How are you feeling?"

"Okay, I guess. Considering I'm back from the dead in someone else's body."

"Oh, yes." Gemma quickly pulled her hand away and scrutinized Holly. "By the way, who am I speaking to? Is it Holly Vince or Vince Vince?"

"It's Holly, you idiot." It was obvious that despite Holly's staying on the phone for an extra half hour last night to try to explain the new situation, Gemma was still having problems making sense of it.

"Hey, that's a bit unfair calling me an idiot when you're the one who managed to get herself into someone else's body," her friend complained.

"My point exactly," Vince piped in. "And for the record, Gemma, I promise I had nothing to do with Holly trying to hit on you at the funeral yesterday."

Gemma laughed, and Holly rolled her eyes. "Please don't encourage him. Vince, don't you have something else to do while we talk?"

"Sure, I'll just go over and grab a cup of coffee. Oh, no, wait. I can't move."

"Ignore him," Holly advised Gemma. "Because we can't afford to waste any more time and— Oh . . . there's Todd. . . ."

Holly sighed as she looked over to where he was striding across the foyer with a paper under one arm and a coffee in his other hand—a decaf skinny cappuccino, not that he ever let on, but Holly knew he was secretly worried about his weight. Probably wanted to look good for their wedding. She sighed again.

"Great, and things just keep getting better and better," Vince growled, but Holly didn't pay him any attention.

"Look at how gorgeous he is. I love the way his hair goes all tousled . . . see . . . like that."

Vince squinted. "It's sort of a weird color, if you ask me. Does he dye it?"

"Oh, well, I guess he gets a few tones and highlights, but there's nothing wrong with male grooming. In fact, some of your colleagues would do very well to take a page out of Todd's book."

"I'll be sure to pass that little tip along," Vince said in a dry voice.

Holly continued to stare in Todd's direction. "This is so annoying. I mean, he's my boyfriend and I can't even go over there and tell him how much I love him. And what's *she* doing?"

"Who?" Gemma spun around to see what was going on.

"Rochelle Jackson," Holly said in disdain as she stared at Todd, who was paying an awful lot of attention to the stupid girl. "She is so unbelievable. I feel like going over there and giving that slut a piece of my mind. Is she touching his *butt*?"

"Look, Holly, don't freak out," Gemma said tentatively, as if she were about to reveal some more information.

"Don't freak out about what?" Holly said in a dangerously low voice.

"Okay." Gemma let out a muffled sigh. "I didn't want to tell you before, but Rochelle's been making a play for Todd ever since you died."

"But I've only been dead two weeks. Why, that little—"

"I know she is. But the thing is, Todd isn't remotely interested. Holly, he's really upset about your dying. It's totally thrown him."

"Well, so it should. I mean, we were meant to be— Oh." Holly broke off with a start as something occurred to her. "It was Rochelle who gave me the pills! You were so right when you said that it couldn't have been Tina. Because what would be the point of knocking me out for only one night? But with Rochelle it's different. She wanted to knock me out so she could have Todd all to herself at the ball."

"You're right." This revelation had made an impact on Gemma. "We both know that Rochelle doesn't stop at anything to get what she wants, so making you fall asleep for the night certainly wouldn't be beyond her. Unbelievable."

"I'll say. That girl does not know how to take no for an answer. She definitely has boundary issues. And why is she still touching him?"

"Well, that's about to change," Gemma said firmly. "As soon as we get proof, then she's history. I think we should start with her office."

"Her and her stupid office," Holly growled. Rochelle liked to mention it at every opportunity, since the rest of last year's graduates were still stuck in cubicles. Word on the street, though, was that she hadn't earned that office at all; she'd gotten it only because she was friendly with the CEO. Real friendly.

And now she had stopped Todd from proposing on the night of the ball. Well, the pills may have worked, but there was no way Holly was going to stand by and let her get away with stealing her fiancé as well. This was war.

Holly could feel the determination rising up through her. Finally they were getting somewhere. At this rate they would catch Rochelle, convince Todd of the truth, and still have time to watch the latest episode of *The Rich and the Restless* before she went back to heaven. *Perfect.*

Gemma nodded. "That girl is toast. We're going to take her down."

Vince folded his arms, and Holly could tell by the way his lips were turning that he was about to frown. "Before you go pointing fingers, shouldn't we be working out *how* she managed to do it?"

"Oh." Gemma paused. "I hadn't thought of that. I guess we'd better retrace your steps first."

Holly pulled out a piece of paper from Vince's pocket. "I do have this. It's a list of all the things I remembered doing the day I died. According to the Internet the tablets could still keep working for up to eight hours, so I've gone back as far as ten in the morning."

Gemma peered over and chewed her lip as she studied it. "You only had one cup of coffee at work, and that was made by Tina, so Rochelle couldn't have spiked your drink. Are you sure you didn't go somewhere for lunch? Perhaps she did it then?"

"No," Holly reluctantly agreed. She'd been particularly busy that day trying to get her presentation ready for Monday, so she hadn't even left the building for a break. "I brown-bagged it and ate at my desk."

"Did you put it in the staff room fridge?" Vince wondered, but Gemma gave a dismissive shake of her head.

"They work on different floors."

Holly stabbed at the piece of paper. "But our fridge was on the blink, so I did go up to the fourth floor to put mine in there. I remember because I had chicken in my sandwich and I was worried about salmonella poisoning." For a moment Holly was struck by the irony, since it wasn't the salmonella she should've been worrying about. On a brighter note, at least it was a start.

"Okay, so what are we waiting for? Let's go," she said, but Vince's feet weren't moving anywhere. If she could've glared at him, she would've. "What? We've got motive; we've got opportunity; now we just need to find means."

"Yes, well, I hate to break up this little *Law and Order* episode, but aren't you forgetting something?"

Holly wrinkled her nose as she lifted up her fingers to start mentally ticking things off. "I don't think so. What do you mean?"

Gemma groaned as she nodded in the same direction as Vince. "He means we've got the company meeting, which is about to start right now."

Nine

Ten minutes later they were standing at the back of the meeting room and Vince's arms were firmly folded. Normally Holly preferred to sit a bit closer to the front, just so everyone could see she was keen and eager to make something of herself, but Vince obviously didn't feel the need to impress anyone and had refused point-blank to go anywhere near "those suited monkeys."

Besides, being at the back meant they would be able to make a quick getaway once the meeting was finished—something Holly longed to do. Still, at least she was closer to getting her issues sorted than she had been yesterday. She knew that pretending to be calm and organized was the right thing to do.

Because it was the beginning of the month, nearly one hundred people had turned up, and Holly was quite pleased to have access to Vince's extra height to check them all out. Particularly since the regional executive sales director, David Harris, was droning on about the company decision to change the paper from ninety-six brightness to ninety-two brightness for internal memos.

She yawned and was just trying to decide if Tina

MacDonald had hair extensions when she caught sight of a poster taped up on the wall. It was for a suicide help line, and Holly knew damn well that it hadn't been there two weeks ago.

Unbelievable. How many times did she have to tell people that she hadn't committed suicide? Surely Baker Colwell had better things to do than put up posters like that, especially when based on such flimsy evidence. She was almost tempted to stomp over there and yank it from the wall, when David Harris suddenly coughed and changed topic.

"And now the next thing on the agenda is that I can finally reveal our top account manager for the last quarter, who at this rate will be on target to beat the company record held by yours truly."

There was a faint sprinkle of laughter from somewhere down near the front, and Holly crossed her fingers. Last quarter Todd had just missed out, and she knew he was gunning for this to help move him farther up the rungs.

"So without further ado I would like to congratulate Jim McKenna."

Holly felt her heart sink. Poor Todd—he must be devastated. Especially on top of everything else he'd had to go through in the last two weeks, though hopefully when she—

"And Todd Harman. It was a tie," David Harris finished with a flourish of his arms, and Holly clapped her hands in excitement as she caught sight of Todd's proud face. She just knew this was a sign that everything was going to be okay.

I'm so happy. You have no idea how hard he's worked for this. And what's David Harris doing, trying to pretend that there was only one person?

Vince immediately shoved his hands in his pockets to stop any more clapping. *Yeah, the crazy-wild side of Baker Colwell. Who knew?* Vince retorted.

Boy, you really are cynical. Well, if you hate it so much, then why do you still work here? Holly demanded, completely forgetting about her own dark thoughts with regard to the poster.

Because they pay better than anyone else and I can use the money. My bank manager tends to send me letters when I don't cover my mortgage."

You own your apartment? Holly said in surprise, since most of her friends owned only credit card debts and too many pairs of shoes.

Vince nodded. *I know it's not in the best area and doesn't have the right sort of stainless-steel kitchen appliances, but it's mine, and as long I keep paying the bank, they can't kick me out.*

Did you get kicked out of houses a lot when you were a kid?

Enough. He shrugged, and Holly suddenly wondered if that was why he had left their school when he did. She'd never really given it any thought, but before she could reply, the meeting finally broke up and Gemma sidled up next to them.

"I just overheard Rochelle saying she had to go up to the fifth floor. I've got to see my boss about some new project, but if you want to search her office, this would be the time to do it."

"That's great." Holly could barely contain her excitement. First Todd's news and now this. Thank goodness the whole thing was proving easier than she'd first imagined. Just went to show what a bit of hard work and determination could really do.

"Yes, because just in case I don't get fired for missing my overtime last night, this should get the job done," Vince retorted.

"What?" Gemma wrinkled her nose. "Was that Vince speaking?"

"Yes, just ignore him," Holly advised. "For the tall, dark, silent sort, he sure is chatty."

"Sticks and stones." He folded his arms.

"You know, it's really weird when you bicker with each other like that," Gemma complained as she hitched her purse over her shoulder. "Anyway, I've got to go, but good luck."

"We're going to need it," Vince muttered as they headed over to the other side of the room. *Hey, where are you going? I thought Rochelle's office was the other way.*

It is, Holly admitted as she glanced over at the poster. *But I just want to ask Martha from reception where that came from. She knows everything. And then some. After that I'll pull the horrible thing down.*

Vince tapped his watch. *I don't want to rain on your parade, but we don't have time to do both, so you'd better decide which criminal activity you wish to engage in, because I need to be back in the workshop in twenty minutes.*

Twenty minutes? Holly groaned.

Yes, well, those posters don't have anything to do with you. You died by misadventure. That's what the coroner said.

Everyone knows that death by misadventure is short-hand for suicide, and the posters weren't here two weeks ago, were they?

I'm sure there are any number of reasons why they're up, but if you want to spend time finding out then we won't have time to go to Rochelle's office.

Fine. She relented as she took one last look at Martha's retreating back before turning in the other direction.

It didn't take them long to make their way up to the fourth floor, though every time someone so much as looked at them, Holly could feel herself freeze up.

You know, if you keep doing that, people are going to think that we shouldn't be up here. Vince unstiffened his spine as they finally made it to Rochelle's office without anyone questioning them.

Sorry. Holly gave her arms a shake to help her relax as they peered over the top of the frosted glass to make sure Rochelle really wasn't lurking around behind her desk. Then they waited until the coast was clear before slipping in.

Holly gagged on the overwhelming scent of perfume that hung in the air as she systematically went through each drawer. For one brief moment she thought she had hit the jackpot as her fingers latched onto a bottle of pills, but on closer examination she discovered they were vitamins. Holly sighed and pushed them back in.

Ten minutes later Vince tapped at his watch, and Holly was forced to admit he was right. They couldn't risk getting caught, so it was better to leave empty-handed than have Rochelle walk in on them. It would be more than a little difficult to explain.

She was just turning to leave when she caught sight of a holiday brochure poking from underneath a Baker Colwell training guide. She reached down and grabbed it.

Holly ignored the Hawaiian palm trees and golden sands on the cover and flicked through it until she came across a photocopied article on how to avoid motion sickness.

For a moment she was speechless as her eyes scanned the article, in which, apart from various homeopathic remedies, there was a suggestion for medication—including the name of the drug that Gemma had mentioned.

"I can't believe it," she finally said, and waved the brochure up in the air. "I mean, thinking it and knowing it are two different things. It's a strange feeling."

"Yes, but we don't really know it," Vince pointed out. "It's not like you've found the pills or anything. Just an article."

"Not yet." Holly spun back around with renewed vigor as something brown caught her attention. Rochelle's oversize Chloe bag, which was hanging from a hook on the back of the door.

How on earth had she missed that thing? For a start, it was the size of a house, and Holly had the feeling that it wasn't just because of fashion, but because Rochelle had so many "sleepovers" during the week that a large bag was essential for her morning-after maintenance.

This knowledge made the idea of searching it unappealing, but the thought of not getting up to see her father in Level Three was even worse. There were things she needed to tell him. Things she needed to say. So she purposely marched toward it.

"You know, I don't think this is a great idea." Vince dug in his heels. "For a start, getting caught going through someone's bag is a bit worse than just being in their office. Then there's my meeting, remember?"

"Two minutes," she assured him as she reached up and unhitched the soft leather straps from the hook. "You know, I still can't really believe it. I guess she just freaked when she found out Todd and I were going to get engaged at the ball. She obviously decided to take matters into her own hands."

"You were going to get engaged to Todd Harman?" Vince seemed stunned as Holly put the bag down on the nearby chair.

"On Friday night." She nodded as she tugged at the zipper. "The thing is, we'd had a bit of a fight over it. I actually wanted it to be more low-key. Which is why I need to speak to him—to let him know that I really was going to say yes and that I didn't kill myself. I need him to know that I love him. That's why this is so important."

"Yes, but *engaged*?"

"Of course, engaged. That's generally how people do it when they want to get married. Perhaps we should talk about this later, since the quicker I do this, the less chance there will be of getting—"

"Caught?" someone finished the sentence for them. "Too late—you already are."

Ten

"Only joking," the voice continued. "Vince, what are you doing in here? I've been looking for you everywhere. Did you forget you were meant to meet me this morning before work?"

Holly, who had been holding her breath, let it out in a relieved gasp as she looked up to where Amy Jenkins, the company Goth chick, was standing in the doorway with a scary smile plastered onto her darkened lips.

As usual she was dressed in a long black skirt, a pair of spiky boots, and a ruffled Victorian governess shirt. Why had Holly forgotten that wherever Vince Murphy was, Amy Jenkins wasn't far behind?

No wonder Vince was such a geek if he hung out with people like Amy. And a word of advice to the girl: If she ever wanted to rise out of the secretarial pool, then she should lose the long black hair and matching nail polish. Oh, and the attitude.

Holly edged away from the bag and tried to resist the temptation to glance into it. So close, yet so far away. Still, she supposed it could've been worse. It could've been Rochelle standing in front of her. But on the other hand, Amy Jenkins. *Ugh.*

Okay, you can take over here, Holly mentally informed Vince.

Were you really going to get engaged to Todd the night you died? Vince didn't seem to notice that Amy was standing directly in front of them.

Perhaps we could speak about this another time? Holly suggested. Like when Amy Jenkins wasn't undoing the top button of her blouse. *Why don't you talk to your friend and make her go away?*

Vince still didn't speak, and Amy started to pick imaginary bits of stuff off Vince's shirt. Holly barely resisted the urge to shudder.

"Earth to Vince." Amy giggled. "Come in, Vince."

Holly rolled her eyes. Vince was so going to get it later. She took a deep breath as she edged them both back toward the door. "Amy, hey."

"Hey, yourself. So, who were you talking to just then? I couldn't believe it when I heard your voice coming from this office. I've been looking for you everywhere."

Note to self. Must speak to Vince only in head, not out loud. "Oh, no one." Holly tried to grunt in a Vince-like manner. When she was faced with someone she didn't want to speak to, it was surprisingly easy to replicate.

"So what are you doing here?"

Hmmm. That's a good question. "I was just dropping some . . . er . . . printer paper off for Rochelle, but she's not here."

Printer paper. Good one, Holly, especially since

there's no printer paper to be seen. She held her breath to find out if Amy bought it, but the girl in front of her didn't seem interested in anything other than running her long nails over Vince's arm.

Holly took the opportunity to dart out of the door and into the hallway just in case Rochelle returned. Amy was only one step behind.

"Are you sure you're feeling okay? You were acting weird yesterday when we were in the church, and then when I went to find you in the cemetery, you were gone."

Holly blinked for a minute before realizing Amy must've been at her funeral as well. Next time she died she was definitely going to request it be a private service, because quite frankly, it seemed like it had turned into a bit of a free-for-all.

"Well? Are you okay?" Amy pushed back a long strand of hair and touched Holly's cheek.

This was getting worse, and she was sorely tempted to just tell the girl to get lost then and there. Especially since Vince was so determined to get back to his meeting, which meant Holly had only a couple more minutes to search in the bag, where she just knew the pills would be waiting for her.

Where was Vince? But despite her giving him what could only be described as a mental scream, there was no sign of him, and Holly realized she had to choose between covering for Vince or searching the Chloe bag.

She reluctantly answered, "Oh, yeah, I'm fine. I just felt a bit . . . you know . . . like I needed some fresh air, so I decided to bail and go for a walk. . . ."

Amy was looking at her strangely. "Why are you speaking so weirdly?"

Duh. That would be because Vince had gone AWOL somewhere in his own body and had left a dead girl to do the talking for him. What other reason could there possibly be? "Sorry, I guess the funeral threw me a bit," she said instead.

A tight expression made its way across Amy's mouth. "Yeah, well, if you ask me it was pathetic. I mean, all those people pretending Holly Evans was their best friend, and really they didn't give a shit."

"Like who?" Holly demanded before remembering she was meant to be Vince. "Not that I care, of course." *But names and phone numbers on a postcard, please.*

"Oh, you know." Amy gave a vague wave of her hand. "Anyway, I don't want to talk about the funeral anymore. I want to get back to the conversation we were having yesterday."

"You do?" Holly gulped. *Okay, Vince, anytime you want to take over, just be my guest. Like, really.*

"That's right," Amy purred as she ran a long finger up Holly's arm. "It's not fair to tease a girl."

"No," Holly agreed with a croak as she tried to pull her arm away. "That wouldn't be very nice at all."

Excuse me, but did she always carry on like this in the workplace? Because even though Holly and Todd had been dating for a year and were almost engaged, they were very careful to keep the flirting out of the office. As Todd had often said, there had been too many promising careers ruined by a bit of hanky-panky and a tape of hidden-camera footage.

"Why don't you meet me tonight after my evening shift and we can talk about it properly?"

"Shift?"

"God, Vince, you're so hopeless. Remember I started doing a couple of nights a week at the Fix? Just to pay some extra bills."

"That's right." She nodded her head as she suddenly recalled that Amy occasionally worked in the café down by the river. The first time Holly had seen her there it had totally put her off her espresso and biscotti.

"So come in about nine."

"Whatever." Holly gave a Vince-like shrug of her shoulders.

"Cool." Amy seemed absurdly pleased and started to lean in toward her.

Whoa, if Holly didn't know better she would say that Amy was heading directly for her lips. Actually, they were Vince Murphy's lips, but the problem was that somehow Holly was connected to them, and she would rather sit in Level One for all eternity than have to kiss Amy Jenkins.

Holly had plenty of things she could be doing right now, the prime one being to search Rochelle Jackson's Chloe bag. She would even rather be pulling down suicide help line posters. But being kissed by Amy Jenkins? *No, thanks.*

Besides, not that Holly was a big Vince fan, but honestly, there was nothing wrong with the guy that a few manners and a dose of man tan wouldn't fix. But the whole of Baker Colwell knew Amy was a tart with a rough mouth and split ends. He could do much better than her.

Holly had no intention of telling him that, of course. In fact, it would serve him right if she did let Amy kiss her. Perhaps he was shy around girls? Well, if so, it probably didn't matter, since Amy appeared to have enough forwardness for the pair of them. How could he like her?

Now she could feel Amy's breath hot against her chin, and Holly was just trying to decide whether to throw up or faint when the coughing sound came from behind them, and Amy jumped away from her like a demagnetized piece of steel.

"Any reason why you're not down doing the invoices for Mr. Jones?" A woman, who appeared to be Amy Jenkins's supervisor, was staring down at them through an intimidating pair of bifocals. Thank goodness for that. Holly felt like she should be applauding (or perhaps groveling at the woman's feet in gratitude) for her timely interruption and her stern discipline. It had the desired effect, and Amy went scuttling back to wherever Mr. Jones's invoices were faster than Holly could say *ten years of therapy*.

Okay, so that was way too close, and Holly shuddered as soon as the supervisor had gone. "I seriously thought Amy Jenkins was going to kiss me . . . I mean you. . . . And speaking of you, Vince, what's going on? Where are you?"

There was still no answer, and Holly felt a pang of worry worm through her. Why wasn't he answering? As far as she could tell, answering back seemed to be one of Vince's specialties. This silence stuff was a bit . . . well . . . strange.

"Seriously, Vince, could you please say something? Is

it because of Amy? Because if it is then don't worry about it. I completely understand that you didn't want to talk to her. The girl's horrible."

Then another thought occurred to her, and Holly frowned. "You're not being silent because you *did* want to talk to her and were too embarrassed to do it in front of me, were you? Oh, man." Holly hit herself on the forehead. "This is awkward, isn't it? Just because I don't like the girl doesn't mean you should feel bad about talking to her . . . though I've got to say I'm pleased the kissing never happened . . . but, well . . . it's your body. You should've just talked to her if you wanted to."

"It's a bit more complicated than that." Vince finally spoke, and if it weren't for the fact that they were sharing a body, Holly would almost have hugged him.

"You're okay. I was worried about you. And I guess I should apologize. I didn't mean to screw things up. No wonder you've been weird with me. I've been so caught up in my stuff that I didn't really think it all through. It's a bit of a mess, isn't it?"

Holly could feel Vince frowning. "I know this isn't your fault. But you're right . . . it is a bit of a mess."

"It won't be for much longer," Holly promised. "I'm sorry I've been so bossy, but as soon as I'm gone you can talk to anyone you want. Kiss anyone you—"

"Holly," he cut her off in a gruff voice. "It's not like that."

"Well, I'm sorry anyway."

"You will be," Vince retorted as he glanced down at his watch.

"W-what do you mean?" Holly suddenly had an ominous vision that Vince might want to do more than just kiss Amy Jenkins. Which was fine, since, after all, Vince and Amy were both consenting adults, and it was none of her business (despite the fact that Vince could do a lot better). The thing was that she really, really didn't want to be around for anything so . . . intimate.

"I mean that we need to get back downstairs, because you're about to go to your first technical department team meeting. All I can do is apologize in advance."

Compared to the idea of being part of the most bizarre threesome in the world, the idea of a team meeting didn't seem nearly so bad, and Holly, who had been planning to convince him to sneak back to look in Rochelle's bag, found herself nodding in agreement. "Fine, let's go then." She just hoped Vince's other colleagues weren't quite so keen to kiss him.

Eleven

"Vincent, so nice of you to join us," a voice boomed out as soon as they pushed open the workshop doors. As part of finance operations, Holly didn't venture to this end of the building very often, and when she did she always felt as though she had stumbled into *The Land That Time Forgot*.

Gone was the plush corporate interior of the rest of the building. It was replaced by sterile-looking chest-high benches covered in wires, piles of paper, and tools, with the occasional Lara Croft poster randomly pinned up around the place. Vince continued walking toward a group of guys who were sitting around a large table.

Holly recognized most of them from yesterday, and though she still didn't have a clue as to their names, at least today Old Spice had replaced the gym-sock smell. As for why they were all wearing novelty ties, well, that was anyone's guess.

Mickey Mouse Tie stood up and scowled.

That's my boss, Bob, Vince said in her head before unnecessarily adding, *I don't think he's in a good mood.*

Holly was starting to appreciate that Vince was a master of understatement. She stared at his boss and tried to imagine him thinking happy thoughts, but the way his blue eyes were narrowed, it wasn't likely. He should probably watch that blood vessel on his forehead as well. It didn't look healthy.

"So." The red-faced man folded his arms. "Are you going to tell me where you've been this morning? Or, for that matter, last night, when you were meant to be here working on the Laser account? We're a team, remember? Even when the hours are long, we pull together. I thought you understood that."

"I do," Vince assured him.

"So where were you then?"

Vince coughed and studied his hands. "Well, I was at Holly Evans's funeral, and then . . . it's sort of hard to explain what happened next. . . ."

Holly groaned. As far as lies went, that was pretty lousy. Hadn't he heard of the classics before? Food poisoning. Family emergency. Female problems . . . well, perhaps not that last one, but the other two would've worked just fine.

"To be honest, I thought as much, Vincent, but in the future call me first to let me know."

She almost choked in surprise when she saw Bob's face soften. Even the blood vessel stopped throbbing as he gave Vince a hearty thump on the shoulder. What was it with all of this back patting?

"It won't happen again," Vince promised.

"Good," his boss agreed before giving Vince a sympathetic smile. "I know yesterday's funeral must've been tough on you. You and Holly Evans were old school friends, I believe."

What?

This time Holly did start to choke, which only resulted in more back patting.

What on earth did he say that for? she spluttered silently.

"Yes." A sad smile tugged at Vince's lips. "We were good friends. Very good friends."

Vince! she yelped, but he didn't seem to notice as the four other technicians all started to stomp and holler in the most ridiculous way. What were they, teenagers? And to think that a moment ago she'd almost thought they weren't so bad. A moment ago she'd thought Vince Murphy wasn't so bad. She was obviously mistaken.

"Woohoo! Go, Vince. You sly dog, you!"

"Why didn't you say something before, stud? I thought she and Todd Harman had something going."

"I think that's quite enough," Bob said, though he also had an impressed smile on his face. And with good reason, Holly thought mulishly, since it was obvious from the personality deficiencies of these computer technicians that their chances of getting real-life girlfriends were seriously low. "Now, how about we all get on with this meeting?"

Yes, and perhaps you could all stop talking a load of garbage at the same time? Holly muttered in Vince's head.

Oh, well, if you want me to tell my boss the truth I'd be more than happy to. Though I don't think you'd have much luck getting back to heaven if my body's locked up in a mental institution.

Ooooh. Holly didn't know if she was more annoyed at his lies, or at the fact that he was right. What she did know was that Vince Murphy was one very irritating person. And the sooner this business was finished, the better.

Well?

Fine. She turned her attention back to where Bob was now holding up some sort of gadget and explaining that it was a new router. She narrowed her eyes and studied it intently. She had no idea what a router was, of course, but at least it was better than listening to Vince snickering in her head.

For the next hour Holly, who had planned to spend her time working out how she could get access to Rochelle's Chloe bag and then approach Todd and apologize for their fight, ended up being drawn into the meeting.

Of course, she knew the company provided IT and networking services for some of the largest businesses in town, but she'd always looked at it from a financial point of view. Or, when Todd had talked about his many sales conquests, it had been about the fancy lunches and the perks. For some reason she'd never considered how the systems actually worked.

"Right." Bob finally stood up. "Are we all clear on today?" Everyone nodded and the older man continued. "Okay, so, Andrew, you will finish that pricing. Steve, you're doing the bench jobs, and Vince, I need you to get to work on those service contracts."

Vince nodded and waited until the rest of the technicians disappeared to the various laptops that were dotted around the room. *Sorry about that. Probably more than you ever wanted to know about systems and operator codes.*

Holly resisted a smile. *Actually it wasn't so bad. I thought it would be . . .*

All Star Trek *jokes and frothing at the mouth over the newest Xbox software?* Vince said in a dry voice, and Holly flushed at the cliché, which she was forced to admit was what she had been expecting. Not that she was going to tell Vince that. After all, it was one thing to take over his body and ruin his love life; she really had no right to let him know she'd thought he was a geek as well.

So what are these service contracts you have to do? Will they take long?

Most of them I just need to ring up and schedule in. Why, what are you thinking?

I'm thinking we need to get to that Chloe bag.

Holly. She could feel Vince frowning. *I know you found the article, but is this really worth it? After all, you know the truth, and as for everyone else, does it matter what they think?*

According to Dr. Hill, it's a problem, she admitted as she reached into his satchel and dragged a crumpled suicide poster out. She'd managed to yank it off the wall of the elevator on the way back from Rochelle's office. Vince hadn't been pleased. *Not only does it make me do stuff like this, but up in heaven I was . . . well, I wasn't reacting in a positive fashion when it was being discussed. Dr. Hill said if I don't face my issues I can't move up through the levels, so I thought that if I can at least figure out what happened, I will prove it to my subconscious, if nothing else.*

I'm still not sure I understand your logic, but if it really means that much to you, I'll see if I can dodge Bob so we can try her office again.

Thanks. Holly felt surprisingly touched by Vince's attitude. Yes, he could be annoying, but she had to admit that considering the circumstances they were in, he had been understanding. For a moment she wondered if she would have been as generous if the tables had been turned. Then she frowned. Today there were more questions asked than answered.

That's okay. So we'd better get going.

Don't you want to make these phone calls first? Holly asked, suddenly feeling guilty, considering just how inconvenient this whole thing was. But Vince shook his head. Besides, if she made some concessions now, perhaps he would feel less inclined to kiss Amy Jenkins?

They'll keep until tomorrow. It's best we get out of here before someone notices that I'm not doing anything.

Except talking to a dead girl, Holly quipped, and she could feel Vince's mouth turn up in a small smile. For some reason she liked the idea that she could make him smile. When she'd first moved to her new department, she'd made the mistake of telling a few accountant jokes with the rest of the finance operations team. The jokes had gone down like a Big Mac at a vegetarian restaurant, and since then Holly had stopped trying to make people laugh during work hours.

Ah, yes, apart from that, of course . . . Oh, shit. Don't look up or make eye contact, okay?

Holly immediately looked up and made eye contact

with one of the technicians walking toward them. It was the tall guy from last night.

I told you not to do that, Vince scolded.

Sorry. Holly gave herself a mental kick. She always had been too nosy for her own good. *What do you think he wants?*

No idea, but I'll try to make it short. Don't worry; Andrew's a good guy.

"Vince, do you have a moment?" Andrew asked as he fiddled with his Homer Simpson tie. "I have to give the sales department an estimate of how long the wiring and installation of a Bacchus Three Thousand for the new hospital wing will take, but they don't seem interested in the fact that the system won't work."

"Oh, yeah." Vince nodded. "I had the same problem last month when Simon Trimmer was trying to sell one to the dairy board. I thought I explained to them then that the wireless frequency interferes with the machinery."

"I don't suppose you'd come with me?" the technician said in a hopeful voice. "I've already had so many arguments with them that I think they'll probably just blank on me. Besides, when it comes to wireless, you're the most experienced."

No, Holly silently reminded him. *Rochelle. Bag. Searching.*

Don't worry; I've got it covered, Vince assured her before shaking his head at the technician. "I'm sorry, Andrew. I've got a full day. Just make sure you don't let those sales guys walk all over you. If they were given half a brain they'd be dangerous."

A couple of the technicians over by the workbench

snickered, and Andrew sighed. "Yeah, you're right. I'll ring Todd and tell him I'm on my way up to talk about the quote."

"Okay, sorry I couldn't help. But—" Vince started to say, before Holly stopped him. He was going to see Todd? Well, that was just too perfect for words. She beamed in Andrew's direction.

"But . . . actually, now that I think about it, I do have a few minutes. I will go see Todd with you."

What the . . . Vince swore in her mind.

I'm sorry to interrupt you, she immediately apologized. *But don't you see what a great opportunity this is? What better chance am I going to get to talk to Todd?*

I could think of several, and none of them involve Andrew and me being in the office at the same time. Besides, didn't you say we needed to look in Rochelle's whatchamacallit bag?

This is more important, Holly insisted. Privately she acknowledged that he was right about it not being an ideal situation, but since there would be no chance of speaking to Todd alone—in her own body, with her cute new lingerie on—it was stupid to torture herself. *Also, I've just realized how risky it would be to search Rochelle's bag at work, so it might be best to sneak into her apartment this afternoon while she's at step class.*

Now you want to break into her apartment? Vince sounded a little bit aghast.

Yes, but it's not really breaking in because I know where the spare key is, Holly assured him.

I thought you hated Rochelle Jackson. How do you know where the key is?

Of course I hate her. She's a cow. But unfortunately she's a cow who happens to know a lot of the same people I do, so I've heard her mention where it's kept. But even if I have to be nice to her face, it doesn't mean I like her, all right?

Okay. Vince seemed a bit confused by Holly's logic, but she didn't have time to explain the ins and outs of the female mind. *So how do you know the bag will be there? Won't she take it to the gym?*

You really are a boy. Holly rolled her eyes. *No, she won't take her Chloe bag to the gym. She's got a horrible little glittery thing that she'll probably use.*

Fine. I will bow to your superior bag knowledge, Vince conceded in bewilderment. *But I still don't think it's a good idea to see Todd right now.*

Don't be stupid, Holly retorted. *Anyway, he's been working on this project for almost a month. I'm sure he'd want to know if the equipment isn't correct so he can fix it up.*

She didn't bother to add that Todd had already decided his commission check would be going toward his new car. They'd been looking at sales brochures the night he had suggested they get engaged.

Andrew, who had been reading a text message while the mental ping-pong had been going on, slapped Vince on the back. "This is great. I've tried to tell them before it doesn't work, but they just won't listen."

Vince snorted. "That's because they like what the Bacchus does for their profit margin. Anyway, I suppose we should get this over and done with."

"Sure," Andrew said as they headed toward the door. "Thanks again for doing this. I really appreciate it."

So do I, Holly silently added as she tried to calm her nerves at the idea of seeing Todd again. It seemed like ages since she had really talked to him. Touched him. Spent time with him.

There was no way she was going to screw up such a great opportunity. Everything had to be perfect. As Vince strode down the corridor, Holly wondered what her chances were of getting Vince to stop at a mirror so she could quickly check his hair.

Twelve

"What are you doing here?" Todd said the moment they walked into his corner office. It was a lot fancier than where they had just come from, and though Holly had been in there plenty of times, she'd never had this sort of greeting before. For a moment she was stunned.

"Er, I'm here to talk to you about this quote you're doing for the hospital wing." Andrew waved the plans up in the air and smiled in what Holly could only assume was meant to be a positive manner. It ended up looking as if he were constipated, and she wanted to tell him to relax. Todd might be acting a bit fierce right now, but he was hardly going to bite his head off or anything.

"Not you," Todd said in disdain as he pointed a finger in Vince's direction. "I mean him. After what happened yesterday I didn't think you'd dare show your face around me for a while."

Holly, Vince's tight voice echoed in her head. *Is there something else you forgot to tell me?*

Oh. She flushed. *Now that you mention it . . . Todd didn't really like you hitting on Gemma, so he was just trying to look out for her. There were a few words ex-*

changed, but it's only because he had her best interests at heart. That's the sort of guy he is. She sighed and turned her attention back to where Todd was still scowling.

He was in his charcoal suit today and was wearing the tie she had bought him for his last birthday. It was silk, and cost more than a small piece of fabric had a right to, but he had assured her it was exactly what he wanted. He had obviously chosen to wear it today out of respect for her. She tried not to sniff.

"Well?" Todd demanded. "What are you doing here?"

Here, let me handle this, Holly said privately to Vince before giving Todd a smile. "I actually have a few things I need to discuss with you, and I thought this would be the best way." She stared directly at him, willing him to see beneath Vince's exterior to where she was. For a moment his eyes seemed to widen ever so slightly before he folded his arms and arched an eyebrow.

"Really? Because as riveting as that sounds, I don't have time. Andrew over here has already been dragging his heels on this quote, and I'm due to submit it in two hours."

Hmmmm. So much for her mind power.

Yep, that went well. I think I can take it from here, Vince congratulated her before narrowing his eyes and glaring at Todd. "The reason I'm here is because you seem to have problems understanding that the Bacchus system won't work in that hospital wing, so Andrew asked if I could help explain what the alternatives are. The most practical one is to use Sampson routers and run them in conjunction with a two fifty-eight."

Todd burst out laughing, and Holly stared at him. Well, that was a bit rude. Not that she was really looking forward to hearing a long, boring technical explanation herself, but Vince seemed to know what he was talking about, and that was all that mattered. Besides, the sooner they finished this quote business, the sooner Holly could explain to Todd what was going on, and then she could apologize once and for all about their stupid fight. Time was a-wasting.

"I've managed the hospital's account for the last two years, and I think I know what they like. They'd never go for the Sampson because of the price. Not that tech heads like you ever think of anything like that."

"Yes, but since they'll end up spending twice as much in servicing and downtime, it shouldn't really be so hard to convince them."

Todd rolled his eyes. "Maintenance comes out of a different budget, all right? Now, I know you guys like to think you're the only ones who understand how a computer works, but the truth is you're the last link in the chain around here. If it weren't for the sales force then you'd be sitting around twiddling your thumbs and looking at computer porn. So don't try to tell me my job, okay?"

Andrew coughed and waved the paper in the air once again. "With all due respect, you haven't taken into account the frequency modulation the hospital equipment will be using. If you put this system in, then—"

"You'll risk jamming everything in the building," Vince cut in. "Which would really screw up your commission."

"You know, I can hear the words coming out but they're not making any sense. Now, if you two have finished, I've got work to do."

What? Holly yelped to herself as she realized Todd was showing them the door.

No. That wasn't right. She needed to talk to him. Like, now. She had only until tomorrow to get everything straightened out, and while she'd given Todd a bit of time yesterday because she knew how upset he must've been after the funeral, she couldn't afford to keep on waiting. She dug Vince's Doc Martens into the ground.

"Are you coming?" Andrew was looking at them, and seemed unsure of whether to keep going or not.

"Actually," Holly said before Vince had the chance to get a word in, "you go on without me. I have a few things I need to discuss with Todd."

Can I just tell you that this is not *a good idea?* Vince said in her head. *The truth is, this guy has never liked me, and I can't see that changing anytime soon. Especially not after you tried to hit on Gemma yesterday in my absence.*

If you're trying to be funny, then it's not working, Holly retorted. *I don't really have a choice about this. I either get my issues sorted or I make myself comfortable in Level One. Now will you let me do the talking?*

It's just that I don't think you've thought this through properly.

Of course I have.

Yes, but—

Vince, Holly mentally hissed, trying to fight back her disappointment in his attitude. Of course, she knew he didn't like Todd, but he could at least pretend. That was what friends did . . . and, well, after what they'd been through together she was starting to think Vince was sort of like a friend. Not that she was going to advertise it or anything. But still, if she were alive he might've made it to the Christmas card list. Perhaps even the occasional Sunday brunch when her other friends were too busy.

Fine. Vince gave a slight shrug of his shoulder to admit defeat. *He's all yours.*

"So what the hell is this about?" Todd tapped his watch and scowled. "Because I really wasn't joking about getting this quote submitted."

Holly cleared her throat. "Okay, Todd, this is going to sound a bit strange, but I need to talk to you about Holly Evans. I know—"

"Jeez, you've got some nerve. Well, if you think for a minute that it's any of your business what I decide to do for—"

But before he could finish the door pushed open and Simon Trimmer appeared. As another account manager and one of Todd's best friends, he had spent quite a lot of time with Holly. Not to mention the fact that Gemma currently had her eye on him, but before she could say hello he turned and shot a smug look in Vince's direction.

"Hate to interrupt this little powwow, but we're going to be late for our eleven o'clock with the folks from the power company. They've put on a morning tea to say thank-you for all the hard work we did on that job last month. Funny how they never invited you and your mob, isn't it, Murphy?"

Todd grunted and glared at Vince. "You heard him.

I've got to go and act like a winner now. Something you wouldn't know anything about." Then, before Holly or Vince could say another word, Simon unceremoniously opened the door and ushered them out with his arm.

Holly rubbed the bridge of her nose as they headed toward the elevator. *Okay, so I'm still not sure I understand what happened there.*

You heard him—he had a client function to go to.

Yes, but he was so short. He wouldn't listen to a word I said.

What a surprise.

I think I know him a bit better than you, Holly was goaded into retorting. *He's usually lovely. I guess it's because of yesterday's funeral, and it probably didn't help that you tried to chat up Gemma.*

Yes, how could I forget? Vince said in a dry voice.

Still, at least he explained why he couldn't use the other system. Because of the price.

Vince laughed. *The only reason he won't quote it is because there isn't as much profit margin in the system and it's easier to install. It's just not as beneficial for him to sell it.*

That can't be right. Holly shook her head. *If it really was the wrong system then he wouldn't sell it. Baker Colwell has a reputation to uphold. Besides, if Bob Mackay is head of the technical division then surely he'd say something if it was wrong.*

Vince shrugged. *Bob's a great guy, but he's not really a people person. Talking to them gives him hives. Besides, you can bang your head against a brick wall* only so many times, and Todd was right—*we're the bottom of the chain around here. The account managers bring the work in and they get all the credit. What do we know?*

Don't be silly, Holly scolded him. *I'm sure once you sit down and properly discuss it with Todd, Simon, and the other account managers, then they'll understand what you mean. Anyway, you have to remember that Todd's still grieving. If only I'd realized how badly he was taking it, I could've given him a bit more time. Why is this so hard, anyway? When I was alive I never seemed to have these sorts of problems. I was organized and under control. What's going on?*

It's probably the dead thing that's getting in your way, Vince said in a dry tone.

It does seem bothersome, she agreed with a sigh before scowling as she caught sight of yet another suicide poster. She noticed that Vince had stiffened his arm in case she tried to rip it down. *I mean, I have the Chloe bag to search, but I still have to figure out how to make Todd listen to me.*

Once they were safely past the poster, Vince said, *Perhaps Gemma will know . . . isn't that her just up ahead?*

Holly looked up and said a silent thank-you as she realized Vince was right. At least something was going in her favor today.

"Hey, Gem." She raised her arm in her friend's direction, but instead of looking up, Gemma turned and hurried off in the other direction.

What the . . . Holly stared at her friend's retreating back. Had she missed something? But she could tell by the way Vince had tensed his neck ever so slightly that he had noticed it as well. *I can't believe she ignored us.*

She probably didn't recognize the voice. He shrugged in a way that Holly vaguely remembered from their school days when kids teased him about wearing old clothes. Holly felt a defensive shiver run through her. She certainly hoped Vince was right and Gemma had merely not realized.

Do you mind if I make a call? she asked in a taut voice as she reached for his phone. There was no answer when she rang Gemma's number, but her friend returned the call several minutes later just as Vince pushed open the workshop door. She was thankful the place seemed empty so Holly could talk without fear of being overheard.

"Hey, I just got your message," Gemma said. "I've been in a meeting all morning."

"Really?" Holly narrowed her eyes. "Because I was sure I just saw you on the fourth floor."

"No, I've been in a meeting," Gemma said firmly. "This is the first chance I've had to call you. Why, what's going on?"

"Nothing." Holly let out her breath as she realized she and Vince must've been mistaken. Perhaps Vince needed glasses? He should look into it when she was out of his body and he had a bit more time on his hands. "I just made a mistake."

"I guess it's easy enough to do. So," Gemma continued in a rush. "You'd better fill me in on how it went in Rochelle's office."

Holly was immediately distracted. "I did have some luck. Rochelle had a photocopied article about motion-sickness pills on her desk, so it looks like we're heading in the right direction."

"God, that's unbelievable." Gemma seemed to catch her breath. "Did you find anything else?"

"Well, I was just about to search in her bag when Vince's girlfriend—"

"She's not my girlfriend."

"Okay, Vince's *not*-girlfriend, Amy Jenkins, managed to find us and even tried to kiss me. On the lips."

"Ew," Gemma squealed on the other end of the phone. "No offense, Vince."

"Please, just pretend I'm not here," he assured them in a mild voice.

"Anyway," Holly continued, "if her supervisor hadn't appeared then I can't even bear to think about what would've happened."

"Gross." Gemma sounded like she was shuddering, before giving a small cough. "So, what about Todd? Have you managed to . . . well . . . you know . . ."

"Tell him that I'm back from the dead and living in Vince's body?" Holly finished off before shaking her head. "No, it's harder than I imagined. He's still really broken up. You should've seen how strangely he was acting."

Vince made a snorting noise, and Holly rolled her eyes before saying, "That wasn't me, by the way." Then she filled Gemma in on the less than satisfactory meeting they'd just had. When she thought about it, it seemed they'd had a very busy morning yet not achieved much at all.

"You know," Gemma said after Holly had finished, "I think the only way to convince him is if you have a lot of proof with you. So that there's no way he can dispute it."

"Like what? A note from Dr. Hill explaining about my two-day pass from heaven?"

"No," Gemma retorted. "I mean things that only you would know about. What if you showed him the pearls he gave you for your birthday, and maybe even a copy of that mix CD he burned? I know you hated it, but he thinks you loved it. He'd know it was really you because no one else would have a mix CD with such crap music on it."

"That's not a bad idea." Holly nodded her head in agreement. "It wouldn't take us long to pop over to my old apartment and grab what we needed. Then at least I'll know something's gone right in this day from hell."

"I hate to remind you, but while your roommates might be okay with Holly Evans, recently deceased, going back to pick up these things, I'm not so sure they would be as welcoming if I turned up on the doorstep," Vince pointed out.

"You're right." She groaned. How could she keep forgetting? Then she brightened. "But they wouldn't think it was weird if my best friend turned up."

Gemma coughed and sounded fidgety. "The thing is, I've got this project my boss wants me to work on. It's a bit difficult to get out of."

Holly tried to hide her disappointment. "Well, I guess we can try to figure out some reason for Vince needing to visit."

"There's something else." Gemma's voice sounded faint from the other end of the phone.

"What?"

"I'm sorry, Holly. I hate to break this to you, but your stepmother showed up at your apartment on Thursday to collect your stuff. Which means the only way for you to get what you need is to go back to your old house and ask her for it."

Holly clutched at the cell phone. Could today *possibly* get any worse? Surely Dr. Hill was having some sort of laugh here. Perhaps this was the heavenly version of *Candid Camera*? Because if Holly had been forced to list her absolute worst-case scenario, then this would be it. Okay, so that was a lie, since the idea of being stuck in a guy's body back on earth was probably worse. But this was definitely a close second.

"Are you sure you can't do it?" Holly double-checked, but her friend let out a miserable sigh.

"You know I would if I possibly could."

"Perhaps we don't need to go at all?" Vince suggested, but Holly shook her head and tried not to sound glum.

"Gemma's right. You saw what Todd was like. It's going to be hard enough to convince him even when I do have proof. Without it I won't stand a chance. Not that I blame him, of course, since this whole situation is quite ridiculous. We just have to figure something out."

"Oh," Gemma squeaked. "Why don't you clear your desk and take everything around to your stepmother's house?"

"Hey, that's a perfect excuse. Though incidentally, why *is* all my stuff still there? When I sneaked in last night my password had been changed but my desk hadn't been touched."

"That's my fault. I thought Todd was going to do it last week, but then he got caught up in some big quote for the hospital . . . and, of course, your funeral and everything, so I told personnel I'd do it today."

"Well, we can do it now." Holly clutched at the phone. "And then take it to my stepmother's at lunchtime . . . if that's okay with Vince . . . ?"

"I guess that would work," Vince said grudgingly. "But we'd better do it now, because Bob will be back from his management meeting in about fifteen minutes, and if I'm not here making those phone calls, he'll probably have my balls."

Not something Holly was eager to experience, so she said good-bye to Gemma and jumped to her feet. There was no time to lose.

So why isn't anyone asking what I'm doing here? Vince questioned several minutes later as they started to pack away the small picture frames that had been sitting next to her computer.

Holly glanced around and realized no one seemed at all interested in what was happening. Perhaps it was because he was on the technical side? But still, it wasn't as if he were invisible, and he looked quite cute in the blue shirt she had convinced him to wear. The more obvious answer was that it wasn't exactly the friendliest department she had worked in.

I guess I've only been in this new job for a month. They probably only know me as the girl who killed her-

self. Holly sighed as she picked up a flyer that was sitting on top of her keyboard. It was the same as the posters that were everywhere, but in a bite-size version. She screwed it up and put it in the wastepaper basket. She wouldn't be needing that where she was going.

They were probably too busy writing stuff. Are these things compulsory or something? Vince held up a pile of Holly's neatly written training notes that had been hanging all over her computer screen.

Oh, they're nothing much. Just a few pointers to help jog my memory when I'm working on a key forecast.

Jog? Vince glanced over at another pile of them. *I'm surprised they didn't bury you.*

Holly stared at them. She guessed there were quite a few. She'd never really noticed them before. *It's just because I was new to the team. I wanted to try to learn everything as quickly as possible. There's nothing wrong with working hard.*

Vince held up his hands. *I never said there was.*

Well, good. She quickly put her *The Rich and the Restless* mouse pad into the box. Gemma never understood why Holly set her TiVo for it every afternoon, but for some reason she found it relaxing. She had a stressful job. It was allowed, okay?

So why did you move? Vince asked as he held up a coffee cup to see what she wanted to do it with it. Holly nodded and he added it to the box.

What?

Why did you take the promotion?

Because I got it. She shrugged before realizing that sounded a bit lame. *And it was good for my career.*

Vince didn't answer, and they finished clearing the desk in silence. Besides, Holly hardly needed Vince Murphy's approval of her career path. She wasn't embarrassed that she was ambitious and wanted to get ahead, and the fact she was dead by twenty-two was a complete coincidence.

Thirteen

I've changed my mind; I really don't think this is a good idea, Holly muttered an hour later as Vince made his way down the corridor in long, even strides, clutching at the box of belongings. "Perhaps she won't be at home? Or perhaps we should wait until Gemma can do it, or—"

"Or perhaps we can just get on with it?" Vince suggested in his mild voice. "You said you need these things to help convince Todd of who you are, so that's what we have to do."

Technically she knew Vince was right, but while he had made numerous phone calls and answered a mountain of e-mails (had Amy Jenkins really sent him four? Honestly, the girl didn't know when to take no for an answer, did she?), Holly had become less and less keen on the idea of going home. In fact, since they had become so good at sneaking around she had even contemplated waiting until her stepmother was out and convincing Vince to help her break in. Somehow she didn't think he would go for that one. She was starting to get the feeling he was quite honest and upstanding—qualities that she normally admired, but right now they were proving to be a bit problematic.

Then she narrowed her eyes. Why was he playing devil's advocate, anyway? "Since when do you care about my plans to talk to Todd?"

"Trust me, it's not something I'm looking forward to," he assured her. "But from what you said about Level One, you were having a pretty tough time up there, what with not being able to see your parents or anything. That really sucks. So if doing this stuff helps make it easier for you, well, then I've got your back."

Holly sniffed. She hadn't meant to tell Vince what it had been like up in heaven, but somehow it had just slipped out. Of course, if she had known he was going to use it against her, she might have taken greater care not to be suckered in by his laid-back I'm-so-understanding-and-easy-to-talk-to attitude.

"Besides, the quicker we do it, the less painful it will be. Like pulling off a Band-Aid," Vince added.

"I suppose so," Holly reluctantly agreed as they walked up the stairs to the main reception area. It was almost lunchtime and the place was bustling with workers eager to get out into the warm August sunshine. Holly felt an inexplicable urge to join them. Which was stupid, since when she was alive she'd normally stayed at her desk to get through her work. Then she realized it was probably just because she was famished. Having to power six feet of maleness was certainly hungry work.

She wondered what Vince's thoughts were on sushi. He didn't really look like a sushi person, but she was starting to realize there was more to Vince Murphy than met the eye. Besides, this might be her last chance to eat it.

She was so caught up in trying to decide between California rolls or sashimi that she almost jumped in shock when someone tapped her on the shoulder.

"Hey, Vince. You were miles away."

Holly groaned as they turned around to see the tall figure of Andrew standing in front of them. All Holly wanted to do was find out how she died, speak to her almost fiancé, and get back to heaven to try to bluff her way into Level Three where her parents were. But if the road to hell was paved with good intentions, then it seemed the one to heaven was positively covered with really annoying interruptions.

"Oh, hey." Vince nodded his head. "What's up?"

What are you doing? Holly queried. *I thought we were going for the Band-Aid approach?*

We are. That's why, if you stop interrupting me, I can tell him we're in a hurry.

Sorry, she reluctantly apologized as Andrew grinned at them.

"I just wanted to say thanks for trying to talk some sense into the sales department before."

"That's okay," Vince said. "Sorry I wasn't much help. The worst thing is that we'll probably spend the next six months fixing the damn things because they don't work properly."

"Yeah, it's a bitch, isn't it?" Andrew agreed. "Anyway, I didn't get a chance to tell you before, but it's Graham's birthday, so we're all going next door to Bar One for a drink after work. I thought with the funeral yesterday, you might want to join us. Also, there was something else that I—"

"Love to," Holly spoke before Vince got the chance. "I'll see you there then. Anyway, I'd better go. Bye."

What did you do that for? Vince demanded once Andrew had given them a surprised look before making his way back toward the staircase.

Because I want to get this over and done with as quickly as possible, and Andrew there seemed like he was settling in for the day. It was easier to say yes than to take the time to explain why we can't do it, Holly informed him.

I never give them a reason and I never say yes. Vince shook his head. *I don't socialize with anyone from work. That's why he looked so surprised.*

Oh. Holly paused to consider this for a moment. *I didn't know that.* Besides, that wasn't entirely true. He had asked her out when she had first started at the company last year. Not that she'd said yes, since apart from having her eye on Todd at the time, she had no desire to become reacquainted with Vince. Of course, now she knew he wasn't so bad . . . nice, even . . . but still, it just proved that he wasn't adamantly opposed to going out with people from work. So really, she was doing him a favor by trying to improve his social life. Not that they would have time to go, but that was beside the point.

It didn't take them long to cover the short distance to the parking lot, and Vince headed toward one of the many white Baker Colwell service vans. He slid in behind the wheel and they made the journey to Holly's old house in silence, which was good, because the closer they got, the less Holly felt like talking. Or like going in.

She had moved out when she'd gone to college, but had felt obliged to visit once a week to see her stepmother. However, since starting at Baker Colwell she had been so busy between work and Todd that she couldn't even remember the last time she'd been home. She had a funny feeling it might not have been since Easter, almost four months ago.

Are you okay? Vince silently asked once he parked the van and they were standing in front of the door.

Not really. Holly gulped. *Perhaps you were right. I don't really need to do this in order to speak to Todd. I convinced Gemma without resorting to evidence. Surely I could do the same again. And you believed me.*

I had overwhelming proof, Vince reminded her. *As much as I dislike Todd, for whatever reason you've been given a second chance to get things sorted out and say your good-byes. You need to make the most of it.*

Holly, who had been about to protest, closed her mouth as she felt inexplicably reassured by Vince's philosophy. While there was no doubt that this setup made everything a lot more difficult, in some ways she was finding his continued presence a relief from all the changes that had been thrust upon her lately. It was obviously some sort of latent Darwinian survival skill that was helping her to get along with the person whose body she was sharing.

Thank you, she said as she pressed the bell.

It's fine. Are you sure you don't want me to do the talking? Vince asked.

No. Holly gave an adamant shake of her head as she once again went over the cover story they had come up with.

Hello, Mrs. Evans, you don't know me, but I'm a friend of Holly's and I've come here on behalf of Baker Colwell. . . . Cue holding up ID card. *I've just cleared out her desk and thought you might like the rest of her belongings. . . .* Cue holding up the sum whole of her working life: a box containing a coffee cup, some photos, and a dog-eared work diary.

As far as cover stories went, it wasn't very original or believable, but hopefully it would be enough to get them in the door. From there she didn't have a clue how they were going to manage it, but the law of averages suggested that something had to go right for her today. Didn't it?

She was just about to push the button again when she heard the sound of her stepmother's heels tapping along the marbled hallway. The door opened and Holly sucked in a deep breath as she tried to prepare herself to face her nemesis.

"Hello, Mrs. Evans . . ." Holly started to say, but the rest of the words sort of died on her lips as she stared in front of her.

Boy.

It had to be said that her stepmother didn't look too well. Perhaps she'd eaten something that disagreed with her at the funeral yesterday. Fish, perhaps? Because something definitely wasn't right with her pale face and her red-rimmed eyes.

"Oh, hello." Her stepmother blinked as if adjusting

to the bright light of the day. "It's Vincent, isn't it? You and Holly went to school together for a while. Goodness, you look exactly the same."

"Just a bit taller, I guess. I was only about eight back then," Vince said—which was probably lucky, since Holly was pretty much rendered speechless.

Obviously the fish was affecting her stepmother's mind as well. And Holly she was getting a bit sick of Vince pretending they had once been friends. Enough of it already.

"Oh, well, do come in."

"Thanks," Vince once again answered as Holly tried and failed to not feel strange as she crossed over the threshold of her old house.

She'd been born in this house, and her mother had died here only hours later. Despite the pain, Holly had happy memories of growing up, just her and her dad. Besides, how could you miss what you'd never had? Unfortunately her father didn't subscribe to this theory, and she would never forget the first time their domestic bliss was shattered by the appearance of a total stranger called Jill Turner. The onetime meal quickly extended to two nights a week and Sunday afternoons, until there had finally been a wedding.

"I'm sorry I didn't get a chance to talk to you yesterday," her stepmother said as she closed the door behind them. "I did see you at the church, but then things just sort of got away from me, and by the time I went to say hello I couldn't find you anywhere."

Yeah, right. Holly wanted to roll her eyes, since her stepmother had never liked Holly's friends. Not that

Vince was a friend, of course, but her stepmother obviously didn't know that, hence why she was letting them through the front door right now. She supposed she should be grateful. Then Holly realized her stepmother was waiting expectantly for an answer.

"Oh, that's all right. I was feeling a bit strange anyway," she said truthfully as she recalled her sudden arrival back to earth and straight into Vince's size-ten boots.

"It was that sort of day. Anyway . . . sorry the place is such a mess." Her stepmother sniffed as she led the way into the main living room. "I collected Holly's things from her old apartment the other day but haven't had the heart to take them up to her room yet. It all seems so pointless."

Holly glanced around and then turned back to her stepmother. What was she talking about? Holly couldn't remember when she had ever seen the house looking less than spotless. At times it had felt like living in a showroom with nothing out of place. Come to think of it, it wasn't just the boxes of clothing and shoes piled up by the window that seemed strange, but the whole place looked a little . . . *dusty*.

"That's okay." Holly stepped over her old gym bag and followed her stepmother to the kitchen.

"So tell me, Vincent, what can I do for you?"

"Oh . . . well." Holly put the box down on the bench. "I have Holly's personal items from work. I thought you might like them."

Gosh, the things a girl had to do to break into her own house . . . and why was her stepmother dabbing her eyes with a tissue?

"I'm sorry; I thought I'd be better after the funeral, but the smallest thing still sets me off. Thank you for bringing these around. Baker Colwell has been very thoughtful. Did you see the flowers they sent?"

"Holly was well liked," Vince butted in, and her stepmother nodded her head in agreement.

"I can imagine. She was a lovely girl."

What? Holly almost squeaked out loud, because really, this was getting stupid.

"But where are my manners?" Her stepmother seemed to come out of her daze. "Would you like a drink? A cup of coffee or iced tea or something?"

"No, thanks," Holly said before Vince started to cough.

What? she snapped at him.

I could use a coffee.

We're in the middle of a covert operation and you want a drink?

It's been a busy morning.

Fine.

"Actually, Mrs. Evans"—Holly forced herself to give a lighthearted smile—"a coffee would be great."

"Black, no sugar," Vince added.

"That's how Holly had hers," her stepmother reminisced in a sad voice, oblivious to the fact that Vince had taken over. In fact, for some reason Vince was being chattier than normal. Still, Holly supposed it saved her from having to do so much talking.

And could Holly just say it was lucky she loved Todd so much, because this whole idea of coming back to her old house was just weird, with a capital W. Why was her stepmother pretending to do the grieving thing in front of Vince Murphy? It just didn't make any sense, but before she could ponder it further, the phone rang.

"Excuse me," her stepmother said as she picked up the handset. After a minute or so she put her hand over the receiver and gave them an apologetic frown. "I'm so sorry; I might be a few minutes. It's the local paper. They came around the other day to do a small story on Holly, and they just want a few extra details. I think she would've liked to be in the paper."

Well, yes, to be honest it had always been Holly's secret ambition to be in the best-dressed section, or perhaps the most-loved couple, with a photo of her and Todd looking absolutely adorable in matching jeans and white T-shirts (with perhaps even a kitten or a puppy in their laps). In fact, just about anything would have done, except the obituary section.

"I'm sure she would've." Vince once again took over. "While you're on the phone, would you like me to carry those boxes upstairs for you? I don't mind."

Holly groaned. As if her stepmother would ever fall for such an overzealous Boy Scout routine, but a moment later she was proved wrong when her stepmother gave a grateful nod.

"Vince, that would be lovely, but I hate to take up your time. I know how busy you must be. Holly certainly worked hard enough."

"It's nothing," he assured her, and after she told him it was the second bedroom at the top of the stairs, she returned her attention back to the phone and Holly was left blinking.

I can't believe that worked.

Vince shrugged as he walked back to the front room and picked up two boxes. *It seems like she's had a tough couple of weeks.*

Haven't we all, Holly retorted before immediately feeling lousy. Vince was right: Even though Holly didn't like her stepmother, it was obvious she had been left behind to tie up all the loose ends. *Sorry,* she mumbled in a contrite tone. *It just feels weird being back here.*

Don't apologize, Vince said as he took the stairs two at a time. *You're doing okay.*

Thanks. Holly felt a bit taken aback by the unexpected vote of confidence. Vince really seemed to understand how she was feeling, and for a moment she wondered if it was more than just being polite. However, before she could ask, Vince used the base of his shoe to gently push the door open, and Holly found herself face-to-face with her old life.

She couldn't even remember the last time she'd been in there, but was surprised to see it was exactly the same. For some reason she had assumed her stepmother would've turned it into a home gym just out of spite. Apparently not. Though she probably could've taken down the Spice Girls posters. After all, it might be appropriate for a twelve-year-old girl to want to be Posh Spice, but right now, with Vince standing next to her, it didn't seem quite so fitting.

He really was finding out all her dark, dirty secrets after all. While she would've been mortified if Todd ever saw her old room, for some reason it didn't matter that

Vince did. Perhaps it was because she would never see him again after tomorrow?

They quickly dumped the boxes down and headed back down for more. It took five trips in all, and Holly realized that if she weren't dead, she would've been forced to have a serious cleaning out of her closet. Two boxes just to hold summer shoes? It suddenly seemed a bit excessive.

Once they were back in her old room, she knelt down and carefully pulled the tape away from the first box. Although they were labeled, she wasn't sure where her pearls and the mix CD would be.

Holly pulled the cardboard back and felt a jolt go through her, as right at the top was the outfit she had been planning to wear the night she died.

She bit her lip as her fingers touched the delicate silk of the shimmering red dress. How different everything would've been if she *had* managed to come back from the bathroom and slip it on as planned.

The stupid thing was, she hadn't even felt tired or woozy when she first hopped into the steamy water. She had been a little bit jumpy. That was only natural, considering she was going to be become engaged to the man of her dreams later that night. What girl wouldn't be jumpy? Especially since she hadn't managed to apologize to Todd at that stage.

She'd had one other argument with him when they first started dating. It was over something silly, but Todd had ended up being quite mulish about it, and Holly had quickly realized that if you wanted to date a Scorpio, you had to learn to say you were sorry from time to time. Really, it wasn't such a concession.

She thought back to her bath. It was probably the combination of the warm water and the small gin and tonic she'd been drinking to calm her nerves. But one minute she'd been covered in bubbles, reading her bridal magazine, and the next thing she knew she was waking up in heaven.

Dead.

"Hey," Vince said in a soft voice. "Are you okay?"

"I . . . I don't really know." Holly gulped as she chewed on her bottom lip. "I guess I was just having a flashback. But don't worry. I won't ruin your manly image by crying."

"The good thing about being a loner is that I don't have a manly image to worry about. Cry away."

Holly felt a small wobble come into her throat. Again Vince Murphy was turning out to be quite a guy. Even though she was glad he didn't die, if he had, she now realized that she would have definitely become friends with him in heaven. They could've hung out and laughed at the stupid things going on below. It would've been okay.

She gave another little sniffle, but before she could get too weepy, the sound of her stepmother's voice on the phone reminded her they were on a deadline.

"I'm fine." She tried to convince herself. "There'll be time for getting upset later. Right now we've got work to do."

"Lead the way, Sherlock." Vince grinned, and Holly pushed the outfit to one side. Toward the bottom of the carton she finally retrieved the CD Todd had burned her and the black velvet box that held her necklace.

She flicked up the lid and for a moment gazed down at the perfectly round pearls with their intense luster. They were so beautiful, and she tried not to think how much better they would've looked if accompanied by a gigantic diamond engagement ring.

Vince coughed, and Holly snapped the lid shut. "Sorry," she muttered as she caught sight of the stupid stuffed rabbit Todd had given her a few months ago. He had won it at a local fair, but it had a cost him a fortune in attempts to do so. But that was Todd: Once he wanted something he didn't stop until he got it. It was the same determination that made him so successful at work. And so attractive. No wonder that stupid tart Rochelle Jackson wanted to get her French-manicured nails into him.

Holly picked the rabbit up and hugged it to her chest before quickly shoving it in her bag. Then she moved on to the next box, where she found a slinky black skirt and a camisole that had cost her four weeks' wages.

She had been wearing that outfit the day she and Todd went on their first date. If anything would convince him, this would be it. Well, that and a bit of private bedroom information, though with Vince listening in on every word, Holly had decided that sex secrets would be used only as a final resort (and definitely no mention of their first night together, which didn't actually go as planned, but fortunately there had been a vast improvement since).

"You know, just because I don't care about my manly image doesn't mean I want to go around wearing a skirt."

Vince took control of his hand and put the offending item back in the box.

"I don't think you have the legs for a DKNY pencil skirt," Holly retorted as she reached for it again. "Anyway, it's not for wearing. It's for sentimental purposes only."

"I hope you remember that," Vince said as Holly heard her stepmother coming up the stairs.

"Fine," she whispered as she quickly shut the box up. "As long as you're quiet, I'll do anything."

"Anything?" Vince sounded interested.

Stop it, she commanded just as her stepmother walked into the room. *Good grief.* Besides, what on earth did he think she could do when they were in the same body? Then a disturbing thought entered her mind, which she immediately blocked, but not before she felt some sort of movement in the trouser department.

Oh, my God. Vince, she hissed in horror.

Hey, he protested, *I think I know how my body works better than you do, and I can promise it has nothing to do with me.*

Are you saying it's me? She tried to hide her disbelief. *Of all the silly things.*

That's exactly what I'm saying. So what were you thinking about?

Holly blushed. There was no way he was right, of course, but just say for argument's sake he was . . . well, there was even less way she was going to admit to anything. *It's not important,* she said instead. *Besides, here's my stepmother. C-can you make it go away?*

Vince sighed, and while she had no idea what he was

thinking about, she was relieved to feel that . . . things . . . had settled down. Boy, talk about a loaded gun.

Thank you, she said.

Don't mention it. Well, that wouldn't be a problem, since Holly was quite eager to wipe the whole episode from her memory. Completely.

"Here you go, Vincent."

Holly plastered a smile onto her face. "Oh, thanks, Mrs. Evans."

Holly blew on the coffee for a minute, pleased at the distraction. *Just concentrate on the coffee*, she instructed herself. *It's all about the coffee.* Then she took a sip and felt the caffeine snake its way through her. Ah, that was better.

She was about to take another sip when she realized her stepmother was studying her anxiously. *Oh no.* Holly's first instinct was to look downward, but luckily everything was under control. Then she caught sight of Vince's satchel. Perhaps taking the rabbit wasn't such a good move after all?

"I . . . Is everything all right?"

Her stepmother sat down on the bed. "Sorry . . . yes, everything's fine. It was just that phone call. It's so hard to talk about Holly as if she's actually dead."

Holly let out a sigh of relief as she realized the rabbit was safe. "Well, that's okay then . . . I mean . . . uh, did the journalist ask you a difficult question or something?"

"No more than anyone else has asked." Her stepmother blew her nose. "I guess I'm just finding it overwhelming. After Joe—that's Holly's father—died, he entrusted her into my care, and it was the only thing that helped him go in peace. I've made such a mess of it."

Holly stared at her in surprise. Was she for real? Her stepmother had never given a hoot what Holly or her father had thought. She was just in it for the money.

Wasn't she?

"Er . . . well, I'm sure that's not true," Holly said in a diplomatic voice, not quite sure what else she should do.

"It is. You see, I never got along with Holly. Not really. I pretended to for Joe's sake, but she was so . . . I don't know . . . difficult. And I guess I saw her as a threat. Then, of course, by the time I realized how stupid I was acting, it was too late to change. If I hadn't been so insecure, I might've been able to have a better relationship with her. Perhaps stop her from taking her own life?"

"What?"

What?

"Mrs. Evans, no one thinks that. Holly didn't commit suicide. It was an accident. It wasn't your fault," Vince butted in before Holly could even speak.

"Yes, it was." Her stepmother started to sob uncontrollably now, and Holly was getting seriously freaked out. "I shouldn't be telling you this, but Holly had a few . . . troubles . . . after her father died. Anyway, she seemed better, but I never took the time to really check. I just assumed it was because she was busy at her job."

"She was." This time Holly did manage to answer.

Her stepmother looked up, the tears still heavy on the lashes that fringed her dark blue eyes. "How do you know? I didn't think you and Holly were still friends."

They had never been friends. How many times did Holly have to say it?

"Of course we're still friends," Holly assured her, without even bothering to cross her fingers. After all, she'd already seen heaven, and it didn't seem quite so important to ensure her safe passage there.

Her stepmother pulled another tissue out and wiped her eyes. "You really don't think she—"

"I am absolutely, one hundred percent positive that she didn't plan to . . . you know . . ."

"It was hard enough when Joe died. I tried to put a brave face on for Holly, but this time I couldn't even do that. It seemed so unfair that someone so young and lovely could die."

"I know it does," Vince suddenly said in a soft voice, and before Holly could stop him, he put his arm around her stepmother's shoulder and gave her gentle hug.

Hey.

What on earth was going on here? Did Vince have some sort of Mrs. Robinson fetish or something? Why did he just take over like that?

She longed to ask him, but he seemed too busy being nice to her stepmother, and Holly couldn't quite find the words to speak. Did her stepmother just call her lovely again?

"I think it's unfair Holly died as well," Vince was now saying, and even though it was Vince who was doing the hugging, Holly found herself tightening her grip around her stepmother's slim shoulders. She hadn't expected to feel like this.

"I can't bear what people are saying about her," her stepmother sobbed.

"You need to remember it's not true," Holly said before Vince could jump in. "I'm sure people will stop saying those horrible things any day now. You wait and see."

"Thank you, Vincent Murphy. It's sweet of you to try to make me feel better, and I hope with all my heart that you are right."

Well, that would make two of them.

Or was that three?

Fourteen

Holly was still a bit dazed and confused as they walked back into the workshop and sat down at Vince's bench. Had that really just happened? They didn't have time to stop for lunch, so Vince had just grabbed a sandwich on the way through. Holly had been too distracted to even remember about the sushi.

So what did you make of my stepmother? she suddenly asked him. *Because, you know, that wasn't normal behavior for her. When I was younger she was on my case all the time and never cut me any slack at all.*

She seemed pretty genuine to me.

Yes, well, that's what I thought. She did *seem genuine. But that's the weird part, don't you think?*

Yes, completely weird that your stepmother might be upset about your death.

Holly rubbed the bridge of her nose. It was too much to think about right now. Besides, all that really mattered was that she had evidence in Vince's satchel to convince Todd of who she was. It was such a relief, because the way the morning had been shaping up, Holly had seriously started to doubt whether she would even come close to resolving this mess. If anything, thanks to being in Vince's body, she had been worried about going back with more than she came with (and she so wasn't including that embarrassing incident back there in her bedroom, because that was completely *forgotten*).

Now things seemed a bit more promising, and she had to admit she had Vince to thank for that. Who would've thought that under his geek exterior there was such a nice guy? Well, not that he looked like a geek, exactly. Or acted like one. In fact, Holly couldn't quite remember why she had thought he was a geek in the first place.

So what are your plans now? Vince wiped the last of the crumbs away from his mouth. *I've got to reconfigure an operating system and then upgrade a printer for the Dock and Harbor board, but then I should be able to free myself up for the rest of the afternoon.*

Oh, yes. Now Holly remembered where the geek thing came from, and for a moment she smiled. It was sort of cute the way he spoke like that. When Todd talked about work it was always to do with how much money he had made from a particular job.

Speaking of her almost fiancé . . .

I guess we need to talk to Todd, and I'm sure now that we have all this proof it won't be a problem.

Like selling ice to Eskimos.

Look, I know he was acting a bit strange this morning, but it's just because he's so upset about my death.

Vince made a snorting noise, but before he could retort another one of the technicians came up to them. This one was wearing a Donald Duck tie.

"Hey, Vince. Did you see the message Todd Harman

left you?" Donald said, and Holly could feel her eyes widen in excitement.

Oh, wow, a message. Surely that's a sign? She could hardly contain her glee. She just knew that her earlier willpower had worked.

Or it could just be a message, Vince retorted in a deadpan voice before turning his attention back to the technician. "So what did he want?"

"He came in about half an hour ago saying it was urgent. He was a bit pissed you weren't around."

Holly hardly heard him. She had known somewhere deep down that Todd recognized her spirit and that every second away from her was agony.

Definitely a sign, she said to Vince, but he ignored her as he nodded to Donald Duck to continue.

"Anyway, he left you three laptops that he needs you to look at ASAP. He also wants you to get him four more user manuals as well. There's a note."

Vince didn't seem impressed. "Let me guess, for Peterson's?"

The technician nodded. "Of course. Their system hasn't crashed for at least three days; what do you expect?"

What's he talking about? Holly silently asked—not that she really cared, since she was fairly sure the laptops were just a cover for Todd to see her again.

One of your boyfriend's accounts, Vince told her. *A particular trick of the sales department is to undercut on competing quotes by not including a software licensing agreement. Instead they just copy the existing individual user software and network it. Problem is, while it's cheaper, it's not legal or stable. Which is why the system keeps crashing.*

Vince, you've got to stop with all of these conspiracy theories. Of course Todd wouldn't do that, and if there's an omission it's because he doesn't know about it.

Vince stalked over to his workbench and pulled a folder out of an envelope, which he then flipped open. Holly quickly scanned the first page. *Okay, so apparently it's illegal to do,* she conceded once she finished reading it. *But I'm sure there's been a simple mistake.*

Donald Duck coughed. "Are you okay, Vince? You seem a bit distracted."

"Huh?" Vince looked up from the folder and gave an apologetic grimace. "Oh, I was just . . . thinking something through. What were you saying?"

Donald shook his head. "Nothing. It's just that you wandered off; that's all."

Sorry, Holly apologized to Vince. *That was my fault.*

I know.

"Okay. Well, I've got a firewall with my name on it." Donald shot Vince a quizzical glance before heading toward the door, but before he got very far, he turned back toward them. "Don't forget drinks tonight. Andrew said you're coming along. First round on me."

Holly frowned as something else occurred to her. *But what I don't understand is . . . Oh, hang on. I think Donald's saying good-bye.*

Vince blinked and glanced up. "Oh, right, see you later, Donald— Shit, I mean Graham."

Whoops. It was the tie. Holly gulped.

"Are you sure you're okay?" Graham studied them through narrowed eyes.

"Yes, it's just been a *very* trying day," Vince assured him, but Holly couldn't help but feel he might be referring to her.

Vince, I really am sorry. But why do they wear those things, anyway? Does someone come around selling them cheap or something?

For a moment Vince made a strangled sound from his throat, as if he wanted to say something, but then he burst out laughing.

Is that a you-forgive-me laugh or an I'm-going-insane-from-the-pressure laugh?

It's an I've-never-known-anyone-else-like-you laugh, he explained as he sat down and started to listen to his voice mail. (Ew, two more from Amy starting-to-turn-into-a-bit-of-a-stalker Jenkins.) Well, at least he wasn't mad at her, but as to whether it was a compliment or not, Holly couldn't be too sure.

Holly was dying to ring Gemma, but Vince was still doing goodness knew what to the three laptops he had laid out on his workbench. One of the many problems with body-sharing was that she couldn't exactly sneak off for a cup of tea and a flick through her *Bride and Beauty* magazine. Or pick up a phone.

She couldn't even glance around, since apparently Vince couldn't fix the computers and stare at the posters on the wall at the same time. Which meant she had to settle for looking at his hands. Still, at least they were quite nice, as far as fingers went. Strong and lean, and though it pained her to admit it, they were better than Todd's, who had very short nails. She had never caught him chewing them, but she had her suspicions. Still, life was all about compromise, and everything else about him was pretty perfect.

Then she flushed as she realized she had better not think too much about Todd in case the same thing happened that did earlier in her bedroom. She paused for a moment to make sure everything was in a relaxed state and then let out a sigh of relief. She had obviously checked herself in time. There was no way she wanted to go through that again.

She glanced over to the note he had left for Vince. The tone to it was definitely friendlier than their previous meeting, and he had asked Vince to bring the fixed computers up to his office before three thirty in the afternoon. It definitely wasn't a coincidence, since he could've asked any of the technicians to do it, yet he had singled out Vince. Which really meant he had singled out Holly, and—

Holly. Vince silently coughed.

Sorry. She obediently returned her attention back to the computer and stared at the monitor instead. *What is all this stuff, anyway?*

Vince shrugged. *Looks like it's content for Peterson's Productions' new Web site. I'm just making sure I've retrieved all the files.*

Peterson's Productions? Why does that sound familiar?

They produce TV shows. I think this is Lorraine's computer. She's one of the assistants. Anyway, it seems to all be here—

Oh, my God! Holly cut him off before lifting her hand off the mouse to stop him from exiting the window. *Peterson's Productions does* The Rich and the Restless. *That's why the name sounded so familiar. I see their logo at the end of every episode. Why didn't you tell me you did their computers?*

You didn't ask. Anyway, they're Todd's account; why didn't he mention it?

I don't know. Holly paused for a moment, deciding it didn't really matter. The main thing was that now she knew. *So, come on; keep scrolling down.*

No way. My job is to fix these things, not to look at confidential files. It's against company policy.

Vince. This is The Rich and the Restless. Holly pressed down on his finger until the cursor moved onto the next page. *Don't be so stuffy. Perhaps they'll have some new story lines? I haven't seen the show for over two weeks. If God is really so high and mighty, then why doesn't he have cable?*

One of the great mysteries, Vince agreed with a straight face.

Oh, look. They're talking about the end-of-season finale, and here's some stuff on the characters they've killed off in the past. Boy, I wish they really were kicking the bucket, and then I'd be able to hang out with them in heaven. We could have a Rich and the Restless *Is Dead Cool club. How wicked would that be . . . and— Oh. Hang on a minute. That's not right,* Holly said, pointing to the screen.

What do you mean, "That's not right?" There's nothing wrong or right about it; it's just text for the Web site.

I was out there the other day and Lorraine mentioned she had to get everything together for the designers.

That might be so, but the text is wrong. Listen to this. "From 2001 to 2003, Jenny Little played everyone's favorite nurse, Carla Wandsworth, until tragedy struck and Carla was caught up in the dreadful Rich and the Restless *fire of season two."*

And you're telling me this because?

Because Carla is alive and well and living quite happily at number twelve Flamingo Crescent. Yes, she was in the fire, though not in season two; it was season three. And as for dying, that's just a load of baloney. She suffered severe facial burns, but under the careful care of plastic surgeon Guy Sheraton she went on to make a full recovery, and she and Guy married last year. Then Holly sniffed. *They were even hoping to start IVF this season. Their babies would've been beautiful.*

Okay, so, not meaning to change the subject here, but don't we have more important things to worry about than a couple of mistakes on The Rich and the Restless *Web site?*

Holly folded her arms. *Well, I'm not sure if that's the right attitude. This is a much beloved show that people take very seriously.*

Yes, so I can see.

Unlike the person who did this research, she said darkly as she moved her fingers toward the keyboard, but Vince clenched his fist in the air, blocking her so she couldn't.

I was only going to correct the mistakes. She pouted. *I thought you'd be pleased that I'm trying to think about other things besides my problems.*

"I promise I'll e-mail Lorraine and get her to make the corrections."

You know, I still can't believe they're doing a new Web site. Holly clapped her hands in excitement. *I wonder if they're going to have a chat room? That would be great. I know so many people were devastated when Clyde and Sarah broke up; it would be important to have a place where people could share stories of consolation. It would really help the grieving process.*

Holly, you do remember you're dead, don't you? Vince asked as he rose to his feet and started to reassemble the computers. *Now, I suppose we'd better take these up to Todd's office. Are you ready?*

Holly looked at his watch and realized he was right. It was time for her to finally talk to Todd and get everything sorted out once and for all. *Okay, but you won't forget to e-mail that person, will you?*

I won't, he assured her as he hooked his satchel over his shoulder and stacked the computers up in front of him.

Oh, and what about the manuals he wanted? Holly came to a standstill. *It's just that if I'm going to explain to Todd that I'm back from the dead and temporarily living in your body, we might want to stay on his good side.*

Todd knows very well that he can either order new manuals for them or photocopy old ones himself. It's not my job.

Again on the good side, Holly reminded him, and she couldn't help but admire that despite the way his lips twitched, he merely put down the computers and marched toward the photocopying machine. *Thanks, Vince,* she said. *I really do owe you one.*

Holly was surprised they hadn't worn a hole in the carpet, they'd been up and down to the fourth floor so many times today, but at last it was going to happen.

Yesterday when Dr. Hill had thrown her into this ridiculous situation, she had thought that returning to clear things up would be the easiest thing in the world, whereas it was turning out to be incredibly difficult. Still, at least things were finally looking up. They had a chance to sit down and talk to Todd, and tonight after work they could stake out Rochelle Jackson's apartment until the coast was clear. Yes, it was all coming together—

"If you're looking for Todd, he's not here," a voice said from behind them, and Holly spun around (not something that was easy to do when carrying three laptops in your arms) to where Simon Trimmer was standing.

"He wants to take these back to Peterson's with him," Vince explained, but Simon just shrugged.

"Something else came up. He was going to text you to get you to drop them off instead. Apparently it's urgent they get them by four."

"Well, he didn't, and I've got a full schedule this afternoon," Vince retorted before Holly took over.

"Where's he gone?" she demanded.

Simon didn't seem to notice a change of speaker as he folded his arms. "I don't see how that's any of your business."

What? Holly glared back at him. Of course it was her business. She had a lot of explaining and apologizing to do, and it was a bit difficult if the person in question was nowhere to be found.

"Personally, I'm not interested," Vince replied in a calm voice. "I just wanted to let him know that I'm not his delivery boy. If he wants these taken over to Peterson's, he can do it himself or arrange for a courier."

"Too late," Simon retorted. "And I doubt David Harris would be pleased to hear that his good friend Stuart Peterson wasn't getting the service he deserved."

Holly couldn't believe the snicker that was building in Simon Trimmer's voice. Holly might just have to take issue with that, and she would certainly be passing it on to Todd when she finally managed to talk to him. She opened her mouth to reply, but before anything could come out Vince clamped his lips firmly shut.

Just leave it, Holly. I'll get one of the guys to run them over.

Yes, but Simon's acting intolerably. To think that Gemma wanted to date him. I'm just going to have to tell her he isn't suitable.

You're not hearing any arguments from me, Vince replied as they headed back down the hall.

So much for that plan, Holly moaned as they turned a corner. *I really thought I was getting somewhere.* At that moment she caught sight of another suicide help line poster, and she reached out to yank it down off the wall. This time Vince didn't even bother to stop her.

Fifteen

"Okay," Holly said as soon as they got back to the empty workshop and Vince put the laptops on the bench. "So this is not good. Not only do I need to speak to Todd, I need to find him first. I also need to search Rochelle's apartment and tell Gemma not to date Simon Trimmer. Except Gemma isn't answering her phone, which means I'm never going to get anything done and I'll be stuck in Level One forever and never get to Level Two, let alone Level Three, where my dad is, and—"

"Hey." Vince dropped his hand so that Holly could no longer manically tick off his fingers. "The first thing you need to do is stop panicking."

"Yes, but the day is almost over and I've achieved nothing. Nothing. I think I'm going to be sick. Do you feel sick as well, or is it just me? Because I swear that—"

Vince dragged in a lungful of air, and Holly felt the panic start to subside. "Look," he said in a calm voice. "I think we'd better find Gemma. She might know where Todd is. Okay?"

"But—"

"But nothing," Vince cut her off. "Now let's go find

Gemma. Trust me: You'll feel much better when we can figure out a new plan."

"Thanks," she said as layers of calm descended upon her as they headed for the elevator again. Vince was right: She felt better already.

There she is. Holly nodded over to where Gemma and a gaggle of colleagues were standing next to a bulletin board, having an animated conversation. Vince paused for a minute, but Holly didn't want to waste any more time, so she hurried across the office until she was just behind the group.

No one turned around, so she did a polite cough.

I don't think she heard us, Vince commented, as Gemma's back stayed firmly facing them.

"Hey, Gem," Holly said in a clear voice. "Do you have a minute?"

Gemma slowly turned around. "Oh, Vince," she said in an overbright voice. "W-what a surprise. I didn't realize you were there."

Holly stared at the way Gemma was wringing her hands together—a sure sign she was embarrassed.

You know, Holly, perhaps we should just wait until Gemma's finished with work.

We can't afford to waste any more time, Holly reminded him before returning her attention to a mortified-looking Gemma.

"I was wondering if we—I mean if I—could have a quick word with you?"

"A-actually, now isn't such a great time," Gemma said as she raised her eyebrows in the direction of her colleagues. There were four of them, and they were all studying them, with great interest.

Holly lifted her own eyebrows in a telling manner. "Since we're speaking about time, this is rather pressing—"

Before she could finish, Vince gave a small cough and shot Gemma an understanding smile. "So why don't you just call me when you're free?"

A look of relief spread across Gemma's face. "Okay, then. I'll talk to you *later*."

Holly could barely stop her mouth from falling open. Yes, she understood that Gemma might find it slightly odd to be talking to her best friend, who was in the body of a guy, but Holly could hardly understand why Gemma was embarrassed by it all. She had been acting funny all day, and the worst thing was that Holly couldn't say anything about it in front of Vince because there was no way she wanted to hurt his feelings.

At the back of her mind was the realization that up until yesterday she hadn't been interested in spending time with Vince either. But that was different, she thought.

So why didn't Gemma want to talk to Vince?

He was a nice guy. Cute, funny, and okay, perhaps he was slightly moody, but these days, with long working hours and not enough sleep, who wasn't a bit moody? And kind. He was turning out to be a genuinely kind person, and Holly had the feeling he would've taken those boxes up for her stepmother, whether they needed to look in them or not.

Then she realized that somehow her brain had managed to make a little mental trip back to her old bedroom. No, that incident was wiped forever, so her brain could just damn well behave itself. *Okay?*

Are you all right? Vince asked as they got out of the elevator and made their way back to the workshop.

Yes, I'm fine, she hastily reassured him, since she didn't want to let on about her concerns for Gemma. Or anything else that she most certainly wasn't thinking about. *Why do you ask?*

Because you just walked past three suicide line posters and didn't try and tear any of them down. . . .

Holly flushed. She was starting to get the feeling Vince knew her better than she knew herself.

Gemma rang ten minutes later. "Holly, I'm so, so sorry about before."

"That's okay," Holly lied, careful not to give herself away to Vince by clenching her jaw. But she was jaw clenching on the inside.

"You know what it's like when everyone's talking shop."

Hmm. Holly made a stubborn little snort.

"Of course, it didn't help that my boss was right in the middle of the most *boring* lecture ever. He does go on," Gemma continued in a rush, and Holly felt herself unbend a bit. She reluctantly admitted that it was true about Gemma's boss. He was the king of boring lectures.

Perhaps she was just a bit touchy about everything? After all, that was what got her kicked out of heaven in the first place. Man, this was so complicated.

"So, anyway," Gemma charged on, "how did everything go? Did you get the things from your old house?"

"Oh." Holly blinked. That seemed like ages ago now. "I got the necklace, the CD, and a few other memory-jogging items."

"Was she horrible?"

Holly chewed on her lip for a moment. "Actually, she was being sort of nice. If I didn't know better I'd say she was upset."

"You know . . ." Gemma seemed to ponder. "I think you could be right. She looked pretty distressed at the funeral, and then at the wake she kept wanting to talk to me about you."

"I've only been dead for two weeks, but it's weird because I'm not angry at her anymore. She admitted that she didn't like me when I was younger, and all of a sudden everything I had felt for so long . . . well, it just rushed away. I guess I have to admit that I wasn't an angel either. I suppose it was a two-way street."

Gemma paused for a minute. "A lot of stuff happened, Holly, but you can't live in the past forever."

"Sometimes you don't know what you've got until it's gone," Vince added in a thoughtful voice, and Holly, who had been about to laugh at the tried and true cliché, wondered if there was something else behind his words. Actually, there had been a couple of times when he had been more than just understanding about everything. Had his family been a bit dysfunctional as well? She knew his dad was in prison, but come to think of it, he hadn't mentioned his mom yet. She made a mental note to ask him about it later. When her brain wasn't quite so overloaded.

Then she caught sight of Vince's watch and realized

they were wasting time. "I guess the point is, I did manage to get all the things I need. Unfortunately Todd's gone AWOL, and Simon Trimmer won't tell us where he is. Also, we need to get around to Rochelle's house and look for evidence. Did I mention my head hurts?"

"Mine too," Vince agreed as he rubbed his temples.

"Okay, so this is where I come in," Gemma said. "I know I haven't been much help during the day, and I'm really sorry about that. But the good news is that I have a date with Simon tonight."

Holly's life was going down the toilet and Gemma was talking about dating? Not that she wasn't happy for her friend. Well, apart from the fact that Simon was proving to be a bit of jerk. It was just . . . well . . . the timing could've been better.

"Oh, I hope you have a nice time." She tried to sound enthusiastic. After all, just because she was dead didn't mean Gemma shouldn't still have a life. "Though I must say Simon wasn't really that nice when I tried to speak to him before."

"Yes, but he didn't know you were you," Gemma defended. "I forgot to say the reason it's good news is because Simon wanted to know if it was okay to bring Todd along. I think he must be worried about Todd right now. Isn't that so sweet?"

Holly instantly forgot her headache as she clutched at the phone. "This is wonderful news. I should've known you wouldn't let me down. So where are you going?"

"To the Pool Palace at nine o'clock."

"Man, I hate that place," Vince complained. "Do we have to go in?"

"Yes, we have to go in," Holly informed him. "I can't very well speak to Todd from outside, can I?"

"We might have a better chance of not getting hit if we don't go in," Vince pointed out.

"He's not going to hit you once he realizes what's happened." Gemma sounded shocked. "Oh, damn. My boss wants me. Look, I'm probably going to be about another half hour, so why don't you go on ahead to Rochelle's and I'll meet you there as soon as I can?"

"That's fine," Holly agreed, and as soon as she hung up the phone she rubbed her brow. "I feel exhausted. This has been the longest day ever."

Vince got to his feet and slung his satchel over his shoulder. "Yes, and it's not over yet. We still have an apartment to break into."

Once again Holly marveled at his man-strength. If she were in her regular body she probably would've been drooping with exhaustion by now, fit only to collapse on the couch with a glass of wine and her remote control, but he just seemed to feel . . . well . . . like it was business as usual. For the first time since she'd found herself stuck in Vince Murphy's six-foot body, she realized that she could've done a lot worse.

As they made their way back up to the reception area, there was a steady stream of people leaving for the day. Holly was surprised, since she couldn't remember the last time she had finished work on time. She hoped that Rochelle Jackson wasn't being quite so conscientious. If she were, it would be a first.

All she knew was that the sooner they searched Rochelle's Chloe bag for proof, the sooner Holly could start mentally preparing for her conversation with Todd tonight. Most of the day had been spent skating around the edges, but this was almost it. She was going to confront the issues and get herself back up to heaven, past Level Two and into Level Three. Back to her dad. Her real mom. It was where she needed to be, and—

"Hey," she complained as she realized Vince had come to a halt behind a large marble column. "Why are we stopping?"

"Look." He nodded in the direction of the front door. "There're Andrew and the others."

"So? Now that I've spent some time with them, they're not so bad . . . well, apart from the ties, obviously," Holly said before it dawned on her what Vince meant. She groaned. "Oh, no. I said we'd join them for a drink, didn't I?"

"Yup," Vince agreed.

"Why didn't I keep my big mouth shut? No, wait. Don't answer that."

For a moment she could feel Vince's lips twitch. "Don't sweat it. We'll just stay here until they go. Then when the coast is clear we can leave."

"Who knew you were so sneaky?" Holly was impressed—and relieved. The sooner they got proof from Rochelle's bag, the sooner they could go home and prepare for the big meeting with Todd tonight. What did one wear on a date when she was in a man's body?

"I told you I had your back." Vince gave a modest shrug before letting out a string of expletives.

"What's wrong now?"

"I think we might have a bit of a problem at five o'clock."

Holly glanced at her watch. "What are you talking about? It's already quarter past."

"No, I mean look over in the direction of five o'clock," he said as he drew her attention toward the grand staircase over to the right.

"Oh, it's Fluffy. She glanced up as a familiar white-haired dog danced over toward them. "So what's the problem?"

"Fluffy's the problem."

"Fluffy? Don't be silly." Holly rolled her eyes as the little dog hurried over. Technically Fluffy belonged to Martha, the receptionist who knew everything and had worked at the company since the dawn of time. Due to some slight ear problem, she had convinced personnel she could not do her job without her specially trained hearing dog.

The reality was that Fluffy spent more time cruising around the building, begging treats, and generally being adorable than giving his mistress the benefit of his finely tuned audio skills. Not that Martha seemed to mind, since she still never missed any gossip, and she didn't have to pay a dog sitter for Fluffy during the day.

There had even been a stage when personnel had informed Martha that Fluffy could no longer come into the workplace under new health and safety laws. Fortunately that very week Fluffy had been the company mascot at the national Baker Colwell games, and since the head office had gone on to trounce all competitors in an unprecedented victory, Fluffy's banishment had never again been mentioned.

"Here, girl," Holly cooed as she felt around in her

pocket for her normal stash of treats, only to discover it was actually Vince's pocket and that he didn't seem to find it necessary to carry any emergency chocolate or cookies with him. Would she ever truly understand men?

"I really wouldn't do that if I were you."

"Vince, you're just being silly. Fluffy loves me. In fact, she loves everyone and— Oh, my God . . . Fluffy, stop barking." But the sound of Vince's voice seemed to send the small dog into an apoplectic frenzy.

"Well, she might love everyone else, but she doesn't love me," Vince said in a caustic tone. "Perhaps we'd better not speak out loud. It only seems to aggravate her."

You think? Holly glanced down to where the small dog was tugging at Vince's trousers. Then she realized Fluffy's antics were attracting quite a crowd. *Perhaps it's because dogs are really clever and she's got a sixth sense and knows there are two people in one body?*

Yeah, maybe, he said, but he didn't sound convinced as Fluffy continued to yap and jump at his leg. *Though I'm pretty sure it's because she hates me.*

"Shhhh, Fluffy," she hissed in a low voice, which only made the dog jump higher. *Do something, Vince.*

Any suggestions?

I was hoping you'd have some, she said as more heads turned toward them. But before Vince could answer, Andrew and a couple of the other technicians glanced over and waved.

"Hey, Vince. We were starting to give up on you. Come on; the rest of the guys are already at the bar."

We don't have time for this, Holly hissed in Vince's head, but he just gave her a shrug.

Look, we'll just go along and escape as soon as we can. Besides, at least it will get us away from this dog.

Sometimes Holly wasn't even sure why she bothered. Perhaps she should just call up Dr. Hill and put a stop to this ridiculous farce right now. But of course, before she could say anything, Vince was already striding across the reception area to where Andrew was waiting. It seemed today was destined to be one of those days that anything that could go wrong, would go wrong. Perhaps it was Vince Murphy's Law?

Sixteen

I'm not drinking beer. Holly folded her arms so that Vince couldn't pick up the bottle he'd just ordered from the barman. *Do you know how many calories are in that thing?*

Vince glanced down at his lean legs and then reached for the bottle. *Look, when you get back up into heaven you can have Cosmopolitans or whatever it is that young dead career girls drink, but I like beer.*

Holly was about to protest, but after Vince took a long swig she started to feel some of the stress of the day wander off into the corner. *Hmm.* Normally if she had a glass of wine or a cocktail the sensation was a lot sharper. Less smooth. She lifted up Vince's arm to encourage him to take another swig. After all, he was right; it had been a long day, and it wasn't like she needed to squeeze into her skinny jeans anymore. Perhaps they should grab a couple of Hershey bars before the end of the night? Not that she wanted to take advantage of this newly inherited metabolism, but it did seem a shame to waste it completely.

Vince leaned against the bar, and they watched the rest of the technicians laughing at something Andrew said. Holly was pretty sure it had nothing to do with html code. In fact, if she pretended the novelty ties weren't there, she probably never would've guessed they were all from the technical department. Now Graham was telling everyone about what had happened last weekend at his brother's bachelor party. She never would've guessed these guys would be funny, either.

I think this might've been just what the doctor ordered, she told Vince as he lifted the bottle to his mouth and took another gulp. Holly let out a satisfied sigh. She was definitely getting the hang of it now.

Well, your doctor ordered you to come back to earth and get to work, but most regular doctors would probably just suggest a bit of relaxation to alleviate stress.

I wonder if Dr. Hill had any idea how complicated this whole process would be, Holly mused. *It's like we keep taking two steps backward to go one step forward. Anyway, I just wanted to tell you you've been great.*

It's not a big deal. Vince shrugged as he played with the neck of the beer bottle. *I can't imagine how annoying it must be to be so close to seeing your folks and being told you can't.*

I think that's what made me act so crazy up there, Holly admitted. *There's so much I want to tell them. You have no idea—* Holly paused midsentence as she recalled that she'd never gotten around to asking Vince why he was so understanding about this whole situation. Especially when it came to families.

An uncomfortable thought descended on her, and she lifted his arm up to have another drink of beer. This time it didn't taste quite so nice.

Vince, she suddenly asked, *have you ever been very close to a person who's died?*

For a moment he didn't answer as they watched Bob Mackay demonstrate his juggling abilities with peanuts. *My mom died when I was eight,* he eventually admitted, and if Holly had been able to touch him she would've reached out and squeezed his hand. As it was she had to be content with crossing her fingers. She didn't know if it helped, but somehow it made her feel more connected to him.

Why didn't you say something? She tried to keep the horror out of her question. *All this time I've been prattling on about my own problems and . . .* her voice trailed off. Since she couldn't stare at Vince, she stared at the beer bottle. *Eight. That's when you moved away from our school, wasn't it? I thought my life went bad when my dad got remarried, but your mom died.*

Holly, the reason I didn't say anything is because, as you keep reminding me, we're up against the clock, and also it was something that happened a long time ago. I'd like to think that if my mom got kicked out of heaven and put in someone else's body that they'd help her out just the same.

Vince, she started to say, but before she could get any further, Andrew appeared by their side with another bottle of beer in his hand and an embarrassed expression on his face.

"So, Vince," the tall technician said. "I wanted to ask you something earlier, but you were in a hurry."

Yeah, and right now we're having a private conversation, Holly wanted to say. Not that there was anything wrong with Andrew, because he did seem quite decent, but all she really wanted to do was talk to Vince about his mom. Just the two of them. Alone.

"Oh, sorry about that," she heard Vince say to the tall technician, and she realized Vince obviously didn't quite feel the same need to be alone with her. "What's up?"

Andrew gave an awkward cough. "I know you can't stay long, but I was wondering . . . Oh, hell, this is really embarrassing. . . ."

What's he talking about? Holly asked Vince, but he just shrugged.

I have no idea.

Oh no, you don't think he knows that—

That I have a dead girl in my body? Vince queried. *No, I think you're safe there.*

Andrew tried again. "Okay, so what I'm trying to say is . . . well . . . I've noticed that you've been talking to Gemma Gulliven today."

Holly started to cough, but Vince ignored her.

"Sure," he agreed. "Why? Do you know her?"

Andrew began to fiddle with the label on the front of his beer bottle. "I guess I've spoken to her a couple of times when I've had to go up to HR, but I'm not really sure she knows who I am. It's just . . . I was wondering if you and she were . . . well . . ."

Oh. My. God. Andrew, Homer Simpson–tie-wearing technician, has a crush on Gemma? Holly wanted to giggle, but for some reason Vince didn't seem to find it quite as amusing as she did.

"No, nothing like that. I don't really know her that well," Vince said.

"Oh." Andrew flushed. "It's just that I'd been think-ing of asking her out, but if you guys are—"

"Definitely not." Vince shook his head so fast that Holly could feel the beer starting to make her a bit dizzy.

"Well, great." Andrew took a large gulp of his drink and the color returned to his face. "So, perhaps I'll ask her out, then. . . . Anyway, didn't you say you couldn't stay long?"

Holly felt Vince glance at his watch and nod his head. "Yeah, I'd better get my skates on, but good luck with Gemma. She seems like a nice girl."

He's going to need it, Holly silently thought, espe-cially since Simon Trimmer had finally asked Gemma out. Though judging by the downward twist to Vince's lips, Holly decided she had better keep this information to herself.

You can say it, you know, Vince said as he shrugged his jacket back on and lifted an arm in the direction of the rest of the group to say good-bye.

Say what?

Say that Gemma will never agree to go on a date with Andrew.

Vince, I wasn't . . . I mean . . . Holly chewed her lip. *Hell.*

He already knows what the answer is.

So why's he going to ask her out then? Holly wanted to know, before remembering that she hadn't planned to admit that Gemma would in fact say no. With capital let-ters and neon lights.

Because at least then he'll know he'd tried to do something about it.

Holly shook her head as they made their way out of the bar and back onto the street. There was no way she was ever going to understand men, and considering she was now getting firsthand experience, that was really saying something.

"Sorry I took so long."

Holly looked up to see Gemma standing next to the bush that she and Vince were currently hiding behind. They had been there for the last twenty minutes, and whatever weirdness had sprung up between them at the bar had disappeared again.

"Has Rochelle come home yet?" her friend asked.

"She's been in there for ten minutes, and so far there hasn't been any movement." Holly shook her head as she glanced up to the Art Deco–style apartment block where Rochelle lived.

"That's a relief." Gemma joined them in a squatting position so she wouldn't be seen. "My technophobic boss kept changing his mind on what font he wanted on the report he's working on. It took ages. Have you been drinking?"

"Sort of," Holly admitted. "Just a quick one."

Gemma swiped at a bit of dirt near her shoe before frowning. "I'm not sure that was such a good idea, especially since you know what a lightweight you are when you drink on an empty stomach."

"Yes, but I wasn't drinking on my stomach," Holly reminded her. "I was drinking on Vince's stomach, so I feel perfectly okay."

"It's true," Vince agreed. "She only told me three

times that she loved me . . . though I think I'm now her best friend in the whole entire universe," he confided with a wink.

Holly raised an eyebrow. How exactly did Vince know so much about drunken women, anyway? Did he go out to clubs and meet them? She tried to think whether she'd ever seen him out, but she was quite sure she hadn't. Perhaps he went to the sleazy clubs where the women were really free and easy? Well, she hoped he behaved, because he was too nice a guy to throw himself away on just anyone. Not that it was any of her business, of course; she was just saying.

"You *are* drunk," Gemma accused, and Holly forced herself to stop drifting off.

"Honestly, I'm fine. Vince is only teasing you. Apparently he has a sense of humor underneath his dark and brooding act."

"Thanks. I think," Vince retorted.

"Yes, but while it's all well and fine to laugh about it," Gemma said stubbornly, "it's not really funny. Did you realize that alcohol is a depressant and that suicide is the third biggest killer in the fifteen-to-twenty-four age group? So obviously the two are closely linked."

"What?" Holly and Vince spoke as one.

"It's true," Gemma persisted. "Sometimes people don't show the signs on the outside, but it doesn't mean they're not there, and—"

"Gemma," Holly interrupted. "Have you been reading those suicide help line pamphlets that have been scattered around the office?"

"It's just a little bit of proactive information. It's not

like it's aimed directly at you." Gemma gave a defensive wave of her arm.

"That's because I'm dead, and as a rule they don't try to target deceased employees. Anyway, I didn't kill myself, remember?"

"Oh." Her friend started to chew her lip. "Sorry, but don't you think it's creepy how many people feel like killing themselves and no one even knows?"

"Yes, well, perhaps if they knew how awful heaven was, they wouldn't be in such a hurry," Holly retorted, and Gemma blushed.

"You're right. Just ignore me. Anyway, I'm still not clear on why you were drinking in the first place."

"It's a bit of a long story."

Gemma glanced toward Rochelle's closed door. "I think we have time."

"Fine," Holly said as she launched into how they had tried to avoid Andrew and company but had ended up being found out.

"But Fluffy's so sweet and kind." Gemma widened her eyes once Holly had finished her story. "That doesn't make any sense."

"I know; that's what I thought, but apparently Fluffy doesn't like Vince."

Gemma looked shocked. "You don't like Fluffy?"

"Hey. I never said I didn't like Fluffy," Vince protested. "I said that Fluffy didn't like me."

"But why? You know, even though my roommate, Irene, is crazy, she's often said that if a dog doesn't like someone it's because there's something wrong with the person. Like they're evil or something."

"Don't be silly. Vince isn't evil. You're not evil, right?"

"No, I'm not evil," Vince assured them both.

"Well, why doesn't Fluffy like him, then?" Gemma clutched at her purse in panic. "Oh, no, please tell me you didn't kick her, because if so, even if Holly's stuck in the same body as you, I just don't think I'd be able to talk to you anymore."

"Of course I didn't kick her." Vince sounded just a bit outraged.

"Well, what then?" Gemma narrowed her eyes.

Vince let out a reluctant sigh. "I guess it's a positive that I don't have a reputation to worry about."

"Vince, please. Just tell us what happened." Holly tried not to chew on his lip, but for some reason this was important. After all, he was a nice guy. She didn't want to find out he was cruel to animals.

"Do you remember how cold it was last November? Like, really, really cold."

Gemma nodded her head. "Holly used that as a great excuse to buy the most adorable cashmere coat you've ever seen."

"It was gorgeous, wasn't it? Hey, now that I'm dead, perhaps you should have it?"

"Isn't that a bit weird to be wearing a dead person's coat?"

"Of course not," Holly assured her before she realized that Vince was rolling his eyes. She coughed. "Anyway, back to Fluffy."

Vince made a sound that could possibly be construed as a sarcastic snort. "Well, one day when I got to work

Fluffy was doing the rounds of the workshop, wearing a blue sweater."

"And?" Holly was still confused.

"And it had a big F in the middle of it."

Gemma stared at him blankly.

"Well, I thought it was funny. I mean, dogs are covered in fur. It's designed to keep them warm. They don't need clothes to do the job. It's dumb."

Holly could feel her eyes widen. "You laughed at Fluffy?"

"You shouldn't do that. Dogs are very sensitive," Gemma added.

"Yeah, and apparently they have a very long memory as well. Look, can we stop talking about this now? It's embarrassing enough that a twelve-inch dog holds a grudge against me, but it's worse that people know about it now."

"So you're sure you didn't do anything else besides laugh at the sweater?" Gemma double-checked.

"Scout's honor." Vince lifted his hand up in something that made him look more like a Trekkie than a Boy Scout, and Gemma seemed satisfied, but before she could say anything else, the front door swung open and Rochelle Jackson emerged.

She was wearing some sort of oversize pink belt, which was masquerading as a skirt, with an equally nonexistent piece of material on her top half.

For a step class?

And boy, she had enough perfume on to kill flies. Honestly, the girl was a walking tart shop. But the thing that made Holly and Gemma really drop their jaws was the size of Rochelle's hair. It was like a Dolly Parton wig, but without Dolly's spunkiness to pull it off.

"Do you think the fact that Todd's single again has gone to her head?" Gemma whispered.

"Something's gone there," Vince agreed as they slunk further down behind the bush.

It seemed to take Rochelle ages to lock the door and even longer to redo her hair, but finally she walked over to her car, and the minute she finished grinding the gears and driving off down the road, Holly jumped to her feet. It looked like this was it.

Seventeen

"Right," Gemma barked. "Go, go, go. And please, Holly, don't do anything stupid like stop and read her diary or try on her clothes. We want this to be a quick operation. Just go in there, find the pills, and get out. Agreed?"

"Of course. I'm only here for another day. The last thing I want to do is spend my time in Rochelle Jackson's bedroom."

"Okay, then. Well, I'll stay here and keep a lookout, and if I see anyone coming I'll call you."

"Agreed." Holly nodded as she hunched her shoulders and ran toward a group of brightly colored pots. As she lifted up the second one, she turned around and gave Gemma the thumbs-up. As predicted, the key was there. Thank goodness it wasn't like Todd's apartment, where you needed three codes and a swipe card just to get through to the foyer. She was fairly certain that retinal scans were just around the corner.

"You do know this is breaking and entering, don't you?" Vince reminded her as Holly twisted the door open. "Not wanting to be a spoilsport, but if we were to get caught, I'd probably be in big trouble."

Holly glanced down and once again reminded herself that she was in the body of six-foot guy. Vince was right: If the police came around, he would be in big trouble. Of course, so would she, since she would fail in her mission.

"It's all right," she said in a decisive voice. "We just won't get caught."

"Comforting." He sighed. "Very comforting." However, he made no protest when she stepped in over the threshold and shut the door behind them.

Rochelle's apartment was a tribute to too much money and not enough sense, but Holly was thankful she had been there before, so she didn't pause too long to stare at the mock-plaster nude statues that adorned the cream-and-gold hallway. However, she couldn't quite miss the huge portrait of Rochelle that was hanging at the top of the stairs.

It was in a ghastly mix of blues and violets, and the artist had been very conservative with the way they'd depicted Rochelle's rounded belly and fat ass. Holly started to giggle and was almost tempted to grab a marker and add a mustache and some glasses, but remembered Gemma's warning. There was no time to muck around.

She hurried up the stairs and into Rochelle's room. It was full of frills and flowers, and Holly wondered if some of Vince's testosterone was rubbing off on her as she glanced around in distaste.

It didn't take her long to spot the Chloe bag, which had been casually abandoned on the floor. Holly immediately bent down and could barely stop her fingers from shaking as she unzipped it and rattled the contents out in front of them. Makeup, hairbrush, more makeup, ticket stubs, umbrella . . .

No, no, no. This wasn't right. Holly checked again, but there still wasn't any sign of motion sickness pills or even a diary with the specific details of everything leading up to the event. Holly tried to hide her disappointment. She had been so certain it would be in the bag. It had been calling out to her like a beacon.

"I'm sorry," Vince said, but Holly just shrugged as she started to scoop everything up and thrust it all back in.

"It's no big deal. We still have the rest of the room to search, anyway."

As soon as the bag was once again zipped up, Holly headed for the dressing table. There were a ridiculous number of photographs of Todd and Rochelle posing together at the Baker Colwell day out. *What a slut,* she thought, while discreetly slipping one of them into her back pocket. After all, he was Holly's boyfriend, not Rochelle's. And besides, he looked so cute in his dark jeans and white polo shirt.

Vince made a pained noise in the back of his throat, which reminded Holly she was actually putting Todd's picture in Vince's pocket. He could destroy it later, she supposed.

She finished with the dresser and moved on to underneath the bed, but again there was nothing but boxes of winter clothes and a ridiculous number of stuffed animals.

Holly wiped her brow. She was running out of places to look, and she couldn't bear to think about what would happen if she didn't find the proof she needed. Except she knew exactly what would happen: She would just be seen as yet another statistic who chickened out of life and killed herself.

Well, she couldn't fail, because she didn't want to be that person—the sort of person who committed suicide, the sort of person her beloved father would have been ashamed of.

For a moment Holly froze. Where had that thought come from? That was the problem with being dead: It gave her far too much time to think. She turned toward the closet with renewed vigor.

"You know," Vince said half an hour later, "I don't think we're going to find anything."

"Don't say that. We can't give up."

"Holly, you've opened up every tube of lipstick and looked in the pockets of every jacket."

"She could've hidden them," Holly defended.

"In a can of hair spray?"

"It's possible," Holly muttered, but she knew he was right: They had been here for ages, and apart from knowing Rochelle's panties were in as bad taste as her clothes, they hadn't learned anything.

Before she could decide what to do next, Vince's phone rang.

"Hide," Gemma snapped at the other end. "She's back early for some reason, and she's on her way up. *Right now.*"

"Shit," Holly swore as she started to dive under the bed just as she heard the front door open. She desperately tried to wriggle underneath before she finally worked out what the problem was.

"This is no good," she wailed. "Why are you so tall?"

"Sorry, next time we're breaking into someone's house I'll put on my short legs. Come on; we'll have to go in the closet."

She managed to squirm her way back out and throw herself into the closet just seconds before the bedroom door opened.

Holly sucked in her breath, but luckily Rochelle was on the phone and didn't seem to be aware that her bedspread was rumpled or that the closet door was still slightly ajar.

"No, *you* hang up," Rochelle said with an annoying giggle. "No . . . you. I mean it, Tiger. I've got to go and get a shower, unless you want me to be late . . . Oh, behave. Of course I'm not going to tell you what color my bra is."

Holly had to stuff her fist in her mouth to stop from making a vomiting noise.

But could she just say . . . *Gross.*

Had she really come all the way back from heaven to listen to Rochelle Jackson have phone sex?

At least on the bright side it meant that Rochelle obviously wasn't that interested in trying to flirt with Todd if she already had a mystery boyfriend. She must see if Gemma could find out who it was.

So how long do you think she's going to be? Vince shifted uncomfortably in the cramped space.

Well, she doesn't seem in a hurry to hang up on Tiger. Holly sighed. *I guess we should just talk amongst ourselves so that we don't have to listen.*

I'll second that.

Okay, so . . . hey, what are you doing? Holly silently demanded as Vince started to wriggle his leg.

I've got a cramp. Can't you feel it?

Holly paused for a minute. She'd been trying hard not to notice every aspect of Vince's physical body, since it somehow seemed a bit intrusive, but now that he mentioned it, she could feel that his right calf muscle was tightened. He gave his leg another wriggle, and Holly tried to ignore how firm his thigh was. She had the feeling that if someone had been thrust into her body, she would be found wanting, since most nights *The Rich and the Restless* won the battle over the gym.

Vince, on the other hand, had nothing to worry about. He was strong and lean, and unlike Todd, it didn't feel like his muscle had come merely from repetitive weight lifting. Not that Todd didn't have a nice body, of course, but there was something . . . harder . . . about Vince's.

Shit, Holly, you're doing it again. I don't know what the hell you're thinking about, but you'd better stop it, okay?

Crap. Holly glanced down and groaned. What was it with her, Vincent Murphy, and bedrooms? She immediately switched her attention to remembering a boring accounting lecturer she'd had at college, and things soon returned to normal.

Well, apart from the fact that she was well and truly mortified, of course. Fortunately at that moment Rochelle finished the call, and a couple of minutes later Holly heard the bathroom door shut and the pelting noise of the shower being turned on.

Holly wasn't going to wait around a minute longer than she had to, and so she pushed open the closet door and hurried back down the stairs and outside.

Gemma was waiting for her around the corner with a pale face and half-chewed fingernails. "Did she see you?"

"Nope, clean getaway," Holly said.

"Oh, thank God." Gemma blew out a column of air in relief. "I had visions of her finding you and then using her stiletto to chop your body up into little pieces and hiding them under the bed."

Holly shook her head. "No room under there, and besides, I'm already dead. I think that would be like a double negative or something."

"Oh." Gemma paused for a minute to consider this. "Well, perhaps you should've told me that before and saved me all the worry. Anyway, don't keep me in suspense. Did you find anything?"

"Not a sausage," Vince was the one who answered. "Though she did seem to have a strange collection of stuffed teddy bears. Is that a crime?"

"It should be." Holly tried to sound lighthearted, but inside she was panicking. Not only did Vince probably think she had a one-track mind, but there had been no sign of any pills. She'd been so sure there would be. After all, every police movie she had ever watched ended like that. The out-of-favor detective would follow his instincts, no matter what, and it would always pay off.

Whoever said life wasn't like the movies sure wasn't joking. It seemed as though the same went for dying.

"Don't worry," Gemma was saying now. "Holly, we've still got tonight and tomorrow."

"I was just so certain—and what about the photo-copied article she had in her office?" Holly wailed.

"It could've been because she really does get motion sickness," Vince said in a soft voice, and for the first time since Holly had landed in his body, she started to realize there was a good chance she would fail in her mission. The thought made her feel ill. It was bad enough dying, but to die and know that her parents were two levels above her was something she could hardly bear to think about. She had so much to tell them, so much to say, and if she never got out of Level One then she would never get the chance. . . .

"We still have time," Gemma said firmly.

"You're right." Holly sucked in a lungful of air and tried to compose herself. "I just need to keep focused and work out what I'm going to say to Todd. I'm sure as long as I can get everything sorted out with him, it will be okay."

"That's the attitude." Gemma nodded her head in approval.

Vince coughed. "There's just one problem."

"Technically there are two problems," Holly corrected, since, in addition to the Todd situation, she still hoped to find out how she died. "But—"

"No." Vince cut her off as he held out his arms. "This is a different problem. Where's my satchel with all of your things in it?"

"Please tell me Gemma was minding it while we went into Rochelle's." Holly could feel her voice wobbling.

Gemma held her own hands up to show they were empty. "I don't think you had it with you. I knew that drinking beer was a bad idea."

Okay, so Holly was pretty sure she was about to have a breakdown. This was so not good. In fact it was very, very bad, and if—

It will be all right, Vince's firm voice echoed in her head, and before she could start to panic any more, he pulled his phone out of his pocket and made a call.

"Andrew, it's me. . . ."

"What's he saying?" Gemma demanded the minute the technician answered. "Is it there? Do they have it?"

Holly let out a sigh of relief as she heard Andrew confirm that the bag was underneath the bar where they had been standing earlier. If Holly wasn't in Vince's body she would've given that guy a kiss next time she saw him. In fact, she would've kissed Vince as well. His Zen-like calm was becoming more than a little addictive.

She gave Gemma the thumbs-up and then waited until Vince finished the call before letting out a large whoop of joy. "Thank goodness your friends know how to party. I was sure they would've left by now," she told him.

"Actually, they are just about to head into town, so if we want to get it we'd best get moving," Vince added. "They said they'll wait for us to show, but we'd better not keep them too long."

"Let's get going."

Gemma hooked her bag farther up her shoulder. "I might just head . . . er . . . home to get ready for my date tonight. If that's okay? I mean I know this is about you and Todd, but I want to look nice for Simon."

"Oh, for some reason I thought we'd get ready to-gether." Holly tried to hide her disappointment before groaning. "Though on second thought, perhaps not."

"I think that might push the weird factor a bit too high today," Gemma agreed as she glanced at her watch and arranged to meet Holly outside the Pool Palace at quarter to nine.

Since Gemma was heading in the opposite direction, they both walked toward the main road and hailed sepa-rate cabs. As theirs headed toward Baker Colwell and Bar One, Holly rubbed her head.

Talk about exhausting. Had it always been like this when she had been alive? Especially the mood swings. She wasn't sure if it was Vince's testosterone or her own blind panic, but it seemed like she'd spent most of the day on a wildly teetering seesaw. It really wasn't good for the nerves.

Vince, who as usual seemed to pick up on her every thought, sent a wave of reassurance through her.

"Are you okay?"

"I think so." She gulped. "I guess we just have to work on the assumption that nothing else could possibly go wrong?"

"Whenever they say that in the movies, it's just a link to the next disaster."

"This is hardly a movie," Holly reminded him as Vince dug into his pocket and paid the driver before opening the back door and getting out. "And it's true. The day's almost over and we're back to the beginning, so how on earth could things possibly get worse?"

"Well, since that spiritual realigner guy of yours seems to be walking toward us, I'd say that was a good indication. I sure know my life takes a dive every time he's around."

Holly felt sick as she realized Vince was right: Here came Dr. Hill. *Oh, great.*

Eighteen

Holly stared at him. He still had the same red hair and chubby fingers, but he sort of looked different this time. Less fuzzy. And instead of the white garb, he was wearing a regular pair of Levi's and a multicolored shirt, while in his hands were several familiar-looking bags. Had he been shopping?

"What are you doing here?"

"I've come down to give you your mid–manual purging analysis, of course. Honestly, Miss Evans, you could've at least brought the rulebook with you for a bit of light reading. Then you might be able to follow the state of play a bit better. It's standard procedure."

"My mid–manual purging? You've got to be joking."

"I don't think he's joking," Vince commented.

Dr. Hill pushed his two eyebrows together in surprise. "Why would I come all the way down here to joke?"

"See?" Vince grinned.

"Same reason you've come down here to go shopping?" Holly pointed out.

"Oh." His face turned red as he kicked the bags. "You mean these old things. They're nothing."

"Yeah, right. I might be dead, but I can still tell a designer-outlet end-of-season-sale bag when I see one."

Dr. Hill dropped down onto the nearby bench and raised his hands. "Okay, guilty as charged. So I like my clothes. Really, if you had to do as much interdimensional travel as I do, you'd make the most of the perks as well."

"Preaching to the converted," Holly assured him. "You don't need to tell me the joys of shopping. Just a pity I can't exactly try anything on in this state."

"I'm right here, you know," Vince reminded her.

"Ah, yes." Dr. Hill fumbled around in his pocket for a notebook and a pen. "So how are you both coping with the transition?"

"The transition has been fine, but trying to get anything done has been pretty much impossible. Just for the record, I think it should be known as an oxymoron when you send a girl back in a guy's body in order to sort out her issues, because I'm sure this experience is creating more problems than it's solving."

"I know it isn't an ideal situation," Dr. Hill admitted as he chewed at the end of his pen. "But it's the best we can do. So, anyway, I guess we'd better get on with it then." He put the pad away and pulled out a small electronic device with a red laser light at one end.

Holly eyed the device. "Get on with what?"

"The analysis, of course."

"I thought that's what you were just doing. With the notebook and the questions."

"Oh, no, that's for a sociological paper I'm writing on the side. These days if you don't publish you don't get promoted. The real test is with this machine. It measures the amount of negative and destructive thoughts in your mind and can tell how close you are to shedding your earthly problems."

"You mean there's a machine to do that?" Holly, who had spent her life cheating on the various magazine quizzes she'd done (from "Is That Guy Really into You?" up to "Are You Ready to Push Through the Glass Ceiling?"), looked horrified. Even the Baker Colwell Potential Employee Personality Test had been a breeze once she figured out which were trick questions and which were legitimate qualifiers.

"It's foolproof," he agreed.

"But how does it work when there's two of us in here?"

"Well, actually . . ." Dr. Hill pulled a strange-looking needle out of the machine in his hands. "That's the first thing we need to talk about. In order for me to get an accurate reading, I need to make sure Mr. Murphy isn't around."

"I thought you said that couldn't be done?" She narrowed her eyes. "So what's changed all of a sudden?"

"I'm not taking him out of the body. I'm just going to put him to sleep for a few hours, so that he doesn't interfere with the machine."

"You want to give him that big needle and knock him out?" Holly demanded, and when Dr. Hill agreed she gave a decisive shake of her head. "No way."

"If I don't do it then I can't do the reading," the doctor tried to explain, but Holly just poked out her bottom lip in a mulish expression.

"Look, I might have deserved to be kicked out of heaven, but poor Vince here has been really good to me today, and I've already messed up his life quite enough. He's not having the needle."

"What happens if we don't do it?" Vince suddenly asked. "Will Holly get in trouble for not having this mid-purging analysis thing?"

Dr. Hill frowned. "She won't get in trouble, but it's designed to let her know how close she is to attaining her goals. Without it she's more or less flying blind. It's very haphazard."

"I'll chance it," Holly said firmly.

"Well, I won't," Vince retorted in a surprisingly alpha way. "You hated Level One, so the sooner you're out of there the better. Give me the needle."

"No." Holly shook her head. "Look, Vince, it's really nice of you, but honestly, you've done enough already."

"If you don't get your issues sorted out you might never see your parents again." Vince thrust out his right arm. "Now let's just get this thing done."

"I need your consent as well, Miss Evans." Dr. Hill appeared to be studying her face.

Vince—

Just say yes, Holly. I mean it; I'll be okay, and this way you can make sure you see your dad again. Okay?

Holly sniffed as she reluctantly nodded at Dr. Hill. "Fine, but you'd better make sure this thing is a hundred and ten percent safe."

"You have my word on it."

She winced a bit as she felt the cool tip of the needle bury deep into her skin. "How does it know where Vince is and where I am?" She tried not to notice that her voice was wobbly.

"It's all part of the abracadabra stuff. Mystical medicine is the best way of summing it up." Dr. Hill now put away the needle and picked up the machine.

Vince, are you okay? she tentatively asked, but she already knew he wasn't there. After she'd spent the day with him, it felt . . . odd not to have him with her.

"He's a nice guy, by the way. You were lucky. Now, are you ready?"

Holly held out her hand and the doctor slid a small steel ring over her knuckle. For a minute or so nothing happened before the machine started to make a beeping noise.

"What does that mean?"

"W-well." He didn't quite meet her eyes. "It's not great. You still seem to be struggling to get things resolved."

"Yes, but I'm getting there." Holly tried to nod her head in a positive fashion in case Dr. Hill was up for a bit of Jedi mind trick. "There was a bit of a setback with finding out how the pills got in my system. I was so certain it was Rochelle, but . . . well . . . Gemma and I will retrace my steps again and see what else we can come up with. As for Todd, I'm seeing him tonight. I have a feeling that's going to go well."

"Of course." The doctor gave a supportive smile. "It's just that you've really got to try to get everything in order. I can't stress that enough."

"I know." Holly nodded. "Or else I'll be stuck in horrid old Level One for ages. Well, I suppose there's always that fat guy to talk to," she said with a sigh.

"Miss Evans," Dr. Hill said in a soft voice. "If the

manual purge doesn't work you won't remember who the fat . . . I mean who Mr. Michaels is."

"As if I'm going to forget him and his smart mouth in a hurry."

Dr. Hill started to fiddle with the laser-beam machine before coughing. "The thing is, if this doesn't work you won't remember anything. If we can't separate your earthly issues from the rest of your mind, then as a last resort we erase everything."

Holly rubbed her chin and studied Vince's shoe. "Well, that doesn't make any sense," she finally said. "If you erase my memories then how will I know when I finally get to Level Three and see my father again . . . or meet my real mom for the first time?"

"You won't."

For a moment all Holly could hear was the slight buzz of the insects floating around in the warm air. It was a perfect summer evening. The kind of night that in the past would've had her and Gemma down by the marina at their favorite bar, righting the wrongs of the world over a glass of wine.

The kind of evening that she would never remember.

"Why didn't you tell me sooner?" she finally managed to croak.

"It's all in the—"

"Rulebook," Holly finished off in a dull voice. "They should put a health warning on the front of that thing: 'Don't read at your own risk.' "

"It's not normally such a problem, but for some reason your mind is really blocked to the greater glories of heaven."

"So I'm being punished." Holly could feel her bottom lip wobble. "Is this because I told my boss last month that I had cramps when really I was just hungover? Or is it because I stole the sign to the women's restroom at the Baker Colwell Christmas party? Because, not naming names, Gemma Gulliven was definitely egging me on."

"You still have until tomorrow at one o'clock before anything is decided, and even then it's not as a punishment for past crimes. It's just as a way of helping you to get on track. It's designed to give some peace and open you up to—"

"Please don't say the glories of heaven or I think I'll be sick," Holly retorted.

"I'm not here to give you a hard time. I'm here to help. After all, I'm your spiritual realigner."

"Okay." She gulped. "So if you're here to help, then help me. Tell me what else I can do. I really don't want to lose my memories."

Dr. Hill gave her a comforting smile as he studied the plasma screen on his little machine. "The problem appears to be tied up in the fact that some people think you committed suicide."

"I. Did. Not—"

Dr. Hill inched away from her. "I'm not here to judge," he reassured her. "All I'm saying is that it seems to bother you."

"Of course it bothers me." Holly rummaged around in Vince's pocket for the flyer that he'd tried to hide from her earlier. *Don't Suffer in Silence. Call Suicide Samaritans Now.* "They are all over the company as well," she informed him. "And they weren't the last time I was here."

"Well, that's what you have to do."

"What, clear my name and convince people I didn't kill myself?"

Dr. Hill nodded.

"In case you hadn't noticed, that's what I *have* been trying to do," Holly was stung into retorting. "It's not like I've come back just to go shopping and relax. I've been working my butt off. Do you think this has been easy for me?" she added in a righteous voice.

Dr. Hill lifted an eyebrow. "You went to a bar and drank beer," he reminded her.

Holly winced. "Well . . . okay . . . I guess I shouldn't have done that. Though in my defense it's been a very long day. Did I tell you that Vince's girlfriend tried to kiss me this morning? Which, by the way, definitely isn't making this job any easier. That girl is like a limpet, and honestly, if Vince is too nice to tell her to shove off then I should probably do it for him. It would be my way of saying thank-you for all his help."

"Er, sure. If you say so. But what was your point?"

Holly scratched her head for a moment. Vince being nice? Amy Jenkins being a limpet? Drinking beer? Oh, yes, that was right—she had been going to say how hard this whole thing was. "It's not exactly simple to prove my innocence in this body. You guys sure don't expect much."

"We have no expectations. This is your mind, and it's the one that won't let go. So really this isn't a work project you're being forced to do. This is for you."

Holly thought of all the handwritten notes she'd made herself when she first started her new job. She knew it didn't always come that easily to her, which was why she worked so hard to make sure she didn't fail. But how could she work hard on the biggest project of her life . . . or death . . . when she couldn't convince anyone to talk to her?

She felt another bubble of panic start to rise, but this time there was no Vince around to calm her down.

"Are you all right?"

She took a deep breath and tried to imagine Vince telling her it would all be okay. "I guess so. That memory-wiping thing just threw me for a few minutes. But I'm going to see Todd tonight, and you know, he's a pretty clever guy. I'm sure he'll be able to help."

The little machine made a beeping noise, and Dr. Hill looked up with a smile. "Definitely the right attitude. There's already an improvement in your mind."

"Hey." Holly felt some of the panic subsiding. "Well, that was easy—not as easy as cheating on a magazine quiz, of course—but not too bad."

"Thanks . . . I think."

"That's okay," she started to say, but the rest of the words stuck in her throat as she caught sight of four guys wearing novelty ties walking toward her. They must have gotten sick of waiting for her to come and collect the satchel. Well, when she said *her,* she actually meant Vince. *Oh, boy.*

At least they were too far away to see her lips moving. The last thing she wanted was for them to think she'd been talking to her invisible friend.

And where was Vince when she needed him?

According to Dr. Hill he would be out of it for the next few hours. *Great.* It looked like she was going to have to go this one alone.

"It's all right," Holly said under her breath to Dr. Hill. "I won't give the game away."

"Hey, Vince, we thought we'd come out here and see if we could find you." Andrew passed the satchel over.

"Yeah, and who are you talking to?" Graham added.

"Talking to? I wasn't talking to anyone." Holly gratefully clutched at the bag and tried to sound Vince-like. "Just here. All by myself."

Dr. Hill coughed. Gosh, the least he could do was not try to distract her. Especially since it was his fault Vince wasn't here to help out.

"What about the guy sitting next to you?" *South Park* Tie and Matching Socks said. Holly hadn't quite managed to catch his name yet.

Dr. Hill coughed again.

"Ha. Good one." Holly laughed, still trying to not let him throw her off. Boy, he really wasn't a team player, was he? Not content with sending her to hell, he was now trying to make her look crazy as well. "As if there's someone sitting next to me."

"I thought you had to leave early to do something at home. Are you sure you didn't go to another bar?"

"Of course I'm—"

"I'm not invisible." Dr. Hill coughed again, and Holly turned and stared at him.

"What?" Holly blinked.

The doctor stood up and collected his bags. "Vince, you win the bet. You can stop pretending I don't exist now." Then he turned to the four boys. "He's a joker, isn't he?"

Holly felt her jaw hang open as Dr. Hill disappeared down the road with his numerous shopping bags. Was he laughing? Honestly, that man needed to have his spiritual realigner license taken away from him. He was a mockery.

He had also come bearing particularly bad news, and Holly realized there was no time to lose. She got to her feet, said good-bye to the technicians, and tried to remember just where Vince's apartment was. She needed to make sure her talk with Todd tonight went perfectly. The alternative wasn't worth thinking about.

Nineteen

Ten minutes later Holly fumbled with the keys in Vince's pocket and finally pushed open the door. She dropped down onto the couch and rubbed her pounding temples. She just needed to relax for a few moments and remind herself that everything would be okay.

If the man of her dreams couldn't help her, then who could? Of course, it was a complete coincidence that a *Friends* repeat was just about to start.

So anyway, where did Vince keep his television?

When they'd arrived back last night, Holly had been too dazed and confused to really notice much more than the fact that she was sharing her body with a guy.

However, today, not only had she started to learn that Vince was actually quite sweet and kind, but she'd also discovered that too much thinking was bad for her brain. She needed to switch off for a little while or she might spontaneously combust. And that couldn't be good for anyone.

Okay, and still no sign of any television.

Holly shut the final cabinet (which she'd known had been a long shot, since it was underneath the sink) and felt like screaming. Was it too much to ask for at least *something* to go right today?

How could he not have a television? After all, that was what watercooler conversations were made of. She was just twiddling her thumbs and once again studying Vince's fingers when the phone rang. Holly jumped up to answer it before realizing that since Vince wasn't around it could just put her right back into another land mine of trouble. On the other hand it could be Gemma with more news. Holly picked up the phone.

"Vince?" a woman said, and Holly cursed herself for being so nosy.

"Er, yeah," she answered in a cautious voice. Well, at least it wasn't Amy Jenkins, which had to be something.

"It's Lorraine here."

"Oh, right." Holly racked her brain to see if the name rang any bells. But no. "H-how are you?"

"I've just had the day from hell."

You want to bet? Holly raised an eyebrow. "Really?"

"God, yes." Lorraine groaned. "You know they say never to work with animals or children, but they should definitely add actors to that list. You wouldn't believe what an old diva Monica Edwards was being today."

Holly nearly dropped the phone.

Monica Edwards played Samantha Montgomery, the matriarch and complete bitch of *The Rich and the Restless*. Of course she would be a diva in real life. That was what character acting was all about. It was a small sacrifice to pay for the dazzling performances she gave week in and week out. After all, you didn't get ten Emmys by being halfhearted.

Which meant this was Lorraine of *The Rich and the Restless* fame. Talk about one degree of separation to . . . well . . . the most famous cast in the whole world. Holly tried not to jump up and down with excitement, but she was jumping on the inside.

"Yeah," Lorraine continued. "She was just being an absolute nightmare, which is why I wasn't able to call you earlier."

"Well, you know, perhaps she was just being crabby because it's Thursday," Holly suggested. "Remember she's married to Larry Edwards, the *Great Morning* host, and he's always away during the week. Well, it stands to reason she'd be a bit funny, doesn't it?"

Lorraine seemed speechless for a moment, which Holly took as a sign to keep speaking, especially about the errors she had seen on the laptop earlier. Besides, it wasn't like Vince had prohibited her from saying anything; it was just that he had been worried about the time factor. And rightly so. But since Holly was taking a small break from freaking about her less than chirpy future, it really wasn't a problem.

"Wow," Lorraine said ten minutes later. "You never told me you were a fan before. How do you know all of that stuff?"

"Er, well, I watch the show, I guess." *Or did watch it up until two weeks ago.*

"I know I should watch it more often." Lorraine seemed to be shuddering on the other end of the phone. "But I just find the thought so depressing. I mean, I have a Ph.D. in 1960s French and Italian cinema."

Gosh, that sounded impressive. Not that Holly was

exactly sure whether she'd seen any French or Italian films from the 1960s, but she was sure they would be good. "So if you hate it so much, then why are you doing the job?"

"I thought it would look good on my résumé to have done some television work, but even though I'm supposed to be a production assistant, I seem to spend most of my time organizing Web sites, sorting out fan mail, and making sure that Lewis Webber gets his special vitamin drinks every morning before filming."

Holly let out a wistful sigh. Imagine watching the gorgeous Lewis having his vitamin drink every day. It was a dizzying thought. Especially if he wore his faded jeans in real life as well. A cowboy with a good understanding of nutrition . . . what could beat that?

However, Lorraine didn't seem to be nearly as enamored of such an image. "It's just such a nightmare. Do you know what it's like to do a job that seems absolutely pointless? I mean really, what would happen if *The Rich and the Restless* didn't exist? It's not like people would starve or the world would stop."

Boy, Lorraine really hated her job—that was for sure. Though Holly supposed it would be depressing to work in a job you didn't really love. At least at Baker Colwell she'd had a sense of achievement with everything she did. Well, okay, so there was a lot of paperwork, and sometimes she struggled to understand everything, but that was completely different.

"The thing is," Lorraine continued, "I keep trying to give them some ideas of how to reach a crossover market—you know, like the French and Italian cinemagoers—but will they listen to me?"

Holly shuddered. She certainly hoped not, since the idea sounded ridiculous.

"Anyway, Vince, did anyone ever tell you that you're a great listener? In fact, perhaps we could hook up for a coffee or something one day?"

"Sorry," Holly automatically replied. "I'm seeing someone."

"Oh." Lorraine sounded a bit disappointed. "Well, she's a lucky girl. What's her name?"

Hmm, there's a good question for you. To be honest, Holly had been thinking about Todd, but she couldn't very well tell Lorraine that, and damned if she was going to say Amy Jenkins—after all, one had to be careful about what one put out into the ether. For Vince's sake, of course.

"Er, her name is Hol—"

She cut herself off. Was she insane? She wasn't Vince's girlfriend. She was just the dead person living in his body, and if she were still alive she would be Todd Harman's girlfriend. Just went to show how tired she was.

"Well, Hol is a lucky girl," Lorraine said at the other end of the phone. "So, anyway, the reason I'm calling . . ."

"Yes?" Holly wiped her brow, more than a little pleased to change the subject. "What's up?"

"It's those laptops you were fixing. Apparently Todd Harman told Stuart Peterson you'd be bringing them all back by four this afternoon, along with some manuals."

Holly groaned as she clutched the phone. After discovering Todd wasn't in his office, she and Vince had completely forgotten about them. Well, *she* had forgotten about them. Knowing Vince he hadn't wanted to panic her any more by adding another chore to the list.

"I'm so sorry," Holly said truthfully, since she had no desire to cause Vince any problems at work. "They're all fixed, but then something else came up."

"So they're working?" Lorraine seemed relieved. "That's great news. What was wrong with them?"

Good question. Holly closed her eyes and tried to remember what on earth Vince had said, but to be honest she had been too busy staring at his fingers to pay attention. "Just a couple of . . . er . . . router . . . server . . . operator system . . . errors," she improvised as she threw in every word she'd heard the technicians use. "Can V . . . I mean, can *I* bring them over first thing tomorrow?"

"I don't suppose you could do it now?" Lorraine asked in a hesitant voice. "Stuart was pretty pissed off they weren't here. He's getting a bit sick of the way everything keeps freezing."

"Oh." Holly rubbed her pounding temples. "It's just that I sort of have something to do."

"I know it's late, and honestly I couldn't give two hoots if I never see my computer again. The stupid thing crashes more often than a test dummy, but like I said, Stuart is on the rampage. He's even talking of pulling the account if the computers aren't here by the time he comes back from a location shoot tonight. Though I doubt he'd go that far, but you know what he's like."

Not really.

Which was a bit of a problem.

Holly glanced at her watch. This was not good news. She had just over an hour before she was supposed to meet Gemma at the Pool Palace and figure out how to finally talk to Todd. But there was no way she could ignore this. Vince's job was in jeopardy and it was her fault. What if this Stuart Peterson really did pull the account? She'd never be able to live with herself.

"Sure." She crossed her fingers and hoped she was owed some karma, because that was the only way she was going to pull this one off. "I'll be there as soon as I can." Then Holly put down the phone and tried to overlook the fact that if anyone tried to ask her a technical question then she was screwed. *Oh, Vince, why aren't you here?*

For once Holly was pleased with the excessive Baker Colwell work ethic that kept so many staff at their desks long after their official knockoff time, since the security guards didn't even blink an eye as she swiped Vince's ID card and hurried down to the workshop. This was bad. Very bad. For a start Holly had hoped to grab a shower and perhaps change Vince's shirt before she went to the Pool Palace, but it looked like that was out the window.

The laptops were on the bench, and Holly looked at them doubtfully as she grabbed Vince's address book. She flicked through to P and was happy to see that the studio wasn't too far away. In a day full of failures and setbacks, Holly found it more than a little reassuring that something was going her way.

Now, where were those manuals they had printed out? She was sure Vince had put them next to the laptops, but they certainly weren't there now. Then she looked at his desk and frowned. Not that she'd been paying too much attention earlier, but she was fairly certain there hadn't been a paper explosion on it.

Holly tried not to curse as she sifted through the papers. *Come on, come on,* she kept repeating to herself as her heart beat out a panicked rhythm. Perhaps it wouldn't matter about the manuals? In fact, they would probably be overshadowed by the fact that while she might be able to deliver the laptops, the only technical knowledge she had was how to work her TiVo.

She glanced at her watch again and tried to stay calm. She needed to do this for Vince, but she also needed to get over to the Pool Palace and see Todd to ensure her safe passage to Level Two.

"Hey, Vince. I thought you were going home," a voice said from behind her, and she jumped as she realized Andrew had just walked through the door. He had loosened his Homer Simpson tie and his hair was looking a bit messy. It was definitely an improvement.

Holly studied his face and tried to determine whether his presence was a good thing or yet another bad thing in a day full of disasters. Well, he didn't look threatening or surprised to see her there, so she might as well go with the good-thing version.

"Lorraine from Peterson's called. Todd promised we'd drop these laptops back and I forgot. Now I can't find the damn manuals we . . . I mean I did earlier."

Andrew glanced at the desk. "I see Fluffy's paid you another visit."

Holly stared at him blankly before catching sight of a telltale white strand of dog hair on the computer keyboard. Boy, Vince really hadn't been joking when he said the little dog didn't like him. Perfect.

"Are you all right?" Andrew frowned. "You've gone a bit pale."

Holly rubbed her temples. Her headache had now turned into a rampant jackhammer. "I just didn't need this tonight. I have this . . . well, I have something really important that I need to do, and looking for manuals and delivering computers isn't making it any easier."

"Do you want me to drop them off? I only came back to pick up my tools because I have an early call tomorrow. But I pass right by Peterson's."

Holly felt like throwing her arms around Andrew in delight, but somehow she managed to hold herself back. She'd done enough to ruin Vince's credibility in the last twenty-four hours, so she had to settle for giving him a manly clap on the shoulders.

"That would be fantastic." She beamed just as she caught sight of a bright yellow envelope with *Manuals* scrawled across the front. *Thank you, thank you, thank you,* she silently mouthed as she snatched it up.

"It's no big deal. You help me out all the time."

I do? Holly frowned before realizing he meant that Vince helped him out all the time. That she could imagine, since she was quickly discovering Vince Murphy was an all-around good guy.

"Still," she said in a gruff voice, "I really appreciate this."

"Sure." Andrew shrugged as he scooped up the laptops and Holly popped the envelope on top for him. "Oh, and by the way, about that Gemma thing we were talking about earlier . . . just forget I said anything. I don't think I'm going to ask her out."

"Why not? What's wrong with Gemma?" Holly bristled before she could stop herself.

Andrew knitted his eyebrows together in surprise. "Are you kidding? Of course there's nothing wrong with her. She's gorgeous. I just decided I could do without the humiliation factor right now."

Oh. Holly chewed her lip. "But I thought you were going to give it a try anyway," she said as she recalled Vince's words. Funny, she'd never thought about it from a guy's point of view before.

"Yeah, I was, but Simon Trimmer was in Bar One earlier, and he was boasting about how he was going out on a date with her tonight at the Pool Palace, so there's no point, really."

"Trust me, she won't be seeing that moron for long."

Andrew shifted the laptops around in his arms. "How do you know?"

Because I'm her best friend and I've recently discovered Simon is a loser, Holly was about to retort, before realizing this might not be so prudent. "I just have a feeling," she said instead, before impulsively adding, "You should ask her, just in case."

"I don't know, man." Andrew shook his head and frowned. "Somehow I don't think I'm her type. She doesn't look like the sort of girl who would go for a tech head. I think I was just deluding myself for a while."

"Why, you think she doesn't like nice guys who are smart and have a good job?" Holly raised an eyebrow at him. Of course, he would stand a slightly better chance if he weren't wearing one of those ties, but she decided now was not the time for fashion advice. Especially from Vince Murphy, who seemed to perpetually live in Doc Martens and leather jackets.

"You really think I should?" Andrew sounded as if he were faltering.

"Yes, I do." Holly made a mental note to explain to Gemma why she should say yes. After all, just because Andrew didn't dress in a flashy suit like Simon Trimmer was no reason at all for her to automatically rule him out.

For a moment Holly shifted uncomfortably as something nibbled away at the edge of her mind, but before she could put it under the microscope, she caught sight of her watch. *Phew.* No time for deep and meaningful thoughts.

She said a hasty good-bye to Andrew and then she ran. If she wanted to get back into Level One, memory intact, then this was her best shot.

Twenty

"Oh, you gave me a shock," Gemma yelped as Holly came to a halt where her friend was standing around the corner from the Pool Palace.

"Sorry. I thought you heard me call out." Holly apologized as Gemma quickly shoved her BlackBerry back in her purse. "Are you okay?"

"Of course I'm okay." Gemma flushed as she glanced around and awkwardly fiddled with her hands. "Why wouldn't I be? I just didn't hear you arrive—that's all."

Holly narrowed her eyes. This wasn't the first time Gemma had acted strangely around her today, and she felt a small knot of disappointment form in her belly as she wondered if Andrew had been right about her friend.

Perhaps she didn't want to mix with a technician? Holly hadn't said anything earlier because she didn't want to offend Vince, but he wasn't here now.

"Are you embarrassed to be seen talking to Vince?"

"What?" Gemma squeaked as she clutched at her purse. "That's the most ridiculous thing I've ever heard."

"Is it?" Holly folded her arms. "This morning we saw you on the third floor running away from us, and then later on when we went up to your desk you were acting weird. Plus, you've been jumpy and fidgety all day."

"No, I haven't," Gemma protested as she gnawed at her lip.

"You're doing it now." Holly glared at her. "Gemma, what the hell is going on?"

Her friend let out a long sigh before pulling a flyer out of her purse. She thrust it into Holly's hand.

"What the . . . ?" Holly knitted her brows together as she studied the suicide help line flyer. Then she turned back to her friend. "Why are you showing me this? I've been pulling these things down all day."

"I know, and as fast as you've been pulling them down, I've been putting them up," Gemma said in a miserable voice.

"That was you?"

"Holly, it's not my fault. It's just that after a *certain* incident, my boss thought we should . . . well . . . look into the matter more closely. Perhaps offer support for other staff members in case they're in a similar situation."

"What, in case some pills mysteriously got into their system just before they hopped into what turned out to be a fatal bath?"

"No! Of course that's not what I mean," Gemma wailed. "Look, you know what it's like there. If they give you something to do, you just have to do it. I know one hundred percent that you didn't commit suicide, and the sooner we find out how those pills got into your system, the sooner we can prove to everyone at Baker Colwell that you were tragically taken from us all before you reached the prime of your life."

Holly sniffed. "I was, wasn't I?"

"Yes." Gemma nodded frantically. "Yes, you were, and we're going to find out how, no matter what it takes. And then we're going to say, 'I told you so' to anyone who thought otherwise."

Holly gave another little sniff. Gemma always knew how to make her feel better.

"So are we okay?" Gemma peered from under her lashes, her voice laced with concern.

"Yes." Holly gave her friend a sheepish smile. "We're cool. To be honest, I'm sort of pleased that's the reason you've been acting so funny."

"What do you mean?" Gemma pushed the flyer back in her purse and widened her eyes.

"I thought it was because you didn't want to be seen talking to Vince. I thought maybe you were embarrassed."

"That's ridiculous. Of course I like Vince. A lot," she added in a loud, clear voice.

"It's all right, Gem. He's not here."

"What? But I thought—"

"It's a long story," Holly said as she explained her impromptu visit from Dr. Hill. "But he should be back sometime in the next few hours."

"Oh." Gemma looked relieved. "After everything he's done for you, I didn't want to offend him . . . so is he going to be all right?"

Holly nodded. "Dr. Hill said there wouldn't be any side effects."

"You know, I think it's so sweet that he let himself be knocked out like that so you could have your test. I didn't realize he was so nice. Or so funny."

Holly shot her friend a startled glance. "Don't tell me you have a crush on me . . . I mean Vince?"

"Please." Gemma looked hurt. "That would just be weird on way too many levels. Anyway, I'm going on a date with Simon Trimmer."

"Sorry." Holly flushed as a jolt of relief ran through her. For some reason she didn't like the idea of Gemma having a crush on Vince.

Her friend looked at her strangely. "I just meant Vince was a nice guy. That's all."

"You're right. He is nice. Not to mention clever and kindhearted, and I don't like to boast"—Holly lifted up her shirt and tapped Vince's rock-hard stomach—"but there's nothing wrong with his body, either."

Gemma made a choking noise. "Holly . . . don't tell me *you* have a thing for Vince?"

"What?" Holly spluttered. "That's ridiculous. Of course I don't. How can you even say that when I'm about to see Todd? Remember him, my almost fiancé?" There was no need to mention the two embarrassing bedroom incidents, since clearly they were only the result of not knowing how to handle all of that testosterone. Boy, it was dangerous stuff when in inexperienced hands.

"I know that; I'm just saying . . . oh, never mind. Anyway, we should probably get going. I don't want to be late for my date, and I doubt you want to miss Todd."

Absolutely not. Holly shook her head. It was all about Todd. *Todd, Todd, Todd.* As for Gemma's ridiculous idea . . . well, her friend was just confusing admiration and friendship with something else. Again, it was all about Todd.

"Okay." Holly started to turn the corner toward the understated entrance of the Pool Palace. "Now let's go over the plan one more time."

"Sure," Gemma agreed. "That would be a great idea except there is no plan, which means we're going to have to wing it."

Holly stopped and groaned.

Wing it?

She needed this to work. After all, this was the guy whom up until two weeks ago, she was going to marry.

It was going to be a beautiful wedding as well. Todd's nephew, little James, would be old enough to be the ring bearer by then, and Holly's dress was going to be the most ravishing thing this side of . . . well, anywhere.

It was going to be perfect.

The sun would be shining; the birds would be singing. Most important of all, she wouldn't be dead.

Now that dream was gone and in its place was nothing but a horrible future in horrible heaven, possibly with no memory of any of this. Yet the only way she was going to get a chance to talk to the love of her life was to . . . *wing it.*

Gemma glanced around to check that the coast was clear before reaching over and squeezing Holly's hand. "It's going to be okay, you know. Trust me."

"You're right." Holly felt a positive surge of energy soar through her. "Everything's going to be fine."

✦

Everything about the Pool Palace was upmarket and sophisticated, from the tournament-size pool tables to the cutting-edge leather couches and discreet lighting.

Also, owing to the fact it was right next to the Fix, Holly and Gemma had spent quite a bit of their time there in the past. But tonight Holly felt completely out of place, and she could suddenly see why Vince wasn't a fan. All around her were young and fabulous things with lots of designer clothes and trust funds. Why hadn't she ever noticed that before?

Not that Holly had tremendous wealth growing up, and any designer clothes she had came from discount outlets, but she had been exposed to this environment from a young age. And she'd taken it for granted.

She watched Gemma saunter over to where Simon and Todd were sitting. Her heart did a little flip-flop. Todd looked gorgeous in a navy polo shirt and a pair of beige trousers, and she longed to give him a kiss and snake her arms around his waist, but instead she was forced to slip into an empty booth just near the door.

She glanced over to see what was happening and was pleased that Gemma was already standing on tiptoe to whisper something in his ear. Boy, at times like this Holly wished she'd been taught useful tools in college. Like how to lip-read. It would've certainly been more helpful than knowing the square root of pi.

"Hey, Murphy, what are you staring at?" a voice demanded, and Holly realized Simon was studying her through a pair of narrowed eyes.

Oh, great. Usually she thought it was funny when the guys goofed around like this, but tonight definitely wasn't one of those times. Especially when she recalled the little incident near Todd's office earlier this afternoon. Had it really been only a few hours ago?

"Just minding my own business." She gave what she hoped was a shrug and looked in the other direction.

"Yeah, well, keep it that way." Simon leaned on his pool cue and scowled. "And stop looking at Gemma. Todd told me what you tried to do at the funeral."

Holly rolled her eyes. She'd been accused of killing herself, talking too much, and having a bad attitude. Now she was being told to stop perving on her best friend. *Just great.*

"Hey, what's going on?" Gemma, who had been deep in conversation with Todd, walked over and put a restraining hand on Simon's arm while shooting Holly a pointed stare and nodding toward the door.

"The guy's a jerk, and I don't like the way he's looking at you. Should I do something about it?"

"You could try," Holly retorted as she thought of how rock-hard Vince's biceps were. Not that she knew how to use them, but she was sure she could give it a try.

"Don't worry about it," Holly heard her friend coo. "He isn't bothering me. Though I must admit I think it's kind of cute that you're jealous. . . ."

"Yeah, you think it's cute, do you?" Simon now lost interest in Holly and puffed out his chest in Gemma's direction.

Oh, please. How could she like such a creep? He was pathetic. Really, she was going to have to have a word with Gemma about her taste in men. Andrew was looking better by the second. And why was Gemma still nodding at the door like that?

Holly tried to send a telepathic message to her friend to clarify the situation, but judging by Gemma's face the experiment was a failure, and Holly was forced to watch Simon wrap his arms around Gemma's waist. *Gross.* Why didn't he just club her over the head and drag her back to the Neanderthal cave he'd crawled out from, for goodness' sake?

In fact, Holly couldn't believe she hadn't noticed what a pig Simon was. It just seemed so obvious now.

Perhaps it was because he was Todd's best friend, so he'd always been on good behavior when Holly was around? Whatever the reason, there was no way Gemma could date him; that was for sure.

Holly was just about to try to send another telepathic message when she realized Todd was walking toward her. She clutched at Vince's satchel and tried not to panic. This was it.

She longed to put her hand up to her hair and pat it, but she didn't quite think that six-foot guys wearing leather jackets and steel-toed boots checked their hair on a regular basis.

Which was why, when Vince woke up again, there was no way she was going to tell him about the tiny amount of mascara she had used, just to add a bit more curl and length. Not that Vince really needed it, but she'd seen the mascara tube in Gemma's purse and couldn't resist.

Holly tried to look nonchalant as Todd moved closer toward her. He was so hot. And she loved the way he moved with a slight limp, thanks to that formerly broken leg.

So what had Gemma told him?

Did he know everything?

Then she frowned. Gemma had been speaking to him for only a couple of minutes, so he couldn't know it all. But he must know something or else he wouldn't be coming over. Right?

She had to admit this conversation was going to be a lot easier without Vince making fun of her every step of the way. Some things were better off being done alone: like trying to convince your boyfriend that his dead girlfriend really was alive and residing in someone else's body.

Todd was only one table away now, and she coughed to clear her throat. It didn't help that she could feel her Adam's apple as she did so. Boy, that Y chromosome sure was responsible for some funny inventions.

Almost there. Almost there. And—

"Vince. God, I've been waving from the outside for five minutes. Didn't you see me?" Holly froze at the sound of Amy Jenkins's voice and was then forced to watch Todd walk straight past her table and toward the door. In the background Gemma's eyes were almost bulging, and finally Holly worked out what her friend had been trying to tell her. They definitely needed a better code.

Holly wanted to scream. This could not be happening. It *was not* happening. She was going to shut her eyes, count to three, and Todd would be sitting down next to her, taking hold of her hand, and telling her he'd known all along that she was there because he loved her so much that he could feel her presence.

One.

Two.

Three.

Holly opened her eyes to see Amy grinning. She was dressed all in black and looking suspiciously like she was about to go on a date. Right about now Holly felt like crying.

Twenty-one

"Amy, what are you doing here?"

And Todd, where are you going?

"What do you mean, what am I doing here?" Amy gathered up her black skirt and slid into the booth. "I'm here for our date."

"What?" Holly could barely concentrate as she tried to peer out through the thick glass window to see where on earth Todd was going.

"Our date," Amy repeated and Holly vaguely remembered it being mentioned earlier. "I almost thought you weren't going to show when you didn't come into the Fix, but then I caught sight of you in here. I didn't think you liked this place."

Of course I do, Holly was about to say, before realizing that Amy was talking about Vince. To Vince. *Well, let's just get something very clear right from the start. There will be no kissing.*

Beneath Amy's pancake makeup and the cheap kohl eyeliner, Holly could tell she was still waiting expectantly for an answer.

"I just thought I'd check it out." Holly reached up

and rubbed her temples. Her headache was still pounding away.

"Cool." Amy gave an indifferent shrug. "I mean, I don't mind it. Apart from all of those self-important idiots who like to hang out here."

Holly couldn't help but notice that Amy was staring directly at Gemma and Simon. Well, Holly agreed about Simon, but Gemma wasn't like them. "Some of them are okay."

"Humph." Amy snorted as she dug out her purse. "Anyway, I'm going to get a drink. Do you want one?"

Holly's head was still pounding, and she had a feeling that it wasn't going to get better on its own. "No, thanks. But could you get me a glass of water?"

"Sure." Amy headed for the bar at the same time Simon did, and a couple of seconds later Gemma slipped into the booth behind Holly.

"What are you doing with that skanky ghoul?" her friend hissed while keeping her head firmly pointed in the other direction as if she were waiting for someone. "Todd's gone outside for some fresh air."

"Tell me about it." Holly groaned, also making sure she was looking away from where Gemma was sitting. "I thought he was coming over, and then little Miss Elvira jumped me. But if Todd is outside, then this is my chance to talk to him."

Gemma shook her head. "Perhaps give him a minute or two, because he's in a really funny mood. I think he's still really down about everything."

"Did you . . . you know . . . tell him I'm here?" Holly caught her breath.

"I was about to, but I had to break up a fight. What on earth was that all about?"

"He started it," Holly protested. "You know, I'm not so sure Simon's a nice person. I don't think you should stay with him."

"Yeah, well, if I hadn't, he might have punched you."

"In his dreams." Holly sniggered.

"What's gotten into you?" Gemma demanded. "Simon might have started it, but you were quite eager to carry it on."

"He was pissing me off. I think it might be a guy thing."

"Well, put a lid on it," Gemma advised as she got up and smoothed down her skirt. "You're not here to fight; you're here to talk to Todd. Anyway, I'd better get back, but try to get rid of Amy Jenkins as soon as you can."

"Preaching to the converted," Holly assured her.

"Who's converted?" Amy demanded as she returned with their drinks. "What was that about?"

"Oh, nothing," Holly lied as she dug into Vince's satchel. She was sure she'd seen some headache tablets in there before, and her fingers finally found the container and she twisted open the top. With all this deception it was no wonder her head felt fit to explode.

"Hey, those pills are a weird shape. What are they?"

"Huh?" Holly glanced down at the container and realized she'd pulled out the wrong ones. Would anything go right for her today?

She read the label. Beta-blockers. They were big as well. Where did Vince get them from? A vet?

"Oh, they're for my . . . sinuses." Holly improvised with a casual shrug.

"I didn't know you had sinus trouble."

"I don't when I take my pills."

"Oh," Amy said, looking relieved. "So I'm going to put some music on. How about a bit of Marilyn Manson to piss everyone off?"

"Sure." Holly waved her hand in agreement as she tried to work out why Vince would have a container of beta-blockers. Not that she knew what they were, but they sounded bad. Before she could think about it she was interrupted by a loud *thud-thud* as Amy's musical choice came hammering out over the speakers.

What a racket. If only someone would do them all a favor and turn it off.

Which was when the music abruptly stopped.

What the . . . ?

Holly spun around to see who had taken umbrage to Marilyn Manson and yanked the cord of the old-fashioned jukebox out from the wall, but no one had moved.

As in, no one had moved.

Holly jumped to her feet and ran over to the pool table to where Gemma and Simon were frozen in time while fighting over the cue. She craned her neck. At the bar the espresso machine had stopped midflow so that the liquid was suspended in air.

She put her hands to her eyes and rubbed them. Was this dreadful day never going to end? She was supposed to be talking to Todd, but everything kept going wrong. First Amy, and then Vince with his annoying tablets, and now this. What was—

Someone coughed, and Holly groaned as she turned back around.

Of course. Why was she even surprised?

Dr. Alan Hill.

This time he was sitting cross-legged on top of the table Holly had just vacated. He'd also changed his outfit into a smart two-piece navy pin-striped suit, which made him look surprisingly masculine despite the chubby fingers and red hair.

"You can stop time?" Holly demanded as she made her way over and slid back into the booth.

"I wouldn't call it stopping time exactly." He waved his hand vaguely in the air. "It's a little bit more complicated than that, but now really isn't the place for a lesson in quantum physics."

"No," she agreed. "It's probably better that you get on with it and let me know what other unexpected, disastrous thing is about to overcome me. Oh, and don't forget to pull that face when you remind me it was all there in black and white on page one hundred and twenty-three of the stupid rulebook, which everyone knows I didn't bother to read."

"Miss Evans," he said in a hurt voice. Did he have more shopping bags by his side? "I don't want you to associate me only with bad news."

"How silly of me to think that, when the last two times have been like a basket of cuddly little kittens. So what's happening now? A mid–mid–manual purge analysis? Or a pre-having-the-memories-of-a-lifetime-wiped-away analysis? Or—"

"Actually, this is a more spontaneous visit." He

beamed as he pulled the red laser machine out of his suit pocket. "I come bearing good news."

Holly shot him a skeptical look. "What sort of good news?"

He held the machine up in the air. "You're making progress."

"No, I'm not." Holly scowled at the annoying machine that couldn't be tricked. "I'm going backward. So far I haven't got a clue how the pills got into my system. I can't talk to my boyfriend, and I'm on a date with a girl who dresses like Morticia Addams. There is no progress."

"I beg to differ." Dr. Hill held the machine up to Holly's face. "See those little lines? Well, they indicate a considerable change in the impulsesomatons that are being emitted from your brain."

"Is that even a word?"

"You're dealing with your issues," he explained. "I see that you found out Miss Gulliven had been putting suicide posters up around your building and you reacted in a very calm manner."

Boy, they really were all-knowing.

"Oh, that. Well, I was just pleased that she wasn't being weird about Vince. As far as the posters go, she was just doing her job. It's no big deal."

"But it is a big deal." Dr. Hill clapped his hands. "It's real progress, Miss Evans."

"I don't understand." Holly clutched at her head. It was still banging like a drum, and this conversation wasn't helping matters at all. "Why would that make such a difference? I haven't even spoken to Todd yet."

"I don't know," the doctor admitted. "The mind is a powerful thing. All I know is that something very large was blocking you from being receptive to the normal purging process, and whatever it is has started to disappear."

"So I'll be okay tomorrow?"

"The block is still there, but it has lessened considerably. You just need to keep working on it. Stay positive."

"Wow, this is such a relief. So even if I don't find how the pills got inside me there, if I talk to Todd tonight you think I'll have a chance?"

"The more outstanding things you get resolved, the better it will be," Dr. Hill agreed. "Clearing the air with your boyfriend will make a big difference."

"Excellent, because I'm going to talk to him as soon as I manage to ditch Amy," Holly explained as she resisted the urge to jump up and hug him. She had a feeling that somewhere in the stupid rulebook was a paragraph about patient–doctor conduct. But she was so happy.

There was a chance she would make it back to heaven and eventually to Level Three. Memory intact.

She just needed to do what Dr. Hill said.

First stop was Todd.

"Good," he said just as the music came back on and the buzz of general conversation resumed its normal frequency.

"Hey, what's happening?"

"Oh, did I forget to mention my little trick lasts for only five minutes?"

"You did forget to mention that," Holly agreed

as Amy walked back to the table, nodding her head in rhythm to the music. Holly stared at Dr. Hill and wondered how on earth she was going to explain why there was a red-haired man sitting on top of the table—looking particularly unbothered about it, if Holly could just add.

"Oh, Amy, I suppose you're wondering what's going on here."

Dr. Hill coughed.

"You mean about why you've been acting so strangely?" she asked before she did a scary little half smiley thing with her lips and reached out to touch Holly's arm. "Though I think I know the answer to that."

Holly had always thought Amy Jenkins was two sandwiches short of a picnic, but now she was just being weird.

"I mean about my . . . er . . . friend here."

Dr. Hill coughed again. He should really get that checked out, because it was becoming a bit annoying.

"What friend? Vince, I think that hanging out in this place is getting to you."

"But—"

"Sorry," Dr. Hill whispered with an apologetic shrug. "I might've also forgotten to mention that this time I *am* invisible."

To think that for just a minute Holly had almost liked the guy. She poked her tongue at him as he got up and headed for the door. Then he waited until it opened before slipping out into the night just as Todd walked back into the room—with his arm draped over the shoulders of the biggest tart in the whole world, Rochelle Jackson.

Twenty-two

"Vince, are you even listening to me?" Amy pushed back her long black hair and scowled.

"What?" Holly managed to drag her stunned gaze away from Todd and Rochelle as they sat down in the booth next to them. Though *sat* probably wasn't the right word to use.

Lying on top of each other would be more accurate.

Lying on top of each other looking like complete and utter jerks would be even more accurate.

Unbelievable.

She could see the look of horror and concern on Gemma's face over by the pool table, but the main thing she could see was that her boyfriend—the man whom she one day had intended to love, honor, and wash his horrible dirty boxers for the rest of her life—was sticking his tongue down Rochelle Jackson's throat. In public. As if it were a normal thing to do.

How could he?

She'd been dead only thirteen days. Thirteen. Was she that forgettable? Was there no period of mourning over such things?

Holly could feel the blood thumping in her skull, but this time it wasn't because of her headache. It was because of pure, unadulterated anger.

She wanted to kill him.

"I'm talking about *us,* Vince," Amy clarified, and Holly tried to block out the kissing noises that were coming from the next booth.

What?

What?!

Holly blinked as she realized what Amy was trying to say; yet from what Vince had told her there was no *us* between him and Amy. And certainly since Holly had taken over his body, she'd done nothing to make Amy think that situation was going to change in a hurry.

Perhaps Amy was delusional, or a sucker for punishment?

"Look." Now Amy's hand was sliding along Holly's leg. "Why don't we get out of here and go back to my place? I've got some weed we could smoke, and then, well . . ." Amy finished with a suggestive lick of her lips as she gripped her fingers further into Holly's thigh.

Holly wriggled down the booth.

Gross.

Did Amy Jenkins have no dignity? Holly had been going out with Todd for at least three months before going to bed with him. And she certainly hadn't planned to do it while she was stoned. Or on a weeknight. Obviously Amy hadn't come by her reputation by accident.

"Well?" Amy fluttered her eyelashes, and Holly flinched.

Were all women like this? So determined to throw themselves at the man of their choice that they didn't take time to work out whether the man in question actually had any thoughts on the matter? If Amy Jenkins dared to touch her thigh one more time there was going to be some bitch-slapping.

Take Todd. She could still scarcely believe that he and Rochelle were kissing in the booth right next door. While Holly was hardly going to forgive him or take him back, she knew exactly who to blame for it.

Rochelle.

She was a man-eater. And so was Amy Jenkins, for that matter. Why couldn't they just stick with guys who actually liked them? Not, Holly acknowledged, that it would be easy to find men who liked them, because they were both such tarts, but that was hardly the point.

They had to stop it, because girls like them were ruining lives.

Even if Holly was dead, that didn't mean it didn't hurt to see her boyfriend cheating on her. Holly had had enough. She removed Amy's unwanted hand from her leg. "Look," she said in a tight voice, "I don't want—"

The sound of Rochelle giggling cut off the rest of her words, and Holly swung her head around just as the pair resurfaced and were sitting there looking smug.

She felt her heart lurch as she stared at Todd's beautiful face. His mouth was smudged with Rochelle's bright red lipstick, and his eyes were full of lust.

Holly felt as if she were going to die. Again.

This could not be happening.

"What are you looking at, Murphy?" Rochelle

drawled as she patted down her ridiculous hair. "Just because you're not getting any doesn't mean you need to perv on us. But you always were a bit weird."

"You're disgusting," Holly said in a low voice as all the pain she had been feeling gathered itself into one long, sharp point inside her. The last time she'd felt like this, the only way to get rid of it had been by cutting herself. Since then she'd worked so hard to make sure she never reached that place again, but now it had happened. Except this time Holly didn't need a blade to help her.

Todd, who had his arms spread out along the back of the booth, jolted into a sitting position, and the contented expression fell away to be replaced by one of surprise. "What did you just say to her?" he said in a dangerous voice.

"The same thing I'm saying to you." Holly clutched at the table and tried to contain the sharp heat of her anger. "You're both disgusting."

Over by the pool table, she could see Gemma raising a panicked eyebrow, while Simon was bristling with expectation. There was no way Holly was going anywhere. She was mad beyond belief.

Somewhere in the back of her mind was Dr. Hill's voice explaining to her how important it was that she dealt with her issues, but she blocked it out.

Right now there was only one thing she wanted to deal with: her cheating scumbag of a boyfriend.

Todd now got to his feet. "You've got to be joking me, man. First the funeral and now this? Anyone would think you're trying to pick a fight with me."

"Anyone would think you deserved it," Holly retorted as she stood up as well. Two could play at this game, and she was glad to see Vince was a good two inches taller than Todd, not to mention a good deal broader. "Holly's been dead two weeks and you're all over some tart. You should be ashamed of yourself."

"Who are you calling a tart?" Rochelle squealed in outrage as she looked up from fixing her hair.

"Come on, Vince, let's just get out of here." Amy scowled. "Who gives a shit about Holly Evans?"

"Yeah, Murphy, why don't you listen to your girl-friend for once?" Todd drawled.

"She's not my girlfriend," Holly said through gritted teeth.

"And Holly wasn't *my* girlfriend," Todd retorted.

"What!?"

What?

Holly felt the world stop, and for a moment she thought Dr. Alan Hill was doing his party trick again, but slowly the surrounding buzz of conversation started to ring in her ears, and she realized the world hadn't really stopped at all. It just felt like it had.

"That's right." Todd sneered as he folded his arms in front of his chest. "Not that it's any of your business, but I was about to break up with her the night she killed herself."

"She *did not* kill herself."

Holly stared at him. He was going to dump her the night they were supposed to get engaged? Unbeliev-able. And to think she'd been planning to wear her adorable bra and panties for him. Well, even if she weren't dead, or a boy, there was no way in a million years he was ever going to see them now. And what about her ring?

"What would you know about it?" Todd demanded, his navy eyes looking cruel and hard.

"I know she didn't kill herself," Holly repeated firmly. "How can you even say that when you were going to get engaged to her?"

"My, my. You *have* been sticking your nose in where it doesn't belong." Todd raised a surprised eyebrow before shrugging. "Not that it matters. Yes, we were going to get engaged, but Holly didn't like the idea of announcing it at the ball. Talk about a lucky break, since two weeks ago I had lunch with a client who happened to go to high school with her. Apparently she tried to slit her wrists when she was there. I found out just in time what a nutcase she was. Talk about a close shave."

Holly could feel her cheeks going red with rage. Was this really the same Todd speaking to her? How could he believe those things he was saying?

"It's all worked out for the best anyway, because I was getting sick of just seeing Todd on the side," Rochelle purred as she put a territorial hand on Todd's arm.

Holly started to shake.

"Why would you be giving a shit about this, Vince?" Amy tugged at Holly's shirt. "If you ask me, they deserve each other."

"Shut up, you stupid bitch," Rochelle howled.

"Oh, excellent." Simon Trimmer obviously thought it was time to make his presence felt. "I've been looking for an excuse to kick this guy's butt all night. So can I fight him now?"

"There isn't going to be a fight," Holly said in a calm voice. In the background she could hear Gemma letting out a sigh of relief, but it was a bit premature, thought Holly as she bunched her right hand into a tight fist and took a swing at Todd's picture-perfect face.

The result was instantaneous and spectacular, and as Todd dropped back down onto the seat in pain, Holly turned to Simon Trimmer and shot him a defiant glare.

"What the . . . ?" His eyes bulged.

"Like I said, there isn't going to be a fight. Todd got what he deserved. Now if you want to make something of it, then that's up to you. But I warn you, I'm not in a good mood."

Simon held up his hands and backed away. "It's got nothing to do with me."

"Well, I'm glad we understand each other then," Holly said as she grabbed her jacket and headed for the door. She'd finally realized that while she was Holly Evans on the inside, she was Vince Murphy on the outside. And Vince Murphy could pack quite a punch.

As she left she could hear Todd screaming at her, "You crazy asshole. You'll pay for this, Murphy. You're already on thin ice because you didn't deliver those laptops to Peterson's this afternoon. Somehow I don't think you're going to be working at Baker Colwell for too much longer. I'll make sure of it."

Holly ignored him as she headed out into the night. As she stalked down the road she could see Dr. Alan Hill standing by the bus stop trying to catch her attention, but Holly just kept walking.

Her head hurt, her knuckles stung, and she was about to lose all of her memories. There wasn't anything the good doctor could say that would make her feel any better. So he might as well say nothing at all.

Twenty-three

By the time she got back to Vince's house she was shaking. *Oh, God.* Life—or in her case death—as she knew it was over. Holly couldn't believe it. What had she done?

She'd never punched anyone in her life, but the way she had been feeling toward Todd had just been impossible to get out in any other way.

She'd ruined everything.

Was it really only a couple of hours ago that Dr. Hill had been telling her how much progress she'd been making and how she had a good chance of the manual purge actually working? She'd gone and blown it in one fell swoop by showing that her issues were as unresolved as ever.

Holly wasn't quite sure which point had triggered her to hit Todd. Was it that he had been cheating on her? Or that he thought that she'd killed herself?

And worse, she'd inadvertently dragged Vince into it by making him look like the villain.

To the outside world Vince was just a normal computer geek, but the reality was that he was a really nice guy who worked hard, kept out of trouble, and still found the time to help self-absorbed dead girls sort out their issues. Now she'd just ensured that he might lose his job as well.

Nice going, Holly Evans.

In a way it wasn't so bad that she was going to lose her memory. The more she thought about it, the less she liked a lot of what her life had been like. Well, Todd was certainly a letdown of epic proportions.

Then there was work itself. Up until now Holly hadn't even questioned the rather heavy-handed corporate environment she'd been part of, but stepping back and dying certainly had a way of giving a girl some perspective.

On top of that, it seemed she had misjudged most everyone around her. Well, her stepmother and Vince Murphy for a start.

If anyone was the loser around here, it was her—Holly Evans. Stupid idiot who couldn't even die right.

She had been such a fool.

Once inside the safety of Vince's room, she took his boots off as the full horror of what had happened played out around her like a multicolor plasma screen in her head.

As she had left the Pool Palace she was aware of Gemma's look of horror, Amy's fury, and Rochelle's annoyance that some of Todd's blood had squirted onto her skintight jeans.

She shrugged the black leather jacket off and threw it onto the nearby chair. But she missed and the jacket landed with a thump on the floor.

Man, she thought as she wriggled off the bed to pick it up. It seemed she couldn't do anything right these days.

She was just about to lie back down when she caught sight of the bottle of pills she'd found in his bag earlier.

She'd almost forgotten about them. She retrieved them from the ground and turned them around in her hand.

So what were beta-blockers?

She supposed she could look it up on the Internet, but she wasn't quite sure she would be able to work his state-of-the-art laptop.

"Wake up, Vince; I want to talk to you," she said out loud, but there was nothing.

She got up and headed over to the desk in the corner. It was of no consequence that tomorrow she would have forgotten all of this. Tonight she not only wanted to take her mind off her own problems, but she wanted to know what was wrong with Vince Murphy.

There was nothing else in there apart from some neatly organized stationery and an alarm clock, so she turned her attention to the closet and decided it warranted further investigation.

She stood on a chair and peered in. There was a pile of plain white T-shirts, and next to them was a pile of black T-shirts. Vince had the fashion sense of Simon Cowell. Holly pushed them aside and thrust her hand toward the back. *Bingo*.

Her fingers clutched a large manila folder, which she dragged out and raced back to the bed to study.

At first not a lot of it made sense. It was obviously medical information in the form of graphs. There were piles of them, and Holly frowned as she turned over page after page. It looked serious.

Vince. What's wrong with you?

She kept paging through until she finally came across a photocopy from a textbook, which meant that she might be vaguely able to understand it.

Long QT syndrome.

What on earth was that? Holly scanned the text (helpfully highlighted with a pink marker), which explained that it was some sort of wonky heart rhythm thing. *Ouch.* Well, that didn't sound very nice.

She flicked back through the other files. The strange graphs seemed to date back at least five years. So Vince Murphy had known about this Long QT thing since he was seventeen.

Then she turned back to the article. Gosh, this thing sounded like a pain in the ass. It could cause fainting, prevent you from playing sports, and in some instances Long QT syndrome could cause sudden death.

Oh, no. The purple lights.

Holly blanched as she recalled the small bright blotches that had been dancing around Vince's head like fireflies on the day of her funeral. What if Dr. Hill hadn't made a mistake after all? What if instead of fainting, Vince had been dying, or nearly dying, and for whatever reason he had lived through it? Perhaps the shock of her landing in his body had jump-started his heart back to life?

If Vince had nearly died, then why didn't he say something? Anything?

Why did he let her rant on and on about her problems as if he didn't have a care in the world?

He must have been so surprised when he'd come

around from his near-death experience to find that she was in his body, but did he complain? Well, okay, so perhaps he wasn't exactly a saint in the complaining department, but overall he had been pretty amazing.

"Vince. Did you really walk around for the last five years knowing you might die at any time? How did you manage to keep this big, terrible thing that was happening to you a secret from everyone?"

Again there was no answer, but Holly didn't really mind as she stared at the ceiling in the darkened room. From outside the window she could hear the distant wail of an ambulance, but she ignored it.

Holly felt a chill go through her body and she shivered. "You know, Vince," she said in a hoarse voice, "you're not the only one who has a secret."

She lifted up her arms and stared at the smooth skin of his wrist. "You're so much braver than I am. If you could see my real arm, you would know what I mean. There are still faint scars from where I cut myself."

Holly could feel the tears trickling down the side of her face as she sat still on the bed. "The scars down on my wrist are the worst. Apparently if my stepmother hadn't found me when she did, I would've been dead in an hour. I wonder how she felt having to see me like that. So soon after my dad had died."

An almost hysterical sob escaped from her lips. "I was out of school for over two weeks, and I know everyone was talking about it. I mean, who would be so stupid as to let the razor slip and almost kill themselves?

"But you see, all those whispers were true. It wasn't an accident." Holly felt strangely calm as she spoke.

"That night I just didn't see the point of living without my dad. So I did it. It was easy, you know—the actual cutting—and for a minute I was happy, but then I got to the hospital and I saw him. My dad."

She started to laugh as she tucked her legs in front of her and wrapped her arms around them. "It's not really funny, is it? But now that I'm dead, I know how hard it was for him to visit me. Story of my life, really—finding things out too late."

Suddenly Holly stopped laughing. "But he couldn't hide how disappointed he was in me. You see, he had died after a long, painful battle with cancer, and he had fought it every step of the way. He was so brave and dignified. And what did I do? Get a razor and let the life seep out of me with two easy strokes. That's why, when I survived, I was too embarrassed to tell the truth. Plus I was grateful to be given another chance. To prove to my dad I wasn't a quitter."

Holly realized her eyes were shut, and she opened them up and looked around the room in shock. "That's why I wanted to see him so badly up in heaven. To tell him it was a stupid mistake, and that for the last six years I've worked my butt off. I guess that's not going happen." Holly sniffed. "I don't even know why I've told you . . . well, not that you're here, but I'm pretending you are. Actually, that's another thing I've discovered about you, Vincent Murphy. You're a great listener."

"Thanks," Vince said in his trademark drawl, which caused Holly to fall off the bed in shock.

Unbelievable.

Twenty-four

"Hey," Vince complained. "Don't stand up so quickly. It's making me dizzy. I've been knocked out, remember?"

"I thought you were *still* knocked out." Holly tried to mask her mortification as she reluctantly sat back down again. "How much did you hear?"

"Well, you did mention how brave and strong I was."

"Oh, God." Holly groaned. "I was only saying that stuff because I didn't think you were awake."

"You said I was a good listener," Vince protested.

"I was being rhetorical." Holly gritted her teeth, an action that Vince immediately reversed.

"Well, I thought it was nice. Besides, since you've found out all of my secrets, it's only right I know a few of yours. Is that why you told me?"

"Maybe," she admitted. That and the fact that after tomorrow Holly wouldn't remember them herself, and it seemed wrong just to let Dr. Hill wipe them away. Perhaps it was like a last confession?

She vaguely remembered a long-ago Sunday school lesson where the vicar's wife talked about the dark night of the soul. Well, Holly was guessing she'd had one of them. Though did it count if the body was dead? Also, she had the feeling the person was meant to come out the other end of the experience feeling cleansed and pure, but that wasn't quite going to happen either. Holly was going to come out of this without a clue what her middle name was, let alone whether she liked chocolate (yes), *The* OC (very much), or the Backstreet Boys, first or second time around (as if).

"Hey." Vince groaned, and Holly realized he was looking down at his knuckles. "Don't tell me I've gone from being a womanizer and a criminal to being a thug?"

Holly studied Vince's hand. Boy, Todd's face had really made a dent, and the three middle knuckles were now red, raw, and throbbing. She hadn't even noticed, or if she had, she'd probably found the pain comforting compared to how she was feeling on the inside.

"So I guess you'd better fill me in on what's happened since I've been gone."

Since she'd already told him her darkest secrets, it seemed petty to try to keep him out of the loop. "The short version is that Todd and Rochelle Jackson have been having an affair behind my back, and after he was rather rude to me, I punched him."

Holly could feel Vince biting down on his lip to keep from laughing. "I see," he said in a constrained voice. "You hit Todd."

"In the face," Holly clarified.

"Always a good place," he agreed, and she could feel a small smile starting to tug at his mouth.

"It's not funny," she moaned. "I really messed up. Todd was furious, and that's not all. We forgot to drop those laptops and manuals off to Peterson's, and even though Andrew did it later on, I think it might be too late. What if I've cost you your—"

"Holly."

"But—"

"But nothing. This isn't about me, so stop worrying and let's concentrate on you."

"Your restraint in rubbing it in is a wondrous thing." Holly let out a long sigh. "But as for me, well, it doesn't really matter. If I can punch Todd, Dr. Hill's whizbang machine is going to know I'm not over my issues. In fact, I've probably collected even more emotional baggage since I've been here."

Not least of which was the fact that she kept thinking of how much nicer it felt now that Vince was back. Surely that was a thought that couldn't do anyone any good.

"So that's why you were getting all deep and meaning-ful before, wasn't it?" he said softly, and Holly nodded.

"I didn't mean to go on," she apologized.

"I'm glad you did. I feel like I know you."

"Yes, well, I feel like I know you as well," Holly said as she caught sight of all of his medical notes. "And I want to know more about this heart condition of yours. Why haven't you been taking your medication? And if I'm in your body, then why don't I feel sick?"

For a moment Holly thought Vince was going to swear, but then he just shrugged. "I have been taking the meds. I just made sure you were asleep when I did it, and I didn't mention it in order to avoid a lecture just like this," Vince said lightly. "Besides, all I did was faint; it's been happening on and off for ages."

Holly shook her head. "I don't believe you. Dr. Hill said he made a mistake when he put me into your body, but I don't think he did. I saw the purple lights around your head when I was in heaven. That means you were meant to die. Apparently it says so in the rulebook. Did you know what was happening?"

"To be honest I was more concerned about the dead girl who was in my body when I came around," Vince quipped. "As for why I was fine . . . well, I couldn't tell you. So quit worrying. There's nothing wrong with me, apart from the fact that my heartbeat isn't quite normal."

Holly felt stupid for doing it, but she found herself putting Vince's hand on his knee and squeezing it. "You're heart works better than that of most people I've met. Don't you forget it."

For a moment Vince didn't say anything before suddenly lying down on the bed. "It's been a long day," he said gruffly. "Probably better if we get some sleep."

It was the sound of the birds outside the window that caused Holly to wake up with a start. At first she couldn't quite work out what was going on, but then it all came flooding back to her.

She had punched Todd, which meant she had probably taken three million steps back from what she had set out to do on earth. Even if she did find out what happened and cleared her name, heaven probably wouldn't give her a second chance.

She had really screwed up big-time.

"Hey." She jumped at the sound of Vince's voice. "I've got something for you."

"You have?" Holly fought back the surprise. Perhaps she should've gotten something for Vince as well? A thank-you-for-letting-me-use-your-body gift. Though she must admit that off the top of her head she couldn't think of anything appropriate.

She felt Vince lean over and reach for a packet of photographs. "What are these?"

"I thought you might want to have a look," he said as he opened them up for her. The first one was of him sitting under a tree with his guitar under his arm and a smile on his face. Man, he was pretty hot-looking when he smiled. No wonder Amy had been making such a play for him, unrequited though it was.

Vince paused on it for only a second before flicking through the rest.

"Ah," he finally said. "Here we go." The photo was old. Vince looked only about eight or so, and he was surrounded by a gaggle of friends.

Holly studied it carefully. Was it a birthday party? The next one was the same, but the one after featured him with a small girl who had huge brown eyes and ... Hey ... Holly had a dress just like that when she was a kid ... and the little white shoes sort of looked familiar as well. ...

No way.

She dragged the photo up to her face to study it more closely. But it was true. Here was photographic evidence that she and Vince had been friends. Well, for one day, anyway.

So why on earth didn't she remember it? Boy, look how adorable she had been back then: all brown ringlets and slim legs.

She flicked through the rest of the photographs until she discovered one that looked familiar. It was the same party, and there was a chubby clown holding up a white bunny rabbit.

She remembered.

There had been tiny little cupcakes with bright red cherries on top, and Holly had a nasty feeling she'd gone around the plate and eaten all the cherries before discarding the cakes. There had been more too: music, laughter, and lots of running around.

And Vince. There he was, suddenly coming into focus in her memory. And not just for that day; there had been other days too.

"I remember," she said finally, and for a moment she thought she could feel Vince smile.

"I'm glad," he said before standing up. "Now I guess I should take you to work so you can say good-bye to Gemma, and then perhaps we could . . . you know . . . find out how those pills got into your system."

"The only thing we're doing this morning is groveling until we know your job is safe."

"Holly, I don't care about my job."

"Well, I do. You have your mortgage to worry about."

Vince folded his arms in a we-will-talk-about-this-later sort of way. However he merely said, "So are you ready?"

No, Holly wanted to yell.

She wasn't remotely ready.

She hadn't been ready to die, and she certainly wasn't ready to lose her memory. But apparently what she wanted didn't really matter too much these days, and so she took a deep breath.

"As I'll ever be."

"Nice going, Murphy," someone called out as they walked into the Baker Colwell foyer.

"Yeah. Well-done. That prick had it coming." Holly looked up and saw it was a couple of guys she'd worked with before she'd gotten her promotion.

"Er, thanks," she said, not quite sure what they were talking about. As she walked on a few more people nodded in her direction, but it wasn't until someone started to cheer and said, "Nice shot," that Holly realized they must be referring to Todd. And that she had punched him.

Hey, you've made me famous, Vince teased.

Yes, but why? Holly frowned. Todd was one of the most popular guys in the company. He was young, dynamic, and had *corner office* written all over him, so why were people so pleased Vince Murphy had decked him?

More important, how had they all found out? Holly felt ill. Despite how happy everyone seemed to be at Todd's getting punched, she had the sinking feeling it would be he who had the last laugh. Before she could delve any further into it Gemma came running up, panting.

"Thank God I've found you. I've been trying to call you all night. Why did you turn off your phone?"

"I didn't," Holly said. "I think the battery's gone dead and I forgot to charge it."

"So, are you okay?" Gemma demanded. "I've been sick with worry. You just ran out of there last night without saying anything."

"I'm sorry." Holly winced. "I had to get some fresh air."

There was no way she could tell Gemma the truth about what was going to happen to her now that she'd failed her manual purge, but if she'd stayed around last night, that was exactly what she would have done.

Look at how she'd spilled her guts to Vince. While Holly had been discovering that a lot of things in her life weren't as she'd thought, Gemma wasn't one of those things. She was the best friend a girl could have, and there was no way Holly wanted her to worry about her eternal damnation.

"It's understandable." Gemma gave a vigorous nod of her head. "I still can't believe that Todd and Rochelle were . . . well, you know. I mean, I knew Rochelle was chasing him like crazy . . . but Todd? I never would've expected that in a million years."

"Yeah," Vince said in a typical Vince-like drawl. "Totally never saw that one coming. Todd's always been such a great guy."

"Vince, you're back." Gemma's face broke into a smile as she recognized who was speaking. "I didn't realize. Did you . . . er . . . have a nice time?"

"As far as being knocked out goes, it wasn't too bad. Though it seems I missed all the action, what with Holly decking Todd like that."

"It was unbelievable. She was . . . I mean, you were . . . well, you both were amazing." Gemma gave an expansive wave of her arms.

"He had it coming," Holly said with a sniff. "Though actually I was more upset about the fact that he didn't believe in me than that he was with Rochelle."

"I know. What a bastard. I'm glad you punched him, because otherwise I would've," Gemma said.

"I don't think Simon would've appreciated that," Holly reminded her.

"Actually Simon didn't appreciate much of what I said after you left. Can you believe him? And to think I wasted four months of my life with a crush on that stupid egghead."

"Madness," Vince interrupted before Holly managed to take over. "I'm so glad you don't like him anymore, because neither do I. It's much better to be single than to be with such an idiot."

Gemma blushed and started to fiddle with her clipboard. "The thing is that after you ran out and I argued with Simon and the rest of them, Vince's friend Andrew came in. I guess he was looking for you, Vince. But when he heard what happened, he wanted to see if I was okay."

"Really?" For a moment Holly was distracted from her own problems. As far as she was aware, Andrew had been planning to go home after he dropped the laptops off. *Sly dog.*

"Yes, he seemed to know we'd been best friends and that Todd had been insulting you. He said Todd had it coming, and he was happy to hear that Vince was the one to do it." Gemma gave them a watery smile. "So I sat with him for a while, which was great because you weren't answering your phone, and I swear I'd been thinking about dropping by to see if you were okay."

"Not a good idea," Vince said. "It's not exactly safe on our end of town. Especially at night, when you're alone."

"He's right," Holly agreed. "And Vince has man-strength."

"Yes, he does." Gemma giggled. "I still can't believe you punched Todd. Does your hand hurt?"

"A bit," Holly admitted. "But it was worth it."

"Yeah." Gemma chuckled. "I bet you won't forget the look on his face in a hurry."

"No, I won't," Holly lied as she recalled just how much that punch had cost her. Besides, even if she could remember it for only a few more hours, it was still a comfort.

"So this morning I wrote down the names of a couple more people who might've given you the pills. I'm also going to go around and take down all of those posters. I don't care what my boss says."

Holly studied her boots and didn't say anything.

"What?" Gemma demanded. "Oh, you're worried that I won't be able to get away like yesterday, but I've—"

"She has to go back to heaven at one o'clock, Gemma." Vince said the words that Holly couldn't quite get out.

Gemma's face went pale as she dropped her purse to the ground with a thump. "But surely they won't take you back until tonight? Midnight or something? That's what they would do in the movies. One o'clock is a stupid time. Besides, you haven't tied up your issues yet. You can't go back until that's done."

"I don't think it works like that." Holly gulped.

"No, don't say that." Gemma started to sob. "W-what's going to happen if you don't sort everything out before you go?"

Holly bit down on her lip and forced herself not to cry. "Oh, you know," she said in a bright voice. "I guess they'll stick me into a heavenly self-help group or something. Probably incredibly boring and I'll get told off for talking."

Gemma tugged a tissue out of her pocket and wiped her eyes. "Yeah, that sounds like you. And you'll be back in the regular part of heaven in no time. Hey, when you get through those levels, you can see your dad and your real mom. That'll be good."

"It certainly will." Holly's voice sounded hoarse, even to her own ears. "I can't wait."

"S-so what are you going to do now? We could still spend the morning trying to, well . . . get some answers."

Holly shook her head. "I think we're just going to see Vince's boss and apologize. Vince isn't too wrapped up in the idea, but I can't bear the thought of my actions costing him his job."

Gemma looked pale. "So this is it?"

"I guess so," Holly agreed. "But at least this time we get to say good-bye properly."

"God, Holly." Gemma started to sob again. "I'm

going to miss you so much. Who knows when we'll see each other again."

"Not for a long time, I hope. I don't want you dying anytime soon." Holly bit her tongue to keep from crying.

"Well, in that case you'd better not forget me," Gemma said firmly. "Because if you find out that my next boyfriend is doing the dirty on me or something, I'm counting on you to somehow show me a sign."

"Two thumps on the wall will mean yes," she assured her friend, while trying not to think about the reality— that in a few hours' time she wouldn't know who Gemma was. Before she could get too depressed, a surge of workers came through the door as the large clock hanging on the marble wall turned nine.

"So, I guess this is good-bye." Gemma wiped away more tears before throwing her arms around Vince's torso and squeezing it tightly.

"Hey," Holly said in alarm. "Remember I'm only Holly on the inside; on the outside I'm—"

"Vince Murphy," Gemma finished off in a strangled snivel. "I know. This is for him as well. He's taken good care of you."

"Thanks," Vince said softly.

"Bye, Gem," Holly mumbled before she untangled herself from her friend's embrace and started to jog away before Vince's limited social status tanked even further by bawling like a baby.

Twenty-five

Look, *Graham, Bob, and Andrew are all smiling at you*, Holly said in confusion as they walked into the workshop ten minutes later once she had managed to compose herself. Had the whole building heard about what had happened last night?

Hey, do you realize you didn't call any of them by the characters on their ties? Vince sounded impressed.

Oh. Holly could feel her face flush. *I guess they are all pretty nice guys. You're lucky. I just hope you're here long enough to appreciate it.*

Well, we haven't been hauled into David Harris's office yet. Vince slung his satchel onto the bench and frowned at the mess. *Let me guess—Fluffy paid me another visit last night?*

Oh, yeah. Holly realized she hadn't done a great job of tidying up. *I was sort of in a hurry to get to the Pool Palace, which is why as soon as I found the manuals, I just gave them all to Andrew and legged it.*

I don't know what manuals you gave him, but it certainly wasn't these. Vince pulled a familiar-looking yellow envelope from somewhere in the depths of the mess and held it up in the air.

Holly felt the horror mounting within her. *That doesn't make sense,* she croaked. *I definitely gave him the envelope.*

Vince started to tidy up the pile of papers on his bench. *It could've been anything. I often keep things in envelopes. Especially since Fluffy started making house calls.*

Holly gulped. That wasn't exactly the most comforting news. *So can you tell what's missing?*

Vince gave a quick scan and shrugged. *I wouldn't have a clue. Look, don't worry about it.*

But this is terrible. Vince, what if they fire you? I mean, not only were we late in delivering the laptops and giving them the manuals, but we punched one of Baker Colwell's most successful account managers in the face. I think we need to apologize before—

Holly— he started to say, but before he could get any further, Bob Mackay poked his head around the corner.

"Vince, David Harris wants to see you in his office. Pronto."

Holly was quite sure she was going to be sick.

Okay, so you're just going to have to tell him everything, Holly instructed as they made their way up to the fourth floor.

You mean about the dead girl in my body?

Holly rolled her eyes. *No, Vince, not about me being in here. I mean about Todd springing the laptops on you at the last minute and not even asking if it was okay for*

*you to deliver them. You could also tell them about that
hospital quote.*

*There's no point. The reason guys like Todd and
Simon do so well here is not just because they sell prod-
ucts; they sell themselves as well. It doesn't take a genius
to guess whom David Harris will side with. Especially
considering the fact that we hit Todd last night.*

You mean I hit him, Holly mentally wailed as they
reached the office. The secretary at the front desk nodded
for them to go straight in.

"He's expecting you," the girl said. Holly didn't take
this as a good sign, and that was further confirmed as
they pushed open the door to see Todd sitting in a chair
to the right of the desk looking smug, his swollen eye
proudly on display. Vince was right: Todd was really
going to milk this.

David Harris stood up with a serious expression on
his face. Holly had never had much to do with the Baker
Colwell executives, but she knew that Todd had been out
with him on more than one social occasion. What a way
to repay Vince for all his kindness.

"Thank you for joining us, Vincent. The reason I've
called you both here is because I have some serious concerns that need addressing."

Todd could barely contain his glee, and Holly had to
grip her hands to stop herself from punching him a second time. It was only the reminder that Vince didn't need
any more trouble right now that stopped her. But how
could she have not seen what sort of person Todd was?

Just then the door opened and David Harris nodded
his head. "Thank you for joining us."

Holly spun around just in time to see a short, angry man walking into the room. *W-who's that?*

Stuart Peterson. Owner of Peterson's Productions and number one buddy of David Harris. And Todd Harman.

No, Holly wanted to shout out. Lorraine had told her last night that her boss was on the rampage, but honestly, this was ridiculous. So what if Vince didn't deliver a couple of lousy laptops on time? Was there really any need to go to such great lengths to punish him? Didn't they know there were more important things to life than tormenting a computer technician? Especially such a nice, lovely one as Vince. In fact, she had a good mind to—

"Vincent. Todd." The man nodded as he walked over to the desk and handed David Harris a familiar-looking yellow envelope. On the outside was written, *Manuals,* in Vince's scrawled handwriting; hence Holly's mistake. She still had no idea what was in there, and all she could do was pray that Vince wasn't the downloading-porn sort of guy.

Holly, stop clenching like that, Vince instructed as she realized she'd had her hands balled into two tight fists.

Sorry, she replied. *But aren't you worried about this? I mean, if they're going to all this trouble they must be pretty mad.*

I'm honest and good at my job. If they have a problem with it, well, there's not much I can do.

Yes, but—

But nothing. I have a few more pressing things to worry about than this. You might not be able to resolve

*things with Todd, but there's still time to try to find out
how those pills got into your body. This is just a waste.*

Holly tried not to sniff, but it was hard, because that
was probably the nicest thing anyone had ever said to
her.

"Do you know what's in here?" David Harris held
the envelope up with a flourish.

"I gather it's not the manuals that Vince Murphy
was meant to deliver to our client at four yesterday afternoon." Todd snickered, and Holly could barely contain
her fury. Seeing things through Vince's eyes had certainly
changed her perceptions.

How, how, *how* had she ever liked him? Yes, he had
all the trimmings to make him look like the perfect catch,
but inside he was fatally flawed. Whereas someone like
Vince was . . . *perfect.*

And lovely.

And sweet, and—

Oh, no.

Holly almost groaned out loud as a startling realization struck her: She loved Vince and hated Todd. How
had this happened? She had been with Todd a year and
had been in Vince's body for only under two days, yet
somehow . . . somehow . . .

Somehow she'd made the classic Lizzy Bennet mistake of getting her Darcys and her Wickhams muddled
up.

Oh, lord.

Holly glanced around the room to see if anyone had
noticed a change in her, but to her surprise nothing had
changed. Todd was still smug, Vince was still standing

there like he didn't have a care in the world, and their two accusers were looking very grim.

Holly Evans loved Vince Murphy.

Talk about lousy timing—and what was worse was that Vince had made it blindingly obvious he was being so nice to her only because of his mother's death. It was his way of banking up his karma in case his own mom got kicked out of heaven. Not that she would, since if she managed to create such a wonderful son, she was probably pretty nice herself. Unlike Holly, who was bad and dreadful and about to have her mind wiped because of it.

Stop wriggling, Vince whispered in her mind, and Holly almost melted at the sound of his voice. It was suddenly so precious. But he was right. She didn't have time to be dreamy. Vince's job was on the line. She needed to pay attention.

"That's right." Stuart Peterson was now holding the envelope up in the air. "It's not the manuals that I was expecting. Do you have an explanation for this, Vince?" the man asked and Holly felt Vince shake his head.

"I have no idea what it is," he replied and she groaned. He was the worst liar ever.

Holly could barely look as Stuart Peterson pulled out a folder. "It's an article on software licensing. Do you know what that is, Todd?"

"Of course I do," he replied smoothly, but Holly noticed that his pinkie finger was twitching the way it did when his team was losing a game.

What's going on? Holly wanted to know, but before Vince could answer Stuart Peterson started to speak.

"Yes, it was a very enlightening article. Would you believe that every company is required to document the license for every software program installed on every computer? I certainly had no idea. But, of course, just as I trust my accountant to do my taxes, I was sure Baker Colwell would be looking after my computer needs. It's certainly what I pay them for."

Vince, Holly hissed again, *I have no idea what he's talking about.*

Remember I told you that's why their system kept crashing? Well, it looks like Peterson has just figured it out. I think things could get interesting.

Good interesting or bad interesting? Holly demanded, since her nerves were getting pretty frayed here, and she wasn't quite sure how much more they were up for.

I guess that would depend on whether you intend on trying to sort things out with Todd Harman.

Holly inwardly growled, and she could feel a flicker of a grin spread across Vince's face.

Well, if that's really the case, then I think you might enjoy this, because I have a feeling your almost fiancé is about to find himself in a spot of trouble.

Stuart Peterson scowled. It had to be said he didn't look happy. "So imagine my surprise when I went through the files to find all of this documentation I supposedly needed. Then when it couldn't be found I went through our invoices to see if we'd in fact paid for all of our software licenses. But no, we had not."

"That's when Stuart called me." David Harris folded his arms. "I told him that we would never sell a system that ran on unlicensed software. Which is when I started going through some of your other accounts, Todd. Now I'm starting to see why you've been winning so many quotes. And it seems that's just the tip of the iceberg. . . ."

"As for you, Vince," Stuart Peterson said, taking over, "I'd like to thank you for bringing this to my attention. Your help has been much appreciated."

Holly widened her eyes as she realized Todd was no longer looking quite so smug. So not only had he cheated on her, but he'd cheated on the company and his clients as well. To think she'd spent the last year dreaming of the day she would be Mrs. Todd Harman, all the while unable to see just what a jerk-off he really was.

"Nice work," Martha from reception called out as they walked past fifteen minutes later. Even Fluffy seemed to look a bit less growly. Boy, Holly was still amazed at how many people had disliked Todd, and by the time they got back to the workshop she felt like the Pied Piper, the way a stream of people had tagged along behind them.

Once they were back, everyone wanted to talk about how Todd Harman had been sacked because he'd deliberately kept things off a quote just to come in at the right price. Then there were the other things David Harris had started to list, but Holly had hardly been listening as she realized Vince was still firmly in possession of his job.

Not that she would remember it soon, but it mattered that she didn't leave Vince worse off than when she'd first landed in his body yesterday. Also, a small part of her couldn't bear for him to think ill of her, and who knew what the unemployment line might've done for his memories?

"Well-done, buddy." Andrew grinned. "That guy has screwed too many of us, and he deserves what he got."

Holly would drink to that, and despite her upcoming mind-wipe she felt a small sense of satisfaction as she listened to Vince's colleagues congratulate him. It wasn't until she felt Vince shake his head that she was rattled from her thoughts.

"Sorry, guys," he said. "You'll have to get the rest of the story from someone else. I'm going to take a personal day."

What's that all about? You're the most popular guy in the building right now, probably the planet. You should make the most of it.

I'll let them fawn all over me tomorrow. He shrugged. *Right now my time is your time. So what else can we do?*

Nothing. Vince, it's too late to try anything else. We just need to accept that I screwed up.

There must be something, he growled, and Holly, who was about to shake her head, suddenly paused.

Actually, you're right. There is one thing we could do . . . if you don't mind.

Just lead the way. I'm all yours.

If only that were true. She sighed. Then for the last time in this life or the next, Holly walked out of Baker Colwell.

"Vince, this is a surprise," Holly's stepmother said half an hour later. "Shouldn't you be at work?"

"I've got a day off."

"Oh, that's nice. I'm glad you remember to use them up. Poor Holly never seemed to have any time away from that place. So what is it I can do for you? Did you have some more things from her desk?"

"Sort of." Holly coughed. Eating humble pie wasn't something she'd tried to do many times before. It tasted funny. "I was wondering if I could come in for a minute."

"Of course. You'll be pleased to see I've tidied up. I'm sorry it was such a mess yesterday."

"That's okay," Holly assured her, absurdly pleased to see that the house had indeed been restored to its former pristine neatness. It was something she'd always taken for granted until she'd moved into Vince's body and seen how lucky she had been.

Actually there were quite a few things that Holly had been taking for granted. Hence this final visit to try to make amends. Though she wasn't sure how a ten-minute visit could change much. Still, she was determined to try.

"Would you like a coffee?" her stepmother asked. Although Holly's stomach had started to rumble, she shook her head. She couldn't afford to waste any time.

"No, thanks." She sat down in the chair her stepmother was offering. It had been her father's favorite, and for a moment Holly felt a twang of nostalgia.

"So tell me, Vince. What can I do for you?"

Holly fiddled with the strap of Vince's satchel. "I've got something for you."

Her stepmother looked startled. "You do?"

Holly dug into Vince's pocket and pulled out the birthday card she'd written earlier. When she first came up with the idea of trying to let her stepmother know she was sorry, Holly thought writing a card was the perfect way.

That was until she'd started writing.

Gone was her small, neat longhand, and in its place was a slanted scrawl that she found almost impossible to read. After ruining the first card, Holly had then spent the next ten minutes trying to train Vince's large hand to master her own style. It wasn't exact, but it was as close as Holly was going to get with the time permitted.

Though to give him his due, Vince had been very good about the whole process, and he'd sworn only once. Well, twice, but the second time was when Holly had made him seal it with a kiss. But he had done it, and for the first time in her life, Holly had been jealous of an envelope.

"I found it in the backseat of my work van, and I recognized it from Holly's box of things. It must've fallen out yesterday." She passed the card over.

Her stepmother didn't move from her chair as she studied the envelope before deftly pulling it open. Then her eyes widened. "It's a birthday card, but that's not for another month, and Holly hardly ever remembered it."

"I guess she did this year." Holly gave a casual shrug. "Anyway, I just thought I should bring it over."

"Thank you." Her stepmother's voice sounded choked with tears, and again Holly felt so odd at this complete turnaround. Though she was starting to wonder if it really was a turnaround at all.

It seemed that Holly had spent most of her time grossly misjudging people: Vince, Todd, her stepmother. . . .

Her life was all a bit of a mess, really. No wonder heaven wanted to wipe her memories and start again. It was probably for the best. She didn't even mind so much about not sorting out her issues—though it would've been nice to find out how the pills got there, just so people like Gemma and her stepmother didn't have to live with the stigma of the rumors. And as for her dad, well . . .

Holly noticed that her stepmother's hands were shaking as she studied the card. She didn't read it aloud, but then she didn't have to, since Holly already knew the contents.

> *Dear Jill,*
> *I bet this is a surprise getting a birthday card from*
> *me. I know we haven't always seen eye-to-eye, but*
> *I just wanted you to know that I hope you have a*
> *wonderful day.*
> *Love, Holly*

Actually, the way Holly had been feeling she could've gone a bit sappier than that, but then again, she wanted her stepmother to actually believe it was true, and as Holly recalled their past relationship, she doubted an overflow of sentiment would be very convincing.

Her stepmother finally glanced up from the card with unshed tears in her eyes. "Thank you," she said softly. "I can't tell you what this means to me."

"I'm glad I could help," Holly croaked. She was finding it increasingly hard to remember she was Vince. In a way she would be glad when this whole thing was over.

"And I have to thank you for something else," her stepmother said.

"You do?" Holly blinked. Especially since it wasn't as if she'd even forked out for a present.

"My neighbor's son was in the Pool Palace last night. He told me you had a fight with Todd."

"Oh." Holly gulped as she automatically covered up her swollen knuckles. Boy, news sure traveled fast. "I'm sorry about that," she mumbled.

"Well, I'm not," her stepmother said in a staunch voice before coughing. "Of course, I'm not saying I approve of violence, but from what I heard, Todd was saying some fairly dreadful things about Holly. I really appreciate your standing up for her."

"Yeah." Holly crossed her fingers. "Well, the dead can't speak for themselves, can they?"

"That's right. Which is why it's up to us to protect the memory of the people we loved," her stepmother said, and for a moment Holly thought Vince was going to say something about love as well, but in the end he just made a grunting noise in the back of his throat.

It was no more than Holly deserved, but still, she couldn't help but wish things had worked out differently.

Twenty-six

It was after twelve by the time Holly waved good-bye to her stepmother. She probably hadn't said as much as she would've liked. But she had said enough.

"That was a really nice thing to do." Vince thrust his hands into his pockets as they walked back toward his apartment. Holly knew he meant it. In fact, that was probably why he had been so helpful, because he'd lost his mother and might not have had the chance to say everything that needed to be said.

"Thanks. I guess I just wanted to let her know somehow that I didn't hate her. Well, up until yesterday I did, but things have changed since then."

"Are you okay?"

"I'm fine," she croaked. Holly couldn't cry. She couldn't even bite down on her lip or else Vince would know she wanted to cry, so they went the rest of the way to his apartment in silence.

He turned the key and stepped inside. As she looked at the bathroom, she wondered if she had time for a shower before . . . it happened. Then she vetoed the idea, since she had a tendency to die in water.

She pushed open the bedroom door and was just about to take her jacket off when she realized there was a lump in the bed.

Well, that was odd. She was sure she'd made it before they left this morning. Then she heard a shuffling noise.

"What the—"

"Hi, Vince," Amy Jenkins drawled as she poked her head out from under the comforter and revealed a pair of bare shoulders.

Oh. My. God.

Was she naked under there?

Holly felt her knees start to go weak. Was this earthly life really so unrelenting? Holly had no recollection of things moving at such a roller-coaster pace down here. Where was the peace? Where was the quiet? Suddenly the no-talking-during-a-funeral policy on Level One was starting to make complete and utter sense.

At least the one consolation of knowing she was going to lose her memory was that she would never again be subjected to images of this revolting situation.

Vince, she hollered at the top of her mental voice. *This one's for you.*

There was no answer, and for a moment Holly thought he was going to bail on her again, like he did the first time Amy turned up, but after taking a deep breath he finally spoke.

"How did you get in?"

"I climbed up onto your window. Pretty handy there's a porch roof just below."

Yeah, great.

"But *why*?" Vince's voice was low and cool, and his eyes didn't flicker as he stared directly at the other girl.

"We have unfinished business, Vince, and since everyone was talking about what happened and that you'd taken the rest of the day off, I thought I'd try here."

In his bed?

"You shouldn't have just turned up," Vince said.

"Oh, come on, Vince, don't be like that. We can have some fun together." Amy leered.

Gross.

Holly glanced at the alarm clock. There was never really a good time to find a naked girl in your bed when you were in fact a girl yourself masquerading in a boy's body. But could she just say that when she was about to get sent back to a life of torment on Level One . . . oh, like, any minute . . . the timing was particularly lousy.

Especially since there were things she wanted to say to Vince. Not that he necessarily would want to hear them, but still . . .

"I'm afraid it's not going to happen." Vince crossed his arms in front of his chest.

Go, Vince. You tell her.

"What do you mean, it's not going to happen?" Amy sat up and dragged the sheet around her unclothed body.

"Like I said, it's not going to happen."

A dark look crossed Amy's pale face, and she got to her feet, still wrapped in the sheet. "You're lusting after that stupid cow Holly Evans, aren't you?"

"What?" Holly didn't mean to yell out loud. But *What?*

"Oh, please, Vince. I'm not an idiot. I saw how you used to moon over that stuck-up bitch."

He did?

Holly could feel Vince swearing under his breath, but Amy was too busy struggling with a flowing black skirt to notice.

"Guys like you make me sick. That girl didn't even know you were alive, yet you'd rather not stand a chance with her than look twice at anyone else."

Well, perhaps if you were a bit nicer.

And took off that horrid white makeup.

And stopped breaking into people's houses and getting all naked, Holly wanted to retort. But she wisely kept her mouth shut.

Vince Murphy had liked her?

How had this happened? How long had it been going on, and why on earth didn't she know anything about it?

"Look, Amy—"

"Don't bother." Amy now grabbed at her black blouse and thrust it over her head while Holly snapped her eyes shut. "I can't believe I cut short my shift at the Fix and wasted two hundred bucks buying a dress for that lousy ball just because you said you were going to go. You didn't even turn up, you scumbag. I thought once you got to know me you'd forget about her."

"Yes, well, jumping into bed with someone isn't the same as getting to know them," Holly retorted, and Vince growled at her to let him handle it.

Sorry, she mentally told him in a contrite tone.

"Oh, don't go all moralistic on me. There's nothing wrong with having sex, Vince. If I knew you were such a prude I wouldn't have bothered going to as much trouble as I did."

Trouble. What sort of trouble had she gone to? And had she just said Holly was a prude, or did she mean Vince was a prude? Maybe they were both prudes? There should be more prudes in the world.

Holly could tell by the way Vince had his hands balled into two tight fists that he didn't like Amy one little bit.

She wondered if that had always been the case. After all, Vince was a nice, decent guy, and knowing him, he would have given Amy a chance. And probably another chance after that, but there was no way he would've liked how the girl was all over him. He *definitely* wouldn't have liked the way she was so eager to whip her clothes off and get down and dirty.

If Amy really knew Vince at all, she would've worked that out for herself.

Just as Holly had.

"Vince Murphy, you *are* a loser after all." Amy was almost frothing at the mouth with rage. "You know, when Benny dared me to hook up with you, I laughed in his face at first."

Huh?

Benny? As in the other company Goth who worked in maintenance and looked like he'd been squashed between two trucks after a hard night of no sleep and too many drugs?

"You were trying to go to bed with me for a dare?" Vince narrowed his eyes.

Amy was now lacing up her shoes. "To begin with I was. But you're a hot guy, Vince. The more I hung around

you, the more I became attracted to you. But you weren't
having any of it. Which, of course, only made me more
determined."

"And they say love is dead," Holly said before remembering she was meant to be Vince. *Whoops.*

"You're pathetic. You know that? Anyway, I'm outta
here, and don't try to speak to me again," Amy spit as she
marched toward the door, but just as she was about to
step out, her bag caught on the handle and the contents
spilled everywhere.

"Shit," the girl swore as she dropped to her knees
and started to scoop up the contents. Boy, what was in
that bag? Or more to the point, what wasn't in there?

Even from where she was standing, Holly could see a
tangle of jewelry that made her wonder if Amy indulged
in a bit of five-finger discounting.

Vince, ever the gentleman, bent down and picked up
a makeup bag and diary. Holly was just about to tell him
to let Amy do it on her own when she caught sight of a
packet of pills with an airplane embossed on the front.

What are those? she whispered, even though Amy
couldn't hear their internal conversation.

I don't know. Vince turned them over in his hand
until they could both clearly see the words MOTION SICK-
NESS stamped across the top.

Oh. My. God.

The pills.

Then things started to flash into sequence in her
mind. Amy had started working at the Fix. This was the
place where Holly went practically every other day for a
vanilla coffee—even two weeks ago, when she had fin-

ished work at seven and was running late to get ready for her night out with Todd.

Holly felt her eyes widen. Hadn't Amy just said she'd been working that night but finished her shift early on the chance of catching Vince at the ball? It certainly wouldn't have been hard for Amy to grind up the pills and put them into Holly's take-out drink.

But why?

All she could think was that Amy didn't want Holly to turn up at the Baker Colwell ball and distract Vince. *What a waste,* she thought for a moment. Especially since, as it turned out, Todd had planned to dump her, which meant Holly probably would've spent most of the night in the restroom, crying and trying to figure out what had happened.

"Give me those." Amy snatched them away the moment she saw them in Vince's hand. "Thanks for nothing, loser."

"Wait." Vince started to run after her, but Holly stood firm.

"What are you doing? She's getting away. Holly, you've found out what happened."

"Look at the time." Holly lifted his arm up so he could see the face of his watch. It was five minutes to one.

"I don't understand."

Holly made him stand by the mirror. "Amy freak-show Jenkins might have ruined my life once, but I'm not going to let her do it again, and I want to look at you before I go."

"But if we don't catch her, you'll be stuck on Level One."

"Vince, I'm stuck there anyway. After what I did to Todd I doubt that machine is ever going to say I'm purged, so it doesn't matter. To be honest, I don't even care anymore. Just tell Gemma and my stepmother about this newest development if you get a chance."

"Sure." Vince's voice sounded gruff. "If that's what you want."

Holly wanted to laugh hysterically. The way this scenario was playing out was so far from what she wanted that it wasn't funny. If she had her way she wouldn't be dead. She would be alive and she would be with Vince.

She reached out and touched his face in the mirror. How had she never noticed how gorgeous he was? But it wasn't his blue eyes and full lips; it was his inside that was gorgeous as well. Okay, so not the literal kidneys and heart stuff. But the *other* stuff. That was what counted. If only Holly had understood that sooner.

"About what Amy said . . . that you liked me. Was that true?"

Vince nodded. "Yeah."

"I remember you asked me out when I first started at Baker Colwell."

"You said no," Vince reminded her.

"Well, I haven't been able to resolve any of my other issues since I've been back here, but this is one I might be able to fix." Holly coughed and stared at his face in the mirror. "I didn't say yes then, but I'm saying it now. I just wanted you to know that."

"Thank you," Vince said softly. "That means something."

Holly touched the glass again and willed herself to remember what he looked like before walking over to the dresser and picking up the photograph of them both from when they were eight.

"I'll miss you, Vince."

"I'll miss you, Holly. I won't forget you," he said, and Holly desperately wished she could say the same thing to him as she clutched at the photo he had given her earlier that morning.

And then there was nothing.

Twenty-seven

"Right, Miss Holly Elliot Evans, client number XY4588890. The time is one ten, and this session will commence immediately."

Holly sat up with a start and tried to work out what was going on. She was in a white room, and the man in front of her had red hair and chubby fingers. He looked familiar.

"I know you," she said.

Then she turned her attention back to herself. Her arm seemed strange, and she held it out. It was shorter than she remembered, and so were her legs. A quick check of her hair confirmed it was hanging down her back. Then she glanced down at the photograph that was still clutched in her hand.

Vince.

"Oh, my God." She jumped up from the couch and waved the photograph around in the air as a series of events came tumbling into her mind. "I remember! I did it." She spun back to where the man was still patiently sitting. "You're Dr. Alan Hill, and my name's Holly Evans. My best friend is Gemma Gulliven." She squealed in excitement. "I'm twenty-two years old, and I *love* chocolate. I beat the system. I remember."

Dr. Hill stood up and pulled an apologetic face. "Miss Evans, calm down."

"But this is so exciting." She couldn't stop smiling. "I remember everything. You love shopping, my Level One tutor was Tyrone, and Rochelle Jackson is a big tart whose fingers are so fat that my ring will look *awful* on her. I can't believe it."

Dr. Hill raised his hand. "*Miss Evans.* Please. Could you just calm down for a minute? There's something I need to explain to you."

"What? That I'm a genius for beating your mindwipe?" She waggled a finger at him and grinned.

"No." He shook his head and walked toward her, his new white loafers squeaking slightly as he moved. "The reason you can remember everything is because you didn't have your memory erased in the first place."

Holly put her excitement on hold for a moment. "What?"

"There was no need to erase your memory because your manual purge was successful."

"No, it wasn't," she told him firmly. "Everyone still thinks I committed suicide, and even though I know Amy Jenkins gave me those pills, it's never going to be proven, is it? I mean, who's going to arrest her just because she owns some motion-sickness pills? I was stupid even to think it mattered. Then there's Todd. Wasn't I supposed to make my peace with him? I was even going to apologize to that son of a bitch. But I remember quite clearly that I punched him instead. And you know what the worst thing is? I don't even care. I'm glad I did it. In fact, I would do it again in a twinkle. So there's no way I passed."

Dr. Hill held up something in his hand. "I've got one machine that begs to differ."

Holly looked at the small device and wrinkled her nose. "I-I don't understand. How's that possible?"

"Let's see, you made amends with your stepmother, you saw your boyfriend for who he really was, and you let go of your hang-ups about suicide. Holly Evans, as of now, you're my star pupil."

"Really?" Holly tried to hide her disbelief as she felt her chest swell with pride. Not that she really had a clue what she'd done, apart from screw everything up, but still, it was nice to be appreciated.

And she had her memories.

She was also completely filled with love for Vince. It wasn't just a feeling. It was more. It was part of her, and she certainly had never had anything like it with Todd. Okay, so it would've been a million times better to be with Vince now, but at least she could remember him, and perhaps if she played her cards right, she could spy on him from time to time. Would that be breaking some sort of heaven/earth privacy policy? She might have to check up on that one.

"Really," Dr. Hill agreed.

Then something occurred to Holly. "So if I managed to get everything right only by accident, wasn't it a bit risky to let me go back to earth to solve the wrong issues? I might not have made it."

"That's always a risk," the doctor admitted. "But if

I'd told you to go down there and speak to your step-mother, or to ignore Todd altogether because he was a cheating bastard, would you have done it?"

"You knew he had been cheating on me?"

"Er . . . well, that's really beside the point." Dr. Hill squirmed in his chair before shooting her a hopeful smile. "Did I mention you're my star pupil?"

Holly glared for a moment before her body was once again taken over by happy feelings. "I guess it all worked out in the end," she conceded.

Dr. Hill wiped his brow as he stood up and started to pace the room. "I'm pleased you understand. It really was the best way for you to dig down and find out what's important. So the question is, what should we do with you now?"

"Give me a nice reward?" Holly said hopefully, and the doctor smiled. "Preferably gift-wrapped."

"Actually I was thinking more in terms of your future with the Company."

"The Company?" Holly wasn't quite sure she was following the program here. "Are we back in heaven or am I having a weird dream?" she asked.

"Oh, I forgot; you haven't read your rulebook yet. The Company is what we call Level Two."

"I've reached Level Two? One more level and I can see my parents?" It was more than she had dared hope for.

"That's right." He nodded as he continued to pace. "However, to get to Level Three requires a vast amount of work. Some people get there quite quickly, like your father, while others spend an eternity trying to reach it. It all depends on your service record."

Holly scratched her head. "You know, I'm still not really following you. What's a service record?"

"Why, it's the record of how you perform for the Company. The better your performance, the better your record. Obviously a job with a high degree of skill will improve your record."

"Right, so you're saying I need a job if I want to get there quickly?" To be honest, Holly felt a little bit disappointed. After she'd gone back to Baker Colwell, it had become increasingly obvious that corporate life wasn't for her. Yet apparently she was going to have to join the rat race again.

"Er, yes. More or less."

"Fine, so where's the human resources place in this joint?"

Dr. Hill picked up the machine again. "We can set you up with a job through this. It analyzes you and works out what you're mentally suited to."

Oh, curses. Not that blinking thing again. "And what did it say?" Holly asked cautiously, not liking the look on Dr. Hill's face.

"The thing is, Miss Evans, not all jobs are glamorous—or comfortable. But remember what I was saying before: High risk means high reward."

Not glamorous? Not comfortable? Was he talking about working down in a mine pit or something? Even if she couldn't feel anything but divine happiness right now, she was pretty certain that once she broke her first nail it would all be downhill.

"Fine, tell me what the stupid thing says then. I know you want to," she said in a resigned voice.

He shot her a pained look. "It seems to think you'd be a good mole."

She knew it. He freaking well wanted to send her down into a mine. *Unbelievable.* Just because she'd been a big, muscley boy with a rock-hard stomach and biceps to kill for was no reason to think she liked digging. Or getting dirty, for that matter.

She was getting punished, after all.

"I know it's not everyone's idea of a dream job," he admitted, obviously reading the disappointment on her face. "But if you want to see your parents sooner, it might be worth considering."

"You're right," she said with a sigh. "Tell me the worst."

"The thing is, you have to live on earth. . . ."

"What?"

What?

"I told you it wasn't ideal. Especially since you've only just been purged. Most people can't even consider the thought of losing their celestial happiness and being turned back into a corporeal body again. All the messy emotions, the pollution, the politics. But the machine has calculated that you have an eighty-five percent chance of adapting to the transition. The highest percentage ever recorded is eighty-seven, so you can imagine why my bosses were so keen for me to discuss this with you."

"Whoa, whoa, whoa." Holly narrowed her eyes and stared at him. "Are you making fun of me?"

"Of course not." The doctor looked confused. "Why would I do that?"

"I don't know, perhaps the same reason you sent

me back to earth in a guy's body. While the guy was still in it."

He looked hurt. "I thought we'd been through that."

"We have, but I'm not sure why else you are acting like this is a horrible job."

Dr. Hill ran his chubby fingers through a red curl and studied her face. "You mean the idea doesn't repulse you?"

Oh, now she understood. It was a trick. "I can't believe you almost got me." She groaned. "There's a catch, isn't there? I can only go back as . . . a tree . . . oh, no, wait—a zebra. Well, I'm not falling for that one again."

"Miss Evans, I think you'd better sit down and let me explain what a mole does. Perhaps it would be a good idea if you don't interrupt."

Holly sat and listened, and despite his predilection for large words, she didn't find herself losing interest at all.

"So let me get this straight," she said when he finally finished. "You're telling me that a mole is like a heavenly secret agent who lives on earth as a human."

The doctor nodded his head.

"Most people don't want to do this because they would rather not give up the warm, fuzzy feeling they get after their purge," she continued.

"That's right."

"Okay, so if I were to be a mole, I could go back as Holly Evans, age twenty-two years old and living at Thirty-four Windsor Street."

"That's right." He didn't seem to notice her incredulity. "And your main duties would be just to live a normal life, while keeping us updated on certain things."

"What sort of things?" Holly shot him a doubtful look. "I mean, I'm not that hot on politics, and I don't think I'd be able to break a secret code if it were spelled out to me in a *Cosmo* magazine, so I'm not quite sure what I could do."

Dr. Hill smiled. "The Company gathers all sorts of intelligence. Anything from eating trends, to whether family values are changing, to the latest fashion collections."

Holly shook her head. "I still don't quite understand. You're giving me the chance to go back and live a normal life, without death?"

"Well, of course, you won't die when you're already dead. You will age normally but there will be some point when you move on to another position in the Company, or even another level. But in earth years it covers more than a natural life span."

"I'll take it," Holly blurted out.

Dr. Hill widened his eyes in surprise. "Generally people like to spend some time thinking it over, or at least reading the rulebook. Then there is the question of your parents. Even on the accelerated program, you do realize it might still take time before you can see them?"

"While I was down there I was determined to clear my name so that my dad didn't think I'd tried to commit suicide again. I wanted him to know how hard I'd been working to make amends. Of course, I should've realized that I didn't need to tell him any of that stuff. He already knows, doesn't he?"

"So proud." Dr. Hill sniffed as he fanned his face with

his hands. "You really *are* my star pupil, and yes, you're right. Your father knows exactly what kind of person you are, Holly, and I think that you finally do as well."

Holly grinned for a moment as she clutched her photograph. "Yeah, I think I do. . . . And now, about this new job of mine. Send me back already."

Twenty-eight

The scalding coffee burned her tongue as she forced herself to swallow it. Well, wasn't that just typical of heaven? They were clever enough to send her back through time to the day she died, and even went to all the trouble of wiping everyone's memory but her own. But did they think to stop Amy Jenkins from slipping her the motion-sickness tablets? Er, no.

"Holly, should you really be drinking so much caffeine before the ball tonight? You don't want to be jumping around like a grasshopper." Her stepmother appeared from the living room, clutching a camera as she raised a questioning eyebrow at the three other empty cups sitting on the kitchen bench.

Holly took another gulp of steaming-hot liquid. "I've just been feeling a little bit tired. I thought it might wake me up," she improvised.

"I see. Well, it was nice of you to stop by before you go out. I wasn't expecting it. You used to like spending all your time in the bath to get ready for a big night out."

"I guess I just thought it's been a while since I've seen you. I should've come sooner," Holly said as she tried to ignore the fact she did feel like a long soak in the tub, especially after the day she'd just had. Except until the pills were out of her system she had decided it was probably safest not to. Technically, Dr. Hill had said she couldn't die again, but since she still hadn't had a chance to read the rulebook yet, she wasn't taking any chances with the fine print. *Been there, done that, and almost got kissed by another girl to prove it.*

"I know you've been busy." Her stepmother smiled. "You don't have to explain. I hope you don't mind if I take a photograph of you, though. You look wonderful. Todd's a lucky guy."

Oh, that freak-faced waste-of-space loser.

She sucked down the last dregs of coffee and tried not to screw up her nose at the bitter aftertaste. "Actually, Todd and I broke up this afternoon."

"Oh, Holly." Her stepmother's face was now a picture of genuine concern, and again Holly wondered if she'd been the only one to change.

"It's all right," Holly quickly reassured her. "In fact I feel great about it."

"But what happened?"

Well, let's see. I died the day we were meant to get engaged, only to find out he was cheating on me with a stupid tart named Rochelle Jackson while I was sitting at the next table in the body of a boy.

"Oh, you know, normal reasons. It's no big deal."

"That's all right," her stepmother said quickly. "You don't need to tell me if you don't want to. I didn't mean to pry."

Gosh, had Holly really been so supersensitive before that her stepmother couldn't even ask a normal question without worrying about the reaction she would get?

Wait, don't answer that.

"You're not prying," Holly said instead. "I guess I started to realize that I was with Todd for all the wrong reasons. Just because he has a perfect résumé doesn't make him the right guy for me. I suppose I didn't like who I was becoming when I was around him."

Her stepmother put down the camera. "It takes a big person to admit that."

"I sort of had it spelled out for me," Holly reluctantly confessed.

"Well, all the same. You might not be able to change the past, but you can always try to make tomorrow better," her stepmother said, and for a moment Holly wondered if Dr. Hill had really managed to purge everyone's memory because if she didn't know better, she would say her stepmother was talking about more than just Holly's disastrous relationship with Todd.

"Anyway . . ." Her stepmother gave her a shy smile. "Now's hardly the time for this; you've got a big night ahead. Who knows? You might even meet the man of your dreams."

I hope not, Holly wanted to retort since there was only one man she was interested in right now. And he hadn't been a dream. He'd been all real.

"Can you believe what Rochelle Jackson's wearing?" Gemma demanded as a group of them stood at the back of the glittering ballroom and checked everyone out now that the free champagne had helped lower some of the staff members' inhibitions.

Holly could very well believe it, because she'd seen the exact same dress hanging in Rochelle's closet the other day. Though somehow it looked even smaller and tighter than before.

"It's gross," she agreed.

"Look at how she and Todd are dancing. That's so disgusting. You guys only broke up this afternoon, and yet she's all over him like a rash."

Holly glanced over to the dance floor, where Todd and Rochelle were both looking smug. "To be honest, I don't think we can blame this one all on Rochelle. It takes two to publicly grope on the dance floor. Despite how drunk Todd is, he doesn't look like he's protesting too much."

"How can you be so calm?" Gemma demanded. "I mean, this must be freaking you out. I'm still not sure I even understand where all that came from. One minute you were the Baker Colwell dream couple and now . . . well, you're not. Actually you're looking a bit pale. Have you eaten something funny?"

"I think I might have had a cup of coffee that didn't agree with me," Holly admitted.

"As if there's such thing as sketchy coffee." Gemma rolled her eyes. "Seriously, Holly, there must be some explanation for all of this."

"I guess I got a sudden vision of what life might be like in the future, and let's just say that I didn't like the picture. Besides, somehow I don't think Todd and Rochelle will last." Holly wasn't too sure how karma worked in situations like this, but she was pretty confident that Todd's dodgy sales practices would come and bite him on the butt at some stage. Would it be wrong of her to hope it was sooner rather than later?

Rochelle Jackson might act (and dress) like a bimbo, but the truth was that she was as ambitious as Todd, and Holly would've bet her heavenly rulebook that Rochelle would drop him faster than a figure-disguising caftan when his double dealings finally caught up with him.

"That's all very well, but it's still a lot of change. I'm not sure I can keep up with it," Gemma complained. "First you break up with Todd, and now you decide to get another job."

"Shhhhh." Holly glanced around to make sure no one was listening. "Besides, I haven't gotten it yet. I won't know more until I see them next week."

"Of course you'll get it. Especially after you recited the family tree of everyone in *The Rich and the Restless* to them over the phone and they said that you knew it better than the scriptwriters. But you still haven't told me how you heard about it in the first place."

A small smile tugged at Holly's lips. She had a feeling that calling *The Rich and the Restless* studio just as Lorraine had been forced to deal with another Monica Edwards diva tantrum might possibly come under the Insider Trading Act. But since no lightning had struck her down—or more important, no Dr. Hill had mysteriously appeared as Holly had asked the harassed production assistant if it would be okay to send in her résumé for a job—she figured that heaven didn't have a problem with Holly moving into the dazzling world of daytime television. Which was why, when Lorraine had positively *begged* her to come in for an interview next week, Holly couldn't help but feel excited about it all.

"It was just in passing, really." Holly shrugged. "I met someone who knew the production assistant and found out she hated her job. So it was just a fluke."

"Well, I guess you are perfectly suited to it," Gemma grudgingly admitted. "But it's going to be so weird without you."

"I know, but we'll still be moving in together. The sooner the better, considering the way Irene's going," Holly reminded her.

"I suppose so, but it's not the same. Especially since I've become less impressed with some of the people at work. Especially Simon Trimmer. Look at how drunk he is. I don't know what I saw in him."

Holly peered over to where Simon Trimmer and some others had taken their bow ties off from around their necks and tied them around their heads as they threw a flower bowl around as if it were a baseball.

"I've been wondering the same thing about Todd. Perhaps we're growing up? Hey, and look at Simon. He's going to hurt someone if he keeps doing—"

"Holly, watch out," Gemma shrieked, but before Holly could even work out what was going on, she felt a pair of arms wrap themselves around her and push her to the floor just as a large glass bowl went skimming past her head, landing with a thud on one of the chairs lined up along the wall.

"Are you all right?" a familiar voice asked, and Holly peered up to see Vince Murphy almost lying on top of her, his blue eyes full of concern. Look how gorgeous he was in a dinner suit. Had he rented it? It must have cost him a fortune. But it was sooooo worth it.

"Hey, Murphy. I think you can get off her now," Gemma snapped as she thrust out a hand to help Holly up. Vince quickly scrambled into a standing position, and Holly thought how much nicer it had been when he was touching her. She let Gemma help her up.

"Holly," Simon slurred as he appeared from the crowd. "Sorry about that. Was aiming for the banner." Holly looked over to where a large Baker Colwell banner was hanging from the wall—on the other side of the room.

"Well, maybe you should get out of here and practice your aim then?" Vince said in a cool voice.

"Are you speaking to me?" Simon blinked in bemusement before lurching slightly to the left.

"Yes, and you'd do well to listen. I heard that the regional director is still around here somewhere, so I suggest you and your drunken friends get out of here before you end up demoted to the mailroom."

For a moment Simon looked as if he were going to say something smart. Perhaps with his fists? But as Vince's cool, steady gaze continued to remain fixed on him, he seemed to change his mind, and his hands dropped back to his sides. Without another word he spun around, and he and the other account managers staggered toward the door.

Good riddance.

"Hey, Murphy, that was pretty cool," Tina MacDonald purred. "Do you want a drink?"

Puhlease. Had Rochelle been giving her lessons?

"No, thanks. I just wanted to see if Holly's okay."

"She's fine." Gemma put a protective arm around Holly's shoulders and started to drag her to one side. "Thanks for your help."

"Actually, Gem"—Holly wriggled free—"I sort of wanted to say thank you to Vince myself. That was a close call."

Gemma was about to open her mouth in protest when Holly saw a familiar-looking guy walking toward them. "Hey, isn't that Andrew, one of the technicians? I think he's coming to ask you to dance."

"I can't dance with him," Gemma protested.

"I think he's kind of cute." Tina fluffed her hair and hitched up her skirt some more. "Maybe he's coming to ask *me* to dance?"

Holly's lip twitched. "No, I think it's definitely Gemma he wants. You should go for it, Gemma."

"No, I couldn't. Could I? Is he really looking at me?" Gemma suddenly started to fiddle with the ring on her finger. "The thing is, I never told you this before, but I've actually talked to him a couple times when he's come into the department for . . . well . . . actually I'm not sure what it was for, but he was quite nice. Bad taste in ties, though."

"You definitely shouldn't judge a man by his tie," Holly assured her. "I think nice is often underrated in guys."

"Okay," squeaked Gemma as she nervously started to walk toward him. "I just might."

"So, are you all right?" Vince's blue eyes caught hers. "That was a pretty close call."

Holly felt her stomach do a series of flip-flops as she returned his gaze. And could she just say how much nicer it was to be able to look at him properly rather than just through a mirror?

"I'm fine," she croaked. "Thanks. I think I would've missed the rest of the ball if you hadn't pushed me out of the way."

"I just happened to be in the right place at the right time." He gave her a familiar shrug, and Holly longed to touch him.

"You have a habit of doing that," she said without thinking, and then blushed. Gosh, already the weight of a double life was sitting on her shoulders. Definitely time for a subject change. "S-so I didn't think you normally came to this sort of thing."

"I don't," Vince said in a wonderfully familiar gruff voice. "In fact, I'm not sure why I changed my mind. I guess the guys I work with finally managed to wear me down into saying yes."

"R-right, so you're not here with anyone else then?" Holly tried to sound casual but was sure she was failing miserably. Still, if she didn't ask she would go mad. "I-I heard you and Amy Jenkins were . . ."

Vince gave an adamant shake of his head. "Definitely nothing between us. Didn't you know?"

Holly looked at him in surprise. "Know what?" That Amy had been sent away to an institution as punishment for an unhealthy habit of trying to poison people with motion-sickness tablets?

"She got transferred for a year. To the Outer Mongolia office."

Holly giggled. Well, it wasn't justice at its best, but there was a certain amount of satisfaction to be had from it. To think she had doubted that heaven didn't know what they were doing when it came to divine retribution.

"So how about you?" Vince's voice sounded deeper than ever. "Are you here alone? I saw Todd dancing with Rochelle Jackson, and then someone said you guys—"

"Are over." Holly wondered if it would be too forward to stop all of this chitchat and just kiss him. After all, she'd lived in his body for two days and now knew him better than she knew her best friend. Surely certain formalities could be waived in such circumstances? Just a pity Vince was showing no signs of remembering any of it. Trust Dr. Hill to finally get something right.

"Really?" Vince sounded pleased, and Holly's heart did an absurd little leap. "Because I was wondering if you'd like to—"

"Yes, please," Holly said before he could even finish, and she winced. She'd become so used to knowing what he was going to say, she'd forgotten he didn't have any memory of it.

As he reached out for her hand to lead her toward the dance floor, he didn't look too unhappy about the situation.

It wasn't exactly a slow song. In fact, over the sound system Green Day was belting out lyrics at a hundred miles an hour, but Holly didn't care. Vince Murphy had asked her to dance with him, and dance she would.

She slipped her hands around his waist, and after a moment of surprise she felt his arms wrap tightly around her shoulders. Ah, this was better. Ever since she'd been back in her body, she'd had a niggling sense that something was missing. Now she knew what: Vince.

She pressed herself tighter. He was probably going to think she was the biggest harlot in the whole world—well, apart from Rochelle Jackson, obviously. But Holly didn't care. She had been dead for two weeks. She needed a hug.

The song finally finished, and as a 50 Cent tune pumped through the air, Vince started to say something to her.

"What?" she called out over the music, but once again he was drowned out, and so he shook his head before grabbing her hand and leading her to the darkened side of the room.

"Couldn't hear a thing," he explained as he leaned against the wall. "There was something I wanted to ask you."

"Yes?" Holly gulped, reverently hoping it would involve the words *kissing* and *now*.

Vince fidgeted with his hand, and Holly noticed the swollen knuckles were no longer there. Pity, since it meant Todd never got punched in the face after all. But still, a girl couldn't have everything.

Then he shook his head. "Actually, don't worry. It would just sound stupid."

"What would sound stupid?" *If you were going to ask me out, that wouldn't sound stupid at all. Or if you wanted to kiss me—definitely not on the stupid side. . . .*

He thrust his hands into his pockets, and Holly's heart went into overdrive. Was he just the hottest guy who had ever lived?

"I never should've opened my mouth," he said.

"Yes, well, you did, and you can't not tell me now. It wouldn't be fair. I'm a woman. We are curious by nature. It's part of the job description."

He blew out a column of air and rolled his eyes. "Fine, but can you at least keep your laughing to a minimum when I say it?"

"How do you know I'll laugh?" she protested.

"Because in my dreams you seemed to laugh at me a lot."

Holly felt her heart start to thump. "Your dreams?"

"See, I told you it was going to sound crazy." He shook his head and looked off into the distance. "Okay, I think I'm just going to go. . . ."

"No." Holly grabbed his arm. Well, that was a mistake, and she shivered as all sorts of nice tingly feelings went whizzing around her body. "Please don't go. I want to hear more about these dreams."

He dropped his head so he was now looking directly at her. "You just seemed to be in them. A lot. Which is stupid, right? Since we hardly know each other."

"We did used to play together as kids," she croaked, unable to drag herself away from Vince's gaze.

"I didn't think you'd remember that."

"You'd be surprised at what I remember." She could tell her voice was husky now. "You're not as invisible as you'd like to think, Vincent Murphy."

She watched his Adam's apple move slightly—a clear sign he was nervous. "So do you think we could perhaps go out one night?" he said.

"I'd like that." She bit her lip in excitement. "I'd like that a lot."

"Great," he said in a hoarse voice, but instead of kissing her, he straightened up and looked like he was about to join Graham, Bob, and the other technicians over by the bar. "So, I suppose I'd better let you get back to your friends. They're probably all freaking out that you're even talking to me."

"I only came with Gemma." Holly shook her head. "But since she seems a bit preoccupied with a complicated technical question, I don't think you have much to worry about."

"Are you sure about this?" He studied her from under the lids of his blue eyes, and Holly nodded as she leaned farther into him.

"You wouldn't believe me if I told you how sure I was."

"You could try," he murmured, but before she could answer, she felt his hands gently reach down to the belt of her dress and pull her toward him.

Then he kissed her.

Boy, did Vince Murphy know how to kiss, and suddenly Holly could see just why Amy Jenkins had gone to such lengths to try to capture his interest. Of course, as Holly found herself returning his kiss, she was certainly pleased Amy had failed. First because she didn't like sharing, and second, because kissing Vince was to die for. Literally.

About the Author

Amanda Ashby was born in Australia and studied English and journalism at Queensland University. Since graduation, she has worked in sales, marketing and travel before discovering that she was no good at any of them and so decided to turn her attention to writing instead. She is married with two young children and has recently returned from the UK to live in New Zealand.